GJ Moffat has been fascinated by courtroom melodramas starring the good and the bad guys since he was a boy. Although he became a lawyer, he always had the urge to write and his debut thriller brings these good guys and bad guys to life in glorious Technicolor.

He is married with two little angel girls and is struggling to learn the electric guitar (hitting more bum notes than good ones).

Praise for *Daisychain*:

'Positively crackles from first page to last . . . An astonishingly accomplished debut with Grisham-like elan . . . If you read just one thriller this year, make it this one'   *Daily Mail*

'Don't even think about stopping half-way through because this is a strictly one-sitting, white-knuckle adrenalin ride that will undoubtedly be one of the best debuts to hit the thriller shelves this year'   *Daily Record*

Daisychain

GJ Moffat

hachette
SCOTLAND

First published in 2009 by
HACHETTE SCOTLAND, an imprint of
Hachette UK

First published in paperback in 2010 by
HACHETTE SCOTLAND

Cataloguing in Publication Data is available from the British Library

ISBN: 978 0 7553 1852 0

Typeset in Monotype Fournier by Ellipsis Books Limited, Glasgow
Printed and bound in Great Britain by Clays Ltd, St Ives plc

Hachette Scotland's policy is to use papers that are natural, renewable
and recyclable products and made from wood grown in sustainable forests.
The logging and manufacturing processes are expected to conform
to the environmental regulations of the country of origin.

HACHETTE SCOTLAND
An Hachette UK Company
338 Euston Road
London NW1 3BH

www.hachettescotland.co.uk
www.hachette.co.uk

For my three angels – Kay, Holly and Lucy

Acknowledgements

To my parents, Christine and Jimmy, I give thanks for the genes and the unconditional love and support that made me who I am (for better or worse, depending on whom you ask).

My big brother, Kevin, for the stuff about guns – it's okay, he's not a criminal or anything (at least in so far as I'm aware). He learned it all in the RAF and he's a damn fine shot if he does say so himself.

Also huge thanks to George McIntosh, money-laundering compliance officer par excellence and retired Lothian and Borders CID, for his time on the police procedural stuff. If it's inaccurate, far fetched or even a little bit too glamorous at times, it's all my fault and nothing to do with George. If it seems realistic, thank George.

Thanks to my publisher at Hachette Scotland, Bob McDevitt, for eventually getting round to picking up my submission and being fantastically enthusiastic about it ever since. Also thanks to Wendy McCance for expert guidance through the editing – hope there's enough secks and violins in it for you?

Many others assisted or supported me in some way in getting to this point. In no particular order (and apologies for any omissions), they are: everyone else at Hachette Scotland, Peter Buckman, Katrina Whone, Tania Gillespie, Alix Bearhop, Suzie Lyons, Beef and Tee (you know who you are), Claire Kennedy, Sergeant Larry Subia of the Denver PD, Simon Leila, Jim McLean, George Kynoch and Doctor Mike Kynoch (for Stella).

Prologue

Her vision blurred red.

He hit her again.

She tried to breathe and it sounded like a baby's rattle filled with syrup as blood gurgled deep inside her lungs. She coughed a fine red mist into the air.

The crunch again of metal on bone.

Something in her broke and she began the long, slow fall into the void. As she fell, an image stirred in her shattered mind and she saw the face of a man, a boy really, no more than twenty years old.

A dream, she thought. A beautiful dream.

No, not a dream, a memory.

What a thing to remember at the end of it all. Why did it have to be this? She wanted something warm to grab on to and hold tight as she fell into the cold embrace of her death. But death is not a friend to warmth and she died drowning in the memory of her own tears.

They sat at the end of the bed with the red cotton throw wrapped tightly around them, making silent bets on the threads of rainwater racing down the window. Two of the threads merged as one, becoming greater together.

She started at a loud crack from the logs burning in the open fireplace. A single glowing ember was spat out on to the old floorboards, scorching the wood black.

Tell him.

She rested her head on his shoulder, her breath a warm caress on his damp skin and his sweat like seawater on her lips. Her heat penetrated deep inside him, settling down in the marrow of his bones. She slipped her hand into his and squeezed hard as the branches of the oak tree raked against the outside wall of the flat.

Tell him.

He turned to her and saw something fleeting in her eyes, something that aged her for a brief instant well beyond her years.

'What?' he asked.

'Nothing,' she said. 'It's nothing.'

As if repeating it would make it true. He sensed that it was not true, but his fear stopped him from asking the questions that he should have asked. He shifted his doubts to the same place he kept his feelings about the growing distance between them in the last month. If he didn't think or talk about it, how could it be real?

How different would things have turned out if he had forced her to open up? She wanted him to do it. To push her down on to the bed and shout at her to let it out, to tell him what it was that was forcing them apart. But he never did.

They could hear the growing din of rush-hour traffic outside on Byres Road and lay back on the bed. The cotton throw fell away leaving them both naked. He turned on his side and traced his fingers over her shoulders and then down over her breasts and on to her stomach. She put her hand on top of his and pressed it hard into the flesh of her belly. She wanted to push his hand down through the layers of skin and fat and muscle until he was inside her womb and could feel the pulse of new life growing there.

Tell him.

He sensed her muscles straining and mistook it for desire. He leaned over and opened his mouth on hers, his tongue sliding over her lips and entering the warmth of her mouth.

Tell him and it will be all right, she thought. Then she almost laughed at the naïveté of the thought. They had both just graduated from Strathclyde University, confident about the future in their chosen careers of law and architecture. And it was a career she wanted, not a husband and a child – she knew that it was selfish but she still found herself pushing him away. How would they bring up a child?

And now, as the distance between them continued to grow, she convinced herself that she was not even sure that he was the one she wanted to make a life with. She knew in her heart that it was the fear and uncertainty driving them apart and not just the natural atrophy that a dying love endures before the end. But she willed herself to ignore that, to make bearable the decision to leave him and end the pregnancy.

Tell him.

Instead, she guided his hand down between her legs, pushed up to meet him and lost herself to him.

Make it good, she told herself. Make it the best and he'll hold it dear, like a photograph that fades with time but never disappears.

It was.

Later, he stood in the door to the street with his hands in the pockets of his jeans and watched her run through the rain to the underground station, water kicking up off her heels. The street lights buzzed to life along the road and glowed dirty yellow in the late afternoon gloom of a Glasgow winter.

He raised a hand to wave as she stopped at the station entrance, lifting the wet hair up out of her face and smiling. He was too far away to see that the smile never touched her eyes, too far to distinguish the tears from the rain.

Was it good enough, she wondered? Then he stepped out into the street, his bare feet splashing in the puddle outside the door. The rain quickly soaked his shirt, moulding it to the contours of his body so that he appeared naked to her. He cupped his hands to his mouth and shouted.

'I love you, Penny.'

Tell him.

Tell him.

Tell him.

Her insides twisted and screamed and she took an unsteady step back towards him, towards life and away from the ugly death waiting for her down the years. But he did what he always did and stepped back inside and out of sight.

'I never want to see you go,' he told her once when she asked why he did that. 'No long goodbyes.'

The moment was lost for ever, her tears coursing away with the water in the gutter and falling into the sewer drain beneath the street. She stood alone in the rain.

'Till a' the seas gang dry,' she whispered to the space where he had been.

It was how she always responded when he told her that he loved her – a poet's way of telling him it would be for ever.

She paid for a single at the ticket booth and waited on the narrow central platform for the distinctive orange train. She stepped on and the doors hissed shut behind her. The train rattled and lurched forward, taking her into the black of the tunnel.

And she was gone.

Day One

1

Monday, 5.00 a.m.

As an associate lawyer in one of Scotland's biggest firms, Kennedy Boyd, Logan Finch didn't get nervous about the big deals any more. But confidence had come slowly and he still remembered the days when he would have to bolt to the bathroom in the early hours of a crucial day to deposit the dinner of the previous night.

He looked at things now from a business perspective; the long nights he endured as a sort of down payment on his future as a corporate lawyer. And now, not far off his thirty-fourth birthday with the biggest deal of his career looming, he felt in control. It had been a price worth paying.

Things change.

He opened his eyes in the dark of his flat, still half asleep and caught in a dream. As the mental residue slowly bled away and reality seeped back in, he was surprised at how real the dream had seemed, at the raw emotions it touched off deep in his chest. He put a hand to his breastbone and felt his heart thudding quick and hard.

Penny.

He hadn't thought of her in a while, and now this dream of their last time together in his old flat. He wondered where she was in the world today. Hong Kong was the last he'd heard from Bob Crawford, but that was probably more than a year ago now.

'Jesus, Logan,' he said aloud. 'Get over yourself.'

His voice sounded too loud in the quiet of the room. He swivelled his feet out on to the wooden floor and lifted a complicated-looking remote control panel from his bedside table. He touched the screen and it glowed a soft blue. Still rubbing sleep out of his eyes, he fiddled with the remote for a bit, said fuck a few times and then found what he was looking for. There was a low-level electric hum and the curtains started to slide back from the floor to ceiling glass panels that made up the exterior walls on two sides of the flat.

He padded barefoot to his wardrobe and pulled on a skanky old sweatshirt, jeans and a woollen beanie hat. Then he walked to one of the windows and pulled the door back, still amazed at how light such a big piece of glass and steel felt on the slick runners. He stepped on to the wooden decked balcony sixteen floors up and looked out to the south side of Glasgow from his place in the Pinnacle building at the end of Bothwell Street.

He loved this flat, even though the mortgage was crippling

him and he'd had to sell his beloved old Merc to finance the deposit. Driving a five-year-old Ford Focus wasn't quite his thing. But you had to make sacrifices in life.

'I hope you're not putting yourself on Queer Street with this mortgage,' his mum had said.

Logan wasn't quite sure where Queer Street was, geographically speaking, but it had certainly felt as if he was on it each time he'd checked his bank statements since he moved in six months ago.

He leaned on the steel railing and blew a long, white breath out into the frigid February air. He was glad for the hat but his toes tingled as the frost on the deck melted under his feet.

The old feelings stirred by the dream bubbled just beneath the surface and Logan drew in a sharp lungful of the cold air to clear his head. He pulled the hat off and ran a hand over his close-cropped hair, turning when he heard the cat's claws clicking on the deck. The old girl jumped on to one of the wooden patio chairs and curled into a ball.

'Coffee, Stella?' he asked.

The cat eyed him contemptuously, purred heavily and then went to sleep.

'Suit yourself.'

He smiled at the memory of the day the cat had wandered into his old garden flat through the open back door while the boys were round for the football. After a six-pack of Stella Artois each, she had her name.

Logan walked to the open-plan kitchen area and turned the coffee machine on, then picked up his acoustic guitar and went through to the living area to wait for the coffee. He'd wanted to learn how to play when he was a teenager but never had the patience back then. He'd started taking regular weekly lessons about a year ago and could now at least play a tune and even throw in a bit of a solo. Sitting on the couch, he strummed through a few bars of a Kings of Leon song and then got up to have his coffee.

He filled a big mug with coffee and milk and went back out to the deck. His attention was drawn to the Kingston Bridge on his right where two marked police cars were whipping over the River Clyde below with their blue lights strobing out into the dark of the morning. It was eerie watching them without the accompanying sirens and he guessed they didn't need them when there was no traffic around. He followed the blue pulse of their progress south and sat on the chair next to Stella. The cat half growled, half purred (grurred?) when he stroked her head.

'Looks like somebody's in trouble,' he said to the disinterested cat.

2

5.15 a.m.

'Shutthefuckup.'

That was how it sounded to her, like one word. She tried to breathe but it hitched in her throat and another sob broke free.

'Shutup. Or I hit you again.'

He had a strong accent but she didn't know where he was from – not any of the places she'd been with her mum. She tried another breath and almost retched on the stink of sweat and blood in the van.

They killed my mum.

She squeezed her eyes tight shut, trying to block out the things in her head – the sickening sound as they hit her mum again and again and blood splashed on the floor. She's dead, she thought. She'd never seen a dead person before but that didn't mean she was wrong.

They killed my mum.

The van hit a hole in the road and she felt the jolt through her broken ribs. The left side of her face was swollen and the numbness in her cheek and around her eye was now giving way to an overwhelming, throbbing pain. The swelling was growing by the second and her left eye was starting to close up.

They killed my mum.

She closed her eyes and tried to tell herself that it would all be okay, that her mum was just hurt like she was. She would get better, the police would catch these men and everything would be back to normal. Or what passed for normal in their nomadic existence.

'I don't like Glasgow,' she'd told her mum when they stepped out of the airport and into the grey drizzle.

'This is my home,' her mum had said. 'This is where I was born. You'll love it when you get to know it, Ellie. I know you will.'

She had cried a lot since then. She missed her old friends in Hong Kong. She missed the heat. And now she was alone.

She blacked out from the pain.

Time passed.

She woke again and her head ached whenever she moved, the swollen part of her face feeling five times its normal size. She could hear one of the men in the front of the car, the driver, speaking into a mobile phone in a foreign language. When he finished, he threw the phone at the passenger and they started arguing loudly in the same language. Sometimes they slipped back into English but she couldn't make out enough to follow what they were saying. It seemed to her as if the driver, who was shorter and fatter than the other one, was mad at the taller one for something.

The tall one turned to look at her, resting his hands on the top of his seat. She saw that her mother's blood had dried on his hands and it was now crusted and broken. He was the one who'd caused her mum to scream and choke and she hated him more than she'd ever hated anyone. He saw her looking at his hands and lifted them from the seat, waving them at her. The driver punched him hard in the arm and said something again in the foreign language. He turned round and she was glad that she couldn't see her mum's blood any more.

The two men fell silent and after a while she realised that there was something curled in her right hand. She opened the hand and touched the glossy paper of the photograph with the fingers of her other hand.

Dad.

It was the picture of her dad that her mum had given her when she was six, nearly six long years and a different life ago. She'd had it on the table beside her bed in the house at May Terrace. It was all she had of him. She remembered grabbing it when the man came into her room and she heard her mum screaming across the hall. She'd held it tight in her fist even when he hit her and hit her and hit her.

Silent tears spilled out on to her cheeks. She was a smart girl, that's what her mum had told her. She learned fast.

Lesson one: you make a sound and they hit you.

Lesson learned.

3

6.40 a.m.

'Get the phone, Becky.' Tom Irvine nudged his wife in the back as the phone's shrill tone sounded again. 'Quick, before it wakes the wee man.'

'Okay, okay.'

Detective Constable Rebecca Irvine's stomach dropped out of her body so far she swore she heard it thump on to the floor beside her bed. She grabbed at the phone, missed it, and knocked it loudly into her alarm clock before getting hold of it and putting it to her ear. It was a civilian operator from the operations room at the Strathclyde Police HQ on Pitt Street.

Oh, Jesus. Not on my first day.

'DC Irvine?' a male voice asked.

'Yes.'

'I have a request for CID assistance from a uniformed officer responding to a 999 call at number seven, May Terrace. That's in Giffnock, on the south side.'

Irvine groped in the dark for the notebook she had left on the table before realising she must have knocked it on to the floor when she tried to grab the phone.

'Hold on,' she said into the phone.

She cupped one hand over the mouthpiece and reached out with the other to turn on her lamp. Her husband let out a sharp grunt and rolled away, pulling the duvet off her and over his head. It was too early for the heating to have come on and she felt the chill of the February air. She was pissed off at him, again, and tried to pull as much of the cover back over her as she could.

After finding the notebook and pen on the floor, Irvine waited for a few seconds for her eyes to adjust a little to the light before speaking again to the operator on the phone.

'Say that address again, please,' she said.

She wrote the details in the notebook, checked the time on her clock and wrote that down beside the address.

'Okay, what's up?' she asked.

What's up? Real professional.

'The officer reports a suspicious death at the locus and requests CID attend.'

'Right.'

'You and DS Sharp are listed as on call this morning.'

'I know.'

'I'm calling DS Sharp now.'

'Thanks.'

The line went dead and she put the phone back in its charger.

'Tom,' she said to the shape next to her in the bed, 'I have to go. You need to get the baby up and ready for the childminder at eight.'

'Aw, come on. It's your turn, Becky.'

She sighed and dug her elbow gently into his back. Why did he have to be such a pain all the time?

'Tom, it's my first day in CID and I'm on call.'

'So?'

They had discussed all this last night and agreed it and now he was reverting to his standard petulant self, which had been cute and endearing when they were first going out but was not what she needed today. She pulled at the duvet as hard as she could and he turned to her and blinked against the light.

'There's a report of a suspicious death on the south side,' she told him.

He blinked some more and rubbed at his eyes.

'It's probably a murder, Tom. On my first day. On my first call-out.'

She was surprised at the way her voice wavered on the M word.

'Shit,' he said. 'I'll do it, okay. You get going to your big, important job.'

She looked at him and saw how much he was enjoying winding her up and it was all she could do to stop herself from slapping his smug face.

She got up, showered quickly and dressed in a plain navy

trouser suit with a white wide-collar blouse and flat shoes. As she was checking herself in the bathroom mirror she noticed a spot of baby sick on her jacket and wiped at it with her wet towel. It left a faint residue, but it was the best she could do. The whole time, Tom just lay on the bed adjusting to being awake. The muffled sounds of their one-year-old son coming slowly to life leaked through the child monitor sitting on the floor under the bed.

She sat on the bed and told him to get up and see to the baby.

'I will,' he said, making no move to do so.

Irvine had no time for his crap today and left him there in the bedroom without saying anything else.

She walked out of the house pulling on her winter coat and wrapping a scarf around her neck. She looked along the street as life in this part of Scotstoun began to stir. Tom, who unlike her was a native of Glasgow, told her before they bought the Victorian terraced house that it was in the west end. Now that they had been here for just over two years it seemed like it was just plain in the west. Anyway, only Bohemian student types and wannabe yuppies lived in the real west end of Glasgow these days and at thirty-one she was past that stage in her life.

She got to her car just as the mobile phone in her coat pocket buzzed, the screen display telling her it was DS Jack Sharp.

'Jack?'

'Becky. Welcome to Strathclyde CID.' He didn't sound cheerful. 'Where are you?'

'Just leaving home.'

'You know the locus?'

'Yeah. Tom and I looked at a house there before we bought ours. Too expensive.'

'Lucky for you, eh? Okay, I'll be there in about forty minutes. How about you?'

'Depends on the traffic. Probably less than that.'

'See you there, then. Good luck.'

She opened the boot of her car and checked the bag with her kit in it: gloves, tape, evidence bags and production labels. All set.

'You go, girl,' she told herself.

She sat huddled in the car while the blower warmed up and started to clear condensation from the windscreen, looking across the street at the lights going on downstairs in their house and wondering how her life had ended up here. She and Tom had been through a tough time before the baby arrived and she thought he'd maybe even had an affair with someone at his work, though he denied it. She had hoped that the baby might go some way towards solving their problems. Now she realised she should have taken more notice of the advice her (single) best friend gave her – that the baby would more likely kill their relationship than cure it. That's how it felt now, and after Tom's behaviour this morning she couldn't see any way back.

Irvine opened the glove compartment and pulled out a CD, turning it over in her hands and looking at the picture of the band on the back cover. She'd gone out with the singer when she was nineteen and he had just started the band with his mates. She never expected them to achieve anything, but now they were a success and she took a slightly guilty delight in listening to them alone in the car. She never entertained thoughts of having stayed with the singer because she was sure it would never have worked between them, and when she saw stories of his drug excesses in the tabloids she knew she was right. But Tom didn't know about that relationship and playing the CD was one of her few secrets. Every girl needed secrets.

She put the CD in and turned the volume up over the noise of the blower, losing herself for a short few minutes in the soundtrack of her old life as the condensation evaporated and the world outside slowly revealed itself.

4

7.30 a.m.

Logan called Alex Cahill after his shower. Cahill was, as usual, impossibly alert at this hour. Logan thought he bordered on being preternaturally perky and told him so.

'Fuck off.'

Standard issue Cahill response.

'You up yet?' Cahill asked.

'Been up since five. Just couldn't wait to see you again, I guess.'

'So, we all set to meet this guy and take his company?'

'Sure. But this other thing with Bob is set to kick off today, so . . .'

'So you're going to ditch your old buddy with the little deal and chase the big bucks. You really want that partnership so bad you would sacrifice what we have together?'

'Well, yeah. I would.'

'Fuck you. See you outside the office at eight thirty.'

He hung up loudly in Logan's ear.

Cahill was one of Logan's first clients – a Colorado native who decided to make the switch to Scotland when he fell in love with and married a Scots girl. She was a nurse and they met while she was in Denver on a government-sponsored research trip studying American nursing practices. Now she stayed at home full time with their two kids while Cahill ran a security business from pretty swish offices at 123 St Vincent Street.

Logan first met him at a birthday party for Cahill's wife, Samantha, six years ago when Logan was dragged along by his then girlfriend, an old school pal of Sam's. It was just one of those things. They got to talking and the next day Cahill phoned Logan to set up the deal for a small security firm operating out of East Kilbride. It was the first of three such acquisitions for Cahill's fledgling business and the current one was going to be the biggest yet. They were friends first; business came a distant second.

Logan was making the final pass to finish off the knot in his tie when Bob Crawford called.

'Logan. You all set for today?'

He sounded hyper, which was pretty much how he always sounded. Crawford was the youngest partner in Kennedy Boyd and had managed his career with the precision of a laser-guided smart bomb. He made partner in six years and now had all that went with it – kids in private school, a big house in Pollokshields (Glasgow's footballers' wives territory, he would say with pride) and a recently purchased Porsche

Turbo. Logan and Crawford were close to agreeing a settlement on a deal Crawford had brought Logan in to handle – the biggest of Logan's career so far.

'Sure, Bob,' Logan said. 'I have this thing with Alex this morning but give me a ring in the meeting room and I'll make my excuses.'

'Okay. Are you and Cahill still running those tired old power games on unsuspecting lawyers?'

'It works.'

'Good, good,' Crawford said, sounding distracted. 'Listen, I'll see you later.'

'Hey, you'll never guess who was in my bed last night.'

'Who?' His mind was on something else.

'Penny.'

'Are you taking the piss, Logan?'

'Yeah, sort of. I had a dream and she was in it. Kind of freaked me out.'

'It would. I mean, considering how she left you. I'd have gone mental.'

'Anyway, when was the last time you heard from her? She was in Hong Kong or something?'

'That was a while back,' Crawford said dismissively. 'Maybe a year and a half. I don't know where she is now. You should just let it go already, Logan. You hear me? She tore your heart out and you still want to go back for more after all this time.'

'You never forget your first love, Bob.'

'I did. Bitch dumped me for someone else and started sleeping with him before she finished with me.'

'That's harsh.'

'Look, I have to go now. Kids are up and Rachel is screaming at them. See you later.'

Another loud hang-up.

It kind of pissed Logan off that he had to play second string to Crawford, but he knew he couldn't really complain about it. They had been in the same year at university and while Crawford was zeroing in on his career with a frightening level of focus Logan took a gap year after he split from Penny travelling round Europe and Australia, funded by shit jobs in low-rent restaurants. At least he could take some small pleasure from calling Crawford Bob, which Crawford hated. He tried hard to get everyone to use his Sunday name – Robert – but no one ever did.

Logan finished the tie and put on his best suit, five hundred pounds' worth of Hugo Boss's finest. The bill for it was still loitering on his already overextended credit card.

'If you could see me now, Penny,' he said to the mirror. 'You'd laugh your fucking head off.'

He smiled at the memory of her laugh and headed out of the flat.

5

7.40 a.m.

Irvine arrived at the house before DS Sharp. May Terrace was an odd little dead-end street, a short row of early twentieth-century terraced houses facing a railway line and bounded at the rear by a newish-looking sports club. The trees this side of the tracks usually obscured the railway line from view, but in the middle of winter the leaves had migrated and as the commuter train rumbled and clanked slowly past, pasty faces stared out at the grim drama unfolding in the terrace.

Irvine showed her warrant card to a female uniformed officer at the entrance to the street and slowed her car to a stop outside house number three. Another uniform, an older man, was posted at the gate at the foot of the path leading up to the door of number seven.

She was terrified. Not of seeing the body, because most cops in Glasgow got to see a body before too long and almost all had witnessed the results of a serious assault on a standard issue drunken Saturday night in the city centre. What scared her was screwing up.

There was so much responsibility at a murder scene – if that's what it was. The chain of evidence had to be preserved, so anyone coming into contact with an evidence bag had to sign the label. A break in the chain was a serious fault that might be exposed at trial. And the integrity of the scene had to be carefully preserved until the scenes of crime team had completed their examination and the body had been removed.

She reached the gate and held up her ID again.

'DC Irvine, CID.'

The uniform scanned the ID and nodded.

'Were you first to arrive?' she asked.

'Yes.'

'Is someone securing the rear of the property?'

'Yes, PC Wilson. He was with me when we attended in response to the emergency call.'

'Can you tell me what you found, Constable . . .'

'Jones. Well, we arrived and the neighbour from number five who made the call came out and met us in the street. She said she had heard a couple of screams in the early hours and some loud noises. And maybe a diesel car or truck starting up and driving away. She couldn't be any more specific than that. I approached the front door and found that it was unlocked. I knocked on it and called out for someone to respond. There was no response, so I opened the door and entered the inner hallway. PC Wilson was behind me.'

'Okay, what did you do once you were inside?'

'We went into the first room on the left, the living room with the window there.' He turned and pointed at the front of the house. 'I immediately saw the body of a woman on the floor. She was naked and her face was badly bruised and swollen. There was also a large volume of blood on the floor around her head. I asked her to respond and when she did not I checked her for signs of life and found none. Then I called it in.'

Cops always used that over-precise language and Irvine suppressed a nervous impulse to laugh.

'Thanks,' she said. 'Do we have a name yet?'

He fumbled at the notebook in his back pocket and flipped through a few pages.

'Penelope Grant.'

She looked round at the sound of another car slowing up at the entrance to the street and recognised Jack Sharp's battered old motor. She walked towards it as he pulled the car to the side of the road behind hers. Sharp was her senior and would take the lead in the investigation. He was around fifty, slim, bald and very neat – except for his car. It was a shambles inside and out. She didn't understand why.

'Morning, DC Irvine,' he said. 'What do we have?'

She explained it all just the way the PC had done for her. Sharp rubbed his chin, still bearing a little shaving rash, and looked down the street to the house.

'All right then,' he said. 'Tell me what we have to do?'

She rubbed her hands together to heat them up. 'We call the pathologist at Glasgow University to attend and formally pronounce life extinct. At the same time, we notify the scenes of crime lab and request that they attend for an examination. When they're done, we remove the body to the mortuary, and record and take custody of the evidence recovered — clothes et cetera.'

'Good. We also need to set up a log of those going in and out of the house and get an incident room up and running back at Pitt Street. You do both of those things and then we'll be all set. Slow and steady, Becky, and you'll do just fine.'

She knew he was right, but did he have to be such a condescending prick in the process?

'Have you been in the house yet to check the body?' Sharp asked.

'Eh, no. No, I haven't. I thought that, you know, we should leave it intact for the lab team. Shouldn't we?'

Sharp lowered his glasses and peered over the frames at her. She didn't think he could be more of a prick if he tried, but she held her temper in check.

'You trust a uniform to establish that the victim is dead?'

She sure did. More than she trusted Sharp, anyway. He took her silence as compliance.

'I don't either. So we'll double check and then start the process. We don't want the pathologist getting a shock when the victim wakes up and asks why a thermometer is sticking out of her arse, do we?'

Irvine felt he was overfond of the rhetorical mode of questioning. He turned towards the house and she followed him, keeping her head down when they passed the PC at the entrance.

The smell of blood was strong, even in the short hallway. Stairs went up straight ahead to a half-landing where the bathroom was and then curled back round to the front of the house. The hallway on the ground floor continued to the left past the stairs and led to what she assumed was a dining room and kitchen at the rear. The whole house was decorated in white and cream, with original stripped and polished floorboards.

'In here,' Sharp said, opening the door to the living room.

The woman's body was lying on its side with the arms curled up over the head and the legs drawn up into the body – almost foetal. Irvine thought that perhaps she had done this to shield herself from the attack. It hadn't worked.

Sharp bent down and felt for a pulse in her wrist. He looked up at Irvine and confirmed she was dead. He stood, looked around the room and then ushered her back out into the cold morning air.

'Any thoughts?' he asked once they were outside.

'Looks like she was trying to cover up,' Irvine said. 'To protect herself.'

'Not that it did her much good, eh?' Sharp said.

He walked away from her down the path and out on to the street. She stood in the cold feeling smaller than her five foot six and already regretting the blonde highlights and short bob cut she got at the weekend. She thought it made her look too young for the job, more like thirteen than thirty-one.

6

8.20 a.m.

Another coffee was definitely in order and Logan picked one up at the Pret a Manger just along the street from his building. He was sipping at it as he turned and headed up the hill towards the Kennedy Boyd offices on the west edge of Blythswood Square. Glasgow city centre is kind of hilly – like San Francisco without the American west coast glamour and mythology.

He reached the south-east corner of the square and saw Cahill waiting just outside the office entrance, past the small park that made up the centre of the square. It was a nice spot, especially in the summer with all the local office workers taking impromptu picnics on the grass with their M&S sandwiches. Today, the barren park surrounded by Victorian office buildings looked cold and bleak.

Cahill turned and grinned broadly when he saw Logan shuffling along with his coffee in one hand, belching out a stream of white air, and his battered leather briefcase in the other. Logan only kept the case because it was a graduation present from his mum and she'd had a near breakdown when she saw the new, vinyl replacement he bought last year. She never tired of reminding him how much it cost and how little money she and his dad earned. He had grown up on a council estate in Ayrshire, sharing bunk beds with his older brother until they were in their teens, and he was the first member of his extended family to go to university.

'How's it goin', Atticus?' Cahill shouted.

Logan walked faster until he reached Cahill. 'You just can't help yourself, can you?' he said.

Cahill was a big fan of *To Kill a Mockingbird* and when he first found out that his lawyer's surname was Finch it was too good an opportunity to pass up. Logan considered the book a classic and one of his favourites, but wasn't so keen on Cahill's nickname.

Cahill laughed and swept a hand up through his thick, sandy hair. He was ten years older than Logan and three inches shorter at five nine. Logan thought he looked like Robert Redford, circa *Butch & Sundance* – minus the 'tache. But he never dared say so to him. Cahill had a big enough ego as it was.

'Never be ashamed of your heritage in the law, lad,' Cahill said. 'It's what makes you who you are. Not this stuff.'

He flicked Logan's jacket lapel. Cahill invariably wore jeans or combats and a black polo shirt to meetings – like today.

Logan had seen him twice in a suit and wondered why he didn't wear them more often. He looked sharp. Redford again, circa *The Sting*.

'Yeah, thanks, Dad. You stick with your video store outfit and I'll go with Hugo every time.'

'You're so shallow. It's what makes you such a great lawyer.'

'So, we all set for this deal?'

'Absolutely. I know this guy. He's a big fucker but he's got no balls so it should work out just fine.'

Whatever got the deal done.

The ground floor of the office building, several old blond sandstone townhouses combined as one, housed the suite of meeting rooms. The largest one at the front had every gadget you could wish for: a projector and screen recessed in the ceiling, DVD and video players, video and phone conferencing, internet access, wi-fi functionality for laptops, a Linn stereo and a fridge with a couple of bottles of champagne (for those deal-making celebrations) and a whole load of beer (for the late night/early morning negotiations). The others were smaller and less well equipped, but still top drawer.

Megan, the receptionist, was just about the nicest, most chipper person you could want front of house. But that didn't mean you could fuck with her meeting room allocation. That was just wrong.

'Hi, Megan.' Cahill smiled. 'Where are we today, my love?'

'I booked the fancy one, just for you, Mr Cahill.'

'When are you going to start calling me Alex, huh?'

'How about when the Americans elect another Bush to the White House?'

Logan smiled and left Cahill there, heading up to the first floor to see Crawford. He found him behind a pile of paperwork in his office at the front of the building. Crawford was not happy and his face looked pinched. It was not a good look for him, exaggerating his long, narrow face, dark floppy hair and slightly too big nose.

'Look, what time do you think these guys will be in?' Logan asked.

'I don't know. You know how they are. They just said, "See you tomorrow morning," and that was that. I'll let you know, okay. Go have fun with your mad pal.'

Cahill was fiddling with the projection screen remote control when Logan found him in the meeting room.

'I know I said this before, but this would be fucking great for a big action movie.'

Logan told him to stop messing about with the gear – it was expensive.

Their opponents appeared twenty minutes later. The lawyer was a slick guy of about forty with sculpted hair and red braces. Logan didn't like him. It was mainly the hair. His client was a bear of a man, easily six four and with giant shovels for hands. Even so, Logan figured from the frown on his face when he shook hands with Cahill that he lost that particular challenge. Cahill grinned the whole time.

'The offer is totally unacceptable, verging on insulting.'

This was the hair's opening gambit.

Cahill stood and stretched, the muscles in his chest and shoulders barely contained by the cotton polo shirt.

'Fuck off,' he growled.

Jesus, it was starting early this time.

7

10.00 a.m.

Irvine co-ordinated the house-to-house inquiries in May Terrace and the surrounding streets while the scenes of crime team went to work inside. Sharp played the big man and spent a good twenty minutes telling the forensic people how he thought they should do their job. Irvine did not think this was a partnership that was going to last.

Despite having seen this kind of thing before, she felt out of place this morning watching the men and women clad in white full body coveralls move in and around the house while uniformed officers went from door to door. She felt detached from the whole thing, as if she was watching a hideously realistic film. She hoped it was just first day nerves.

The pathologist had arrived just before the scenes of crime vans and spent little time pronouncing death. He then disappeared, mumbling something about letting him know in advance when the body was going to be transported to the mortuary so that he could be ready for the post-mortem.

One of the neighbours, a serious-looking middle-aged woman in a business suit, was serving hot coffee to anyone who wanted it and Irvine was only too happy to take her up on the offer. It seemed to be getting colder as the day went on, as the early low cloud cover gave way to a startlingly blue sky. A mild breeze was picking up and rapidly becoming a nagging, bitter wind.

She sat in her car sipping the coffee with the door open and her feet on the ground. Sharp spotted her and came over.

'You holding up, Becky?'

Everyone called her Becky, but coming from him it was starting to sound like an insult.

'I'm fine, Jack. Thanks for asking.'

'Good. Tell me, how's it going with the incident room?'

'It's going fine. Should be ready by lunchtime.'

'Right. Lunchtime.'

Again with the repeating.

'You want me at the mortuary with you, Jack?'

'No, no. One of us will be just fine. I'd really prefer it if you made a start on processing statements from the house-to-house and instituting inquiries on the victim.'

'Uh-huh. And I'll begin notification of the relatives.'

'Yes. You do that.'

Irvine took a long hit from the coffee and breathed slowly through her nose at the same time, willing herself to relax.

A shout from the house made them both look round to see

one of the scenes of crime team looking at them and gesturing frantically for them to come over. Irvine set her mug on the ground and followed after Sharp at a quick jog. They met the man at the foot of the path leading to the front door.

He pulled his mask down under his chin and lifted a pair of clear plastic goggles from his face. There was a sticker with his name on it on the coveralls – *Black, Murdoch*.

'I thought you might want to see this straight away,' he said, handing over a plastic evidence bag containing a photograph in an antique silver frame. 'We lifted it from the living room.'

A single spot of blood had dried on the frame. Sharp frowned, not understanding what he was supposed to see. Irvine saw it immediately.

'Where's the girl?' she said, deliberately not asking where the girl's body was.

'What?' Sharp said.

'It's her daughter, right?' Irvine asked Black.

'Must be. There's a bedroom made up for a girl and it's a mess too. As if there was a struggle. And we found some blood. Maybe not enough for her to have been killed. Not here, anyway.'

'So this isn't just a murder investigation,' Irvine said, feeling slightly winded. She turned to Sharp. 'It's an abduction. We have a dual crime scene.'

For once, Sharp didn't say a thing.

'How come we didn't get this from any of the neighbours?' Irvine asked no one in particular. 'You would have thought somebody would have said something.'

'Maybe nobody asked,' Black said, shrugging.

How long did we lose, Irvine wondered? She hoped the lost time wouldn't make the difference between finding the missing girl alive and not.

'There's this as well,' Black said.

He gave Irvine another evidence bag, this time with a small white card in it. The side facing her was blank, but soaked in blood. She turned it round and read the front.

Logan Finch
Associate
Kennedy Boyd

'Where did you recover this?'

'Under the victim's body.'

'Did it look as if, um, as if it had been deliberately placed there?'

Black's head tilted fractionally to the side.

'Right,' Irvine said. 'How would you know that? Sorry.'

Sharp found his voice again. 'It would appear we have a suspect.'

Black looked at Irvine expectantly. Fuck it, she thought, I'm not going to let this idiot run this investigation the wrong way, even if he is my boss.

'What we have, Jack, is a line of inquiry. At this stage we can't put it any higher than that.'

Sharp took the bag from her and turned it over in his hand. Irvine realised he was embarrassed and just buying time in front of Black.

'Thanks. You can get back in there now.'

Black turned and went away up the path.

'What do you want to do with this, Jack?'

The force was a political machine and it paid to bide your time and pay your dues. She had made her point and there was nothing to be gained from taking it any further now.

'Let's go visit Mr Finch, DC Irvine.'

Boundaries established. Job done.

8

10.25 a.m.

Ellie Grant realised they must have been driving for hours now, but she was exhausted and found it difficult to track the time. She tried to sleep, but whenever she dozed off she nodded forward and the jagged ends of her ribs rubbed sharply together. Her face still throbbed, but at least the swelling appeared to have stopped. Her eye was in bad shape, but it had not closed up completely. Not yet anyway.

Her only comfort was the crumpled photograph still in her hand. She thought she'd lost it the first time she dozed off, but she found it lying in her lap and had held it tightly ever since.

She felt the van slow down sharply and make a right turn. Having spent all that time in it, she'd learned to recognise changes in the pitch of the engine and the texture of the surface under the wheels. This time there was a big difference and the van's wheels slipped and skidded on a loose surface before finding some purchase and steadying. She heard loose chips clatter against the bodywork.

The two men started talking again, their voices rising and the chatter speeding up. Ellie guessed that they were excited about something. Her first, awful, thought was that they were going into a wooded area somewhere and would kill her there. She'd seen enough stories on the TV news to know what happened to young girls who were taken away by bad men.

They never came back.

Mostly.

Tears welled in her eyes and she felt her stomach tighten and something begin to loosen in her bowels. She swallowed hard against the tears and willed herself to hold it all in. A single drop spilled from her damaged left eye and then the urge to cry subsided.

The road twisted left and right and rose and dipped for half an hour and then the van slowed and stopped. Ellie felt the terror rush back in a black tide and didn't think she'd be able to stop herself this time. Then the men opened their doors and stepped outside. Cold air seeped into the van and through Ellie's cotton PJs, the long sleeves and legs not providing much protection.

She heard a door open, like a house door, and then a different man spoke to the two from the van. It gave her mind something to focus on and she concentrated on the voices and pushed back at the tide of fear.

There were footsteps outside and then the rear doors of

the van opened. She closed her eyes at the light flooding in and smelled the brittle air, recognising the scent of pine trees and cut wood. Strong arms went under her legs and back and she was lifted out of the van. She draped one arm round the massive shoulders of the man carrying her and felt his muscles stiffen at the alien intimacy of the gesture. She knew in that moment that she was not going to be killed here. At least not now and not by this man.

She kept her eyes closed and felt the heat of the interior of a building and smelled cooking: bacon and fried eggs. Her mouth filled with saliva. A woman's voice said something in the language the two men in the van had used.

The man carried her further inside, paused to open a door and then set her down on something soft. She spread her hands out on each side and knew that she was on a bed. The man left her, closed a door and clicked a lock into place.

When he was gone, Ellie opened her eyes and breathed more easily, sitting motionless in the dark for what seemed like an age but was actually only a few minutes. It was a small room, no more than nine feet by seven, with a single bed against the wall opposite the door. The walls were made entirely of wood and the one window was at the end of the bed, boarded up with planks of wood with only thin slivers of light spilling through. There was no other furniture in the room. It smelled damp, as if it had not been used for a while, and there were mildew stains on the ceiling.

She heard footsteps outside the room and shut her eyes when the lock on the door clicked open and someone came in and kneeled by the bed. Ellie blinked and the dark shape in front of her resolved into a man. She couldn't make out his features, and realised he was wearing a cap that shaded his face.

'Hello,' he said.

His accent was not like the others'. She said nothing.

'It's not your fault, you know. None of it is.'

His voice was soft but had a bluntness to it that was unsettling. Ellie tried to look into his eyes but could see nothing there in the dim light of the room.

'It wasn't supposed to be like this, but you have to stay here for a few days. You understand?'

She sat still.

'You can say something. I won't hit you.'

She paused, then nodded – I understand.

'But you must do as I say.'

She nodded again. His voice dropped lower.

'If you do not, I will have to punish you.'

Ellie's breath became shallow and she felt sweat beading on her brow. The man reached up and she shrank away from his touch. He put one hand behind her neck and pulled her head forward. He was strong. He brought his other hand up and placed a cool, damp cloth over the shattered portion of her face. It smelled funny, like at the hospital. Then, after a bit, she felt the pain in her face begin to ease a little.

The man took his fingers from her neck and lifted one of her hands to hold the cloth in place.

'If you would like for me to be this way, you must behave.'

This time Ellie nodded. She thought he was American, but

the words sounded strange, as if he didn't quite know what order they should be in.

The man stood and she smelled pine sap on him.

'What's your name?' she asked.

The man paused for a moment. 'You tell me yours first,' he said.

'Ellie Grant.'

'You can call me Mr Drake, okay.' A smile danced behind his eyes. 'Would you like something to eat now?'

'Yes.'

The man turned and left the room.

Ellie began to cry.

After leaving Ellie's room, Drake went down the hall to the main living area. The woman was cooking at a primitive stove and the shorter of the two men from the car was slumped in an old chair watching her while the tall one stood looking out of the window. Drake lifted a knife from the counter top where the woman was preparing the food and walked quickly towards the tall man. As he started to turn, Drake punched him hard and fast in the kidneys. The tall man went down on to his knees, arching his back. Drake kicked him and he fell to the wooden floor, splitting the skin on his chin. The short man sat impassively in his chair, watching the attack with little apparent concern. The woman knew better than to get involved and continued with her work.

Drake kneeled on the tall man's back, pulled his head back sharply and slid the knife under his chin, pressing it into the skin of his throat until it drew blood. The tall man grunted and squirmed.

'You were supposed to bring the woman back alive, you stupid fuck,' Drake hissed in his native Russian. 'What the hell were you thinking?'

The short man had seen enough now. He leaned forward in the chair and placed a hand on Drake's shoulder.

'He's a fucking idiot, Yuri, but the last thing we need is his corpse stinking this place up while we wait for the situation to get sorted,' he said.

Drake turned his head and stared at the short man, his skin stretched tightly over his face and his cheeks flushed red.

'Don't use that name again. It's only Drake now. And where were you when he was killing her?'

The short man sighed and took his hand from Drake's shoulder.

'Nobody told us about the girl, right? I mean, she had to be controlled so I left him with the woman. It was my mistake, okay. We both know he's incapable of controlling himself when his blood's up.'

'It's not the first time he's done this,' Drake said. 'You should have been watching him. Or maybe there was another reason you went to the girl's room, Sergei.'

Sergei ignored the innuendo, sensing that Drake's anger had peaked. He relaxed back in the chair again, holding his hands up and giving Drake his place as their boss.

After they moved from working the streets back in Russia and joined Gabriel's network, Drake had made the international connections that meant he was the right one to lead this job — but it was turning into such a complete fuck-up that his time at the top was likely to be brief. Drake probably knew it too, and Sergei was happy to bide his time until it was right to step up. Then he'd happily be the one to put a bullet in Drake's skull and take his place, no matter how long they'd known each other. There were no true friendships in their line of work.

'What's done is done,' he told Drake. 'We can't change it now and there's no point killing this idiot over it.'

Drake pulled the knife away and let the tall man's head thud back on to the floor before standing up. The tall man pulled himself up and spun to face Drake, wiping at the blood on his chin and throat.

'Relax, Vasiliy,' Sergei said. 'You screwed up back at the house and you're lucky I didn't just kill you and dump you on the way back. One call to Gabriel and you'd be fish food.'

Sergei knew the reference to Gabriel would annoy Drake, undermine his authority.

'Never mind that,' Drake said, glancing at Sergei. 'One more mistake and I'll bury you both. Understand?'

Vasiliy grabbed some paper towels and held them against the shallow wound at his throat.

'Understand?' Drake shouted.

Vasiliy nodded and then brushed past Drake on his way down the hall to the bathroom to clean himself up.

Drake looked down at Sergei. 'Don't talk about Gabriel again,' he said.

Sergei smiled.

'You think you know how this works, Sergei, but you don't,'

Drake said, jabbing a finger at him. 'I mean, this isn't a democracy. You think you can take my place and Gabriel will welcome you with open arms?' He snorted and turned to the window, looking across the water to the other side of the loch.

'So,' he said, with his back still turned to Sergei. 'How are we supposed to put pressure on Finch to complete the deal now that the woman is dead?'

'The girl will be enough for what we need,' Sergei said.

'How is that, eh?' Drake asked. 'Finch has no connection to her. That's what the woman was for.'

Sergei knew he held the better hand and decided to play it.

'In the car on the way here,' he said, 'the girl was in and out of consciousness. She kept calling for her father.'

Drake turned to him, a frown creasing his brow. 'So?'

'So she's got a picture of him in her hand, her father. The idiot took it from her when she was out cold so we could see what it was.'

He paused for maximum effect, enjoying Drake's frustration.

'She's got it back now, but it's a picture of him,' Sergei said, smiling at his small triumph. 'Finch is the girl's father.'

9

11.00 a.m.

Logan was enjoying the spectacle – Cahill in full flow.

'That's not constructive, Mr Cahill,' the hair said.

'In what way is telling you to get the fuck out of this room not constructive? I'd really like for you to explain that to me, Steve,' Cahill said.

'It's Steven.'

'You said that already, Steve.'

Logan knew he had let Cahill off the leash for long enough and that the others were ready for a deal. They'd already shown their weak hand, because the big man had approached Cahill before the lawyers were even involved and let him know that he was willing to sell out.

'Look,' Logan said. 'If you wanted to walk away from this table you would have done it already. Frankly, no one would put up with Mr Cahill's attitude unless they needed to get their hands on his cash.'

The big man did his level best to hold Logan's gaze, but the blush of red under his collar gave the game away. Cahill tensed in his chair next to Logan, ready for the final assault. Logan rested a hand on Cahill's forearm, letting him know that the game was over and he could relax now.

Logan glanced out of the window on to the square and saw two heads bob up and down as they came up the steps to the front door of the office. He had a brief view of a young woman's face under a blonde fringe, her jaw clenched tight and her eyes focused straight ahead. She was attractive, but there was some steel in her gaze.

Cahill leaned forward in his chair and placed his elbows on the light wood of the table. He stared at the hair.

Logan strained to hear the voices of the two visitors in the reception area after the outside door closed hard, gently rattling the sash windows of the room. He thought he heard his name, and then the phone on the sideboard behind him rang loudly. He had a sudden impulse to go to one of the windows, pull it up and open, drop to the street outside and run. The second shrill ring pulled him back into the room. He twisted round in his seat and lifted the phone. It was Megan and she sounded way too polite.

'Mr Finch,' she said.

She never called him that. Not since the first time he had walked through the door of the firm's offices.

'There are two police detectives here and they would like to speak with you. They seem very . . . insistent.'

'Um, thanks, Megan,' Logan told her. 'Can I just have a minute? We're nearly done here.'

The hair bristled at that and shook his head violently. Logan held up a hand, telling him to just chill.

'I'm guessing a minute is about as long as you've got,' Megan said and hung up.

'Steven,' Logan said, turning back to the table. 'It's now or never. We have to leave in less than a minute. What if I draft up the sale and purchase agreement and put in the figure Alex here was just, you know, screaming at the top of his voice? What do you say?'

Silence. Logan looked at the big man.

'And we'll just call it a deal at that. Right?'

The big man nodded almost imperceptibly and stood. The hair looked disconcerted but followed his client round the top of the table and out of the room.

The door swung slowly shut after them and Logan caught the eye of the blonde detective looking at him from reception as Cahill whooped loudly and slapped Logan hard on the back. The flight impulse almost took hold of Logan again. He had no idea why.

'What?' Cahill asked, reading Logan's face.

'Alex, you trust me, right?'

Cahill frowned, the wrinkles in his forehead betraying his real age as the boyishness was replaced by something far harder.

'There are two detectives standing out there with Megan and they are very keen on speaking to me about something.'

Cahill's whole body went rigid and Logan felt the hum of

violence vibrate in the room, like a tuning fork struck against a wall.

'And?'

'I don't know.'

Logan turned and looked down at Cahill and saw the question in his eyes.

'I haven't done anything,' Logan told him, hating the uncertainty in his voice.

The phone rang again and Cahill picked it up. Logan heard a man's tinny voice. Then Cahill spoke.

'He can't do that now, Bob.'

Cahill hung up, put a hand on Logan's shoulder and told him to sit down. Then he opened the door to the reception area and asked the detectives to come in. Logan tried to stand to meet them but Cahill's hand was back on his shoulder and as stiff as a girder.

The detectives walked round to the far side of the table, took out their warrant cards and placed them in the centre of the table. It looked rehearsed, but wasn't. Cahill leaned over and looked at them and then sat next to Logan. The male detective looked uncertain but the woman sat down confidently.

'I'm Detective Constable Irvine, Strathclyde CID,' she said. 'This is my colleague, DS Sharp.'

She didn't look at Sharp when she said his name, but remained focused on Logan.

Cahill nodded, wondering why the junior officer was taking the lead.

'We would like to speak to you alone, Mr Finch,' Irvine

said. 'We're just making routine inquiries into an incident that occurred this morning, but the details are such that it might be best if you—'

'No.'

She blinked instinctively when Cahill cut her off but didn't look at him.

'It would be better if we spoke to you—'

'I said no.'

This time she did look at Cahill.

'DC Irvine has explained that these are routine inquiries, Mr . . .' Sharp said.

Cahill didn't respond.

Logan trusted his friend more than anyone he knew, but he was uncomfortable and felt that Cahill was not helping. He stayed quiet to see how things were going to work out. Cahill always trusted him where legal affairs were concerned and Logan had a feeling that Cahill was in *his* element now.

'Anyway,' Sharp continued. 'There's no reason for Mr Finch not to speak to us. Is there?'

Logan guessed that was the sign Cahill had been probing for – these were not routine inquiries if they moved so quickly to this kind of approach.

Irvine looked at Sharp as if she wanted to slap him. *DS* Sharp, Logan corrected himself. The man was her superior but she was clearly the one to watch.

'Let's be clear here,' Irvine said, speaking to Cahill but looking at Logan. 'Because I want to get off on the right foot so that everyone knows where they stand.'

'Go ahead,' Cahill told her.

She seemed to relax a bit at that and sat back in her chair. Pissing contest over, Logan thought. It would be blindingly obvious to the detectives that Cahill was not a lawyer, sitting there in his combats looking and sounding for all the world like the Sundance Kid. Yet that didn't seem to matter. Maybe what mattered was that they saw in Cahill that he would not be messed with.

'Okay.' Irvine spoke again. 'We are making inquiries into an incident this morning. For obvious reasons I cannot at this stage disclose details, but the inquiry concerns a suspicious death.'

Logan tried to swallow but his throat just dry-clicked.

'A woman died this morning,' Sharp went on. 'And your name came up during the course of our initial investigation.'

'How?' Logan found his voice. 'What do you mean by that?'

'We found one of your business cards at the scene.'

'Okay. If you tell me her name, maybe I'll be able to help. I mean, all sorts of people have my card.'

Irvine sat forward, as if she was going to speak again. But she just looked at Logan, committing his face to memory.

'Penelope Grant,' she said finally.

Logan's heart stopped.

10

11.20 a.m.

Logan's chest constricted and he closed his eyes. He didn't care how it might look to the two detectives sitting opposite. The sounds of the world around him were sucked out, leaving him in a vacuum, silent and airless. Slowly, he became aware of his heart beating again.

THUMP-thump

THUMP-thump

THUMP-thump

But it was a hollow sound now, each beat echoing in an empty chamber.

Sound leaked back into the room. Someone was saying his name, but it sounded alien and unrecognisable to him.

'Mr Finch.'

Logan looked at the woman sitting opposite him. He saw

the intricate details of her face and clothes: the not quite rubbed clean spot of something on the lapel of her dark suit jacket; make-up collecting in the faint crows' feet at the corners of her eyes; the dark roots of her dyed hair; the downy hair on the nape of her neck. He remembered with absolute clarity the burning ember from the fire on that last day and how it sparked and jumped out on to the wooden floor of his flat. He reached out and tried to pick it up, but his fingers closed on nothing but air on the table top.

'Penny,' he said, at last.

'So you do know her?' Sharp asked.

'Yes. I do.'

He was conscious of Cahill watching him closely.

'Did,' he said, turning to face Cahill.

Logan felt all of the long twelve years since he last saw her well up from deep in the pit of his stomach. The emotion rose through him – a huge, choking ball ascending and threatening to tear his head from his shoulders as it exploded out into the air. But he caught it in his throat, a strangled cough the only outward evidence of its awful, black energy.

'When was the last time you saw her?' Irvine asked.

Logan laughed at the absurdity of the question in this situation.

'What's so funny?' Sharp asked. 'A woman is dead, Mr Finch, and we really need to have some answers.'

Logan ignored Sharp and looked again at Irvine. Her face had softened.

'Tell us,' she said.

Logan wiped at his mouth with the back of his hand. He didn't trust his voice not to break, but spoke anyway.

'Twelve years ago.'

He coughed again and felt some of the pressure in him ease.

'That was the last time I saw her, Detective Irvine. She walked out of my flat on Byres Road. I stood in the rain, shouted to her that I loved her and that was it. We had both just graduated and were . . .' He tried to think of the right word. 'Celebrating.' He smiled unconsciously at the euphemism.

'What happened?' Irvine asked.

'Well, you know, I heard later from one of her friends that she'd been planning for a few weeks to leave Scotland and look for a job overseas. See some of the world. But she didn't really keep in touch with anyone after that. Last I heard she was in Hong Kong working for some big construction firm over there and earning a small fortune.'

'Why didn't you try to find her?'

'Why would I? She made it clear what she wanted, or rather didn't want, out of life. Plus, I was young at the time and too proud to go chasing after her. When I grew up, well, it was too late then.'

He breathed in for what felt like the first time in the last few minutes.

'I guess it's really too late now.'

Sharp started to speak again but Irvine cut across him.

'How did you find out she was in Hong Kong?'

Logan hesitated. He didn't know why. But in that instant

he knew he had lost some of Irvine's sympathy as her cop instincts kicked in.

'I, um, can't remember. Somebody told me.'

'Who?' Her voice was tighter now.

Crawford.

'I really can't remember.'

He saw in her eyes that she recognised the lie, but decided to leave it for now.

'Okay, well, thanks, Mr Finch,' she said, rising from her chair. She took a card from her coat pocket and slid it across the table in front of him.

'We'll be back in touch when we have more information to go on,' Sharp said. 'It's early days yet.'

It sounded like a threat and Irvine looked annoyed with him. She walked to the door and opened it without saying anything more. Sharp looked a little startled and followed her out into the reception area.

Cahill put a hand on Logan's chest to stop him following them and closed the door firmly. The water in the jug on the sideboard trembled at the force of it. Cahill then stepped up into Logan's face.

'What the fuck are you doing?'

Logan momentarily considered trying to bluff it out but any such thought was consumed in the dark of Cahill's eyes.

'Why did you lie to them?'

11

1.30 p.m.

Cahill chewed very slowly on his Frankenstein burger in the eponymous bar on West George Street and stared intently at Logan, who was toying with the chips on his plate.

'It's been . . .' Cahill paused and looked at his watch, 'oh, about an hour since you said more than two words to me, Logan.'

Logan picked up a lukewarm chip from his plate and glanced at the big plasma screen above the bar. It was showing an MTV channel, but the music playing on the bar's sound system didn't match the video. Logan hated that.

He looked back at Cahill.

'We've known each other, what, five years now?' he asked.

Cahill nodded slowly.

'And in all that time, how many serious relationships have I had, Alex?'

'None,' Cahill said, not even pausing to think about it.

'Right. None. And how many girlfriends?'

He had to think about that one.

'Don't know. Six or seven, maybe?'

'Three. And the longest one lasted less than six months.'

'Where is this going?'

'She . . .'

Logan felt that unreleased ball of emotion well up inside him again and his vision blurred. He blinked it away.

'What?' Cahill asked, his patience running low. 'Tell me about it.'

'I never got over her, Alex. I mean, I think she was the one. And I know how corny that sounds but I don't care because it's how I feel. We never talked about kids or anything like that, but I always thought we'd be together for ever, you know? Get jobs in the city, have a few years on our own, get married and have kids. Buy a big house somewhere and park a Chelsea tractor in the driveway with baby seats in it.'

Cahill watched silently as he bowed his head and ran his hands up and over his hair.

'Fuck. Listen to me.'

Cahill pushed his plate away and leaned back in his chair. 'If it was all so good, what happened? Why did it end?'

'I don't know. I really don't. I mean, I knew that something wasn't quite right between us but it just seemed like a temporary thing. Then she was gone. She broke off contact with pretty much everyone she knew. She was an only child and lost both her parents after school so she was always a bit of a loner anyway. But there was just no warning and no explanation.'

'Another guy?'

'No. I don't think so. I would have heard about that. She didn't just leave me, you know. She left the country.'

Cahill paused before he spoke again.

'Logan,' he said, 'why didn't you tell them who told you she was in Hong Kong?'

'I don't know. It's just . . . I just couldn't get the name out and then it seemed like I shouldn't say it. I can't explain it.'

'I don't remember you telling me about it.'

'I didn't. I don't talk much to anybody about her any more.'

'Uh-huh. Who was it?'

'Who was it that did what?'

Cahill leaned forward again. A group of five young lawyers from Logan's firm came loudly into the bar and nodded over at them.

'Who told you she was in Hong Kong?'

'It was Bob Crawford.'

Cahill frowned.

'Bob and I were at university together,' Logan explained. 'I was closer to him back then and we kind of hung out together so Penny was around him and got to know him. We're not so close any more. He said she called him one day last summer. Said she was having a great time over there and how it would be good to catch up next time she came home. That she might think about working over here again and needed to re-establish some ties. Bob told her I worked here and that kind of killed the conversation.'

'You really haven't spoken to her in twelve years?'

'Yeah.'

'Boy, she really fucked you up. Explains a lot.'

'Like what?'

'The whole hermit in the sky crap you've got going with that new apartment of yours. You live with a cat called Stella, for fuck's sake.'

Logan managed a smile. 'I like that cat.'

Cahill relaxed a little and tapped a finger on the table in tune with the music. He looked up at another plasma screen on the other side of the bar, suspended under the mezzanine balcony.

'That's the wrong video,' he said. 'I fucking hate that. Why can't they show the same song?'

Logan started to laugh but stopped when Cahill frowned at him.

'You're a difficult guy to read, Alex.'

Cahill dropped his eyes and took a sip from his bottle of cold beer.

'No, I'm not,' he said. 'Maybe you just don't know me too well.'

'I realised this morning that I don't know the first fucking thing about you,' Logan told him. 'Alexander Cahill, international man of mystery.'

'So why do you come over to my house to watch proper football, American style, drink my beer, eat my food and play with my daughters?'

'Tell me about the girls.'

'What's to tell? You know them. Couple of little tearaways. Scream the fucking house down if Sam tries to put a skirt on them.' Cahill smiled.

'Are you different now, since they were born? Do they change you?'

'Let me tell you something. Having kids changes everything. Your relationship with your wife is never the same again. You can't just slip into the shower and surprise her on a Sunday morning without one of them waking up. It's like they have little sensors built into their brains to detect that shit.'

'I'm not asking about that stuff.'

'I know. Of course they change you. Used to be when I was out on . . .'

Cahill stopped himself and looked away for a second before he continued.

'You can't think about yourself any more. They have to come first. You're responsible for shaping their minds and their personalities. You get to determine who they will be in the world by how you raise them. You can't know how that feels until you go through it.' He lifted the bottle to his mouth and drained the last of the beer. 'There's nothing like it in the world when I open that door at night or after I've been away overseas for a few days and they come running and jump up into my arms. It's a different kind of love that you only get from your kids.'

'But, I mean, doesn't the responsibility scare you?'

'It fucking terrifies me. What if I screw them up and I

don't even know until it's too late? Until they stagger in the door at eighteen, high on some shit and black and blue. But you know what's worse?'

'What?'

'The fear of losing them. I ever tell you how we lost Jodie one summer?'

Logan shook his head.

'We were on a beach in southern Spain with Sam's parents. First day there and just trying to chill, to unwind. I lie back on a towel, pull a Broncos cap over my eyes and doze off for a minute. Sam and the folks are unpacking the drinks and food for lunch. Jodie, she's five then, is playing in the sea with Anna. They're both right there in front of us, ten or fifteen yards away. And it's not a busy beach. A little crescent-shaped cove in early season.'

Logan watched Cahill's eyes lose focus as he remembered.

'Next thing, Sam is shaking me awake and asking where Jodie is. Anna is sitting where she was, laughing as the waves lap up and over her little feet. She was two. Jodie is gone. I'm the calm one, so I get up and tell Sam's dad to go in the water and check to see if he can see her. I don't say it out loud, but she can't swim and my first thought is that she's been caught by a current and dragged under. Your first reaction is to think the worst. You don't think, you know, that she's just wandered up the beach 'cause she saw a donkey a little further down. You think she's gone under the water or that some fucker has snatched her. So I head along the beach a bit and then back the other way, shouting her name. Sam's losing it and some of the other people on the beach are asking what's up and can they help. We form a little posse and everyone goes looking for her. After five minutes my reserve is starting to crack. Sam's crying her heart out and her mom just can't console her. I'm thinking, this doesn't happen to me. I can take care of this shit. It's what I do.'

He stopped talking and Logan wondered if his friend had revealed more about himself in the last ten minutes than in the previous five years.

'I start walking along the beach again, kind of lost now, and I see one of the posse walking towards me waving. He's only fifteen – a skinny kid – but he's got a hold of Jodie and she's bawling. Then she sees me and she runs and grabs hold of me so tight I had bruises for a week. I lifted her up and carried her back to Sam. And you know what the worst of it was?'

Logan shook his head.

'She recovered in about half a minute and ran back to her sister to play in the sea. She hardly even gave Sam a proper hug, and she was a wreck.'

Cahill laughed hard as the waitress serving them set the bill down on the table and went away again.

'What if something had happened to her?' Logan asked. 'What would you have done?'

'I don't know, Logan. I really don't. I struggle to think about how I'd get through the day if we lost one of them. But I can tell you this: if someone had snatched her or had done her harm, I would not rest until I had hunted that motherfucker down and torn him limb from fucking limb. Someone comes after one of mine . . .'

He didn't finish the thought.

Logan began to think that maybe he was better off not really knowing too much about Cahill. He was one scary individual.

12

2.00 p.m.

Ellie woke when the door to her room opened again. She was glad to have had some sleep and a little respite from the pain, but it had been broken and filled with dreams of her mum and the events of the morning. She tried to sit up and the pain in her ribs was like a knife slowly sliding into her flesh. She gasped and lay still on the bed.

Drake – the man she thought must be the leader – came in and set a tray on the floor. He wasn't wearing a cap this time and she could see the sharp contours of his cheekbones.

The tray had a bacon sandwich and a glass of milk on it. There was also a kidney-shaped metal tray with a syringe. She heard voices in the other part of the house – the two men who took her from May Terrace and the woman.

Drake kneeled beside the bed and asked her how she felt. She looked at him but said nothing.

'If you are in pain, I can help. I can make it all better.'

Ellie wanted the pain to go away. 'It hurts in my side,' she told him, her chin trembling with emotion.

'That's all right. I have medicine.'

He reached down and lifted the syringe from the tray. Ellie closed her eyes until he was finished because she hated needles. She clenched her teeth when she felt the cold metal bite into her skin and the drug flowed into her.

'Eat up, now. You have to stay strong. If you do not eat, you will become much more ill. I do not want that to happen.'

Again, Ellie was struck by the oddly precise language he used. She nodded and he helped her to sit up before placing the tray on the bed beside her. Then he stood and left.

She ate quickly, savouring the food and enjoying the gentle high as the drugs now coursing through her bloodstream started to go to work.

'I don't understand why Finch had to get involved in the deal in the first place,' Sergei said. 'I mean, we didn't need him. If he wasn't involved we wouldn't be having to deal with all this crap about where the money comes from.'

Drake sighed, bored at having this same conversation again. He thought that Sergei did it just to rile him, and it worked.

'Like I said before, Sergei,' he said. 'I only met Crawford with Gabriel. Crawford was the one who brought Finch in on it.'

The woman sat beside Vasiliy on the couch, aware of the power struggle going on between Drake and Sergei and tired of it after all these years. It was supposed to have been different when they got off the streets and joined up with Gabriel. But Sergei was never going to be content until he was the leader, and he let Drake know that whenever he could.

She knew Sergei was still scared of Drake, of the level of physical violence he was capable of. But he was growing braver in his challenges of late and it worried her. The last thing she wanted, that any woman wanted, was to be left with Sergei and his . . . appetites. They would all have to be careful to make sure he was never alone with the girl for long, because if they lost her they would have no more leverage.

'Maybe if you had more control over things we wouldn't be in this mess and Gabriel would have his money,' Sergei said.

Drake went to the sink and poured himself a glass of water, trying to keep his anger at his old friend in check.

'It will benefit us all if we stick together and work through this,' he said. 'So why don't you do what you're best at, Sergei, and say nothing. Leave the thinking to me and Gabriel.'

Turning to face Sergei, Drake saw the man's cheeks burn red and sensed the anger rising in him. Go on, Drake thought, try it. Let's see once and for all who's the strongest.

Sergei shifted in his chair but made no move to get up. 'Leaving the thinking to you was what got us in trouble,' he said. 'If we'd kept the money trail simple Finch would never have known and he would not be making problems for us.'

'We had to switch it, Sergei, you know that. If you're

spoiling for a fight, why don't you just say so and we can go outside and settle it like men, the way we used to do.'

Sergei stared at him, but did nothing.

'I thought so,' Drake said, turning the tap on and rinsing his glass under the hot water.

The woman watched Sergei as Drake turned his back on him. She could see his thought process played out on his face as he appeared to relax and slump back in his chair. He saw her watching him and flicked his tongue out between his lips, smiling at her discomfort.

Ellie sat in silence and tried to listen for any sounds that might help her work out where she was. When the men's voices in the other room died down, she thought she heard water. Not flowing like a river, but gently lapping. Maybe she was by the sea, she thought. But she knew the salt smell of the sea, and it was absent.

Then she remembered the smell of the trees when they lifted her out of the van. Trees and water. A lake? Wait, what was it her mum said lakes were called in Scotland? She squeezed her eyes tight shut trying to remember.

The one with the monster in it, what was it called? She remembered that story from when she was little. The monster called . . . Nessie. Loch Ness – that was it. She had loved that story, in awe at the mystery of the monster swimming around down there. She smiled and closed her fingers to form a fist, celebrating the small victory.

She was beside a loch. She was certain of it.

13

4.00 p.m.

Logan wandered into Waterstone's on Sauchiehall Street for a coffee after Cahill left him. It wasn't far from Blythswood Square and had a Costa Coffee franchise in the basement. He felt in need of a pick me up.

It was just past four when he got back to the office. His mobile phone had been switched off since the detectives left him alone with Cahill and when he got to his desk on the third floor he had seven messages from Bob Crawford, becoming increasingly shrill until the last one was no more than a string of profanities.

Logan walked up to the next floor, looking up to see a light rain falling on the ornate domed skylight in the stairwell. Crawford's office was the first one on the next landing, with a view of the square. He gave Logan a black look when he leaned against the doorframe.

'The fuck have you been?'

'Had a bad day.'

'Fuck you, you had a bad day. How do you think mine was when you didn't show for the meeting? Fucking bad day.'

Logan wasn't in the mood for Crawford's bullshit. He decided right away to give him the bad news and fuck him if he couldn't take it.

'I found out this morning that Penny . . .'

His tongue felt thick and swollen in his mouth and he was again surprised at the depth of his feelings so long down the years.

'That Penny what, Logan? I told you to forget her.'

'That she was back in Glasgow.'

No reaction from Crawford. Logan knew then that this was not news to Bob.

'And that she was killed this morning.'

Crawford's face went white so fast that Logan thought he was going to throw up or faint or both at the same time. He slumped back in his chair looking very small.

'Two cops from CID were here this morning to ask me about it.'

Crawford's face stayed white and his brow furrowed in a frown. He looked to Logan as if he wanted to ask something but couldn't quite form the words in any semblance of order.

'How long have you known she was here, Bob? And why didn't you tell me?'

Logan stepped into the room and closed the door. He had

no idea why Crawford was reacting so badly to the news but it sparked a tiny flame of anger deep inside him and the heat from the flame started to burn white hot.

'Did you see her, Bob?'

And the more obvious thought struck him.

'Were you sleeping with her?'

He stepped up to the edge of Crawford's desk and that seemed to pull Bob out of his shock. A little colour came back into his face.

'No,' he said, his voice almost a whisper. 'I wouldn't have. I didn't.'

'But you knew she was here, didn't you? I saw it in your face. Did you forget I used to be a criminal lawyer? I can read a lie.'

Logan saw in Crawford's eyes the rapid calculation of how much evasion he could get away with and it stoked him up some more.

'Don't screw around with me on this,' he shouted, feeling tears welling up again. 'Not on this, Bob.' His voice was hoarse and he rasped out the last word.

'I knew she was here,' Crawford told him.

Logan slammed a fist into the table, splitting the skin across two of his knuckles. He had his dad's short fuse and capacity to endure pain. He looked at the blood beading on the surface of the cuts and then starting the slow crawl down the back of his hand, his face empty of emotion.

'Look,' Crawford said. 'She told me not to tell you she was coming back. She begged me not to.'

'How long have you known?' Logan's voice was flat and

Crawford sensed the anger bubbling just beneath the surface.

'Six months. She's been here for two but she called me before that. I did a bit of advance house-hunting for her.'

'Does your wife know? Does Rachel know, Bob?'

'Jesus, Logan, listen to yourself,' Crawford said, standing up. 'You sound like a jealous teenager. I was not fucking her. And anyway, even if I am—'

'Was,' Logan said. 'Past tense. She's dead.'

Crawford sighed. 'What's the deal with you and her? I mean, she left you – dumped you. It was brutal and I saw what it did to you back then. So why did you carry it for her? I don't understand.'

Logan lifted a tissue from the box on Crawford's table and wiped away some of the blood on the back of his hand. He wasn't going to get into that with Crawford now.

'Maybe you should get in touch with CID,' he said. 'Before they come looking for you.'

'What does that mean? You think I killed her?'

'I don't know. I think it's been a while since I really knew you, Bob.'

'Fuck you, Logan.'

'Yeah?'

'Yeah,' Crawford, said, veins bulging in his forehead. 'Maybe *you* knew she was here. Look at your hand, Logan. Look what you did here. Maybe you never got over her and when you found out she was back decided to go see her again. Didn't go so well, eh?'

Logan felt the flames surge within him and he was

consumed. His vision blurred red and then white and for a moment he thought he might black out. He felt his legs go weak and he sat heavily in the chair beside Crawford's desk. Crawford sat down too and stared at Logan with a mixture of fear and regret swimming in his eyes.

The rain turned from a soft drizzle to a downpour, rattling off the window behind Crawford, and Logan was again transported to the flat on Byres Road. He wondered if he was capable of doing such a thing. Was he losing his mind? What if it wasn't a dream last night and he had gone to see her? Could his mind be so damaged that it shut off the memory altogether? He wondered if the truly insane were self-aware.

A monster headache began to throb behind his eyes and he pressed his palms into the sockets to try to relieve the pressure.

'I'm sorry, Logan,' Crawford said. 'That was out of order.'

Logan squinted at him through the pain. 'Was it? What if I didn't dream about her? What if my head is fucked and I did go to see her and killed her?'

'No. That's . . .'

'What? Crazy?' Logan barked out a sharp laugh. 'CID came to see me because they found a business card at her house. One of mine.'

Crawford's eyes seemed to lose focus and his pupils dilated.

'I think you should go home,' he said.

'You scared of me, Bob?'

'Go home.'

'What about the guys, the deal?'

'I'll make a call. It's my neck, not yours.'

Logan left the room, unsure which of them was in worse shape.

14

7.00 p.m.

The incident room at Strathclyde Police HQ on Pitt Street, just one street behind the Kennedy Boyd offices, was almost empty. Sharp had left for home five minutes ago and Irvine sat at one of the desks looking at the crime scene photographs in the stark light of a halogen desk lamp. She looked up at the incident board in front of the desk but the names, numbers and lists of possible leads bled into one unfathomable mess. She had Finch's business card in her hand and repeatedly turned it over in her fingers.

She went to the lavatory down the hall from the incident room and splashed cold water on her face. She rubbed at the moisture with a cheap paper towel which just moved it around instead of absorbing it. Her face looked pale and drawn in the mirror, with dark circles under the eyes, and she told herself to get her coat and go home. She wondered if she should call Tom and let him know where she was, but she pushed the thought away, not wanting to listen to him complaining again.

Back in the incident room she found the gaffer, Detective Superintendent Liam Moore, flipping through her notes and the photographs. He was the senior officer on the case which meant he would not be involved on active detective work, but would establish and direct all lines of inquiry. The buck most definitely stopped at his door.

Moore was a fifty-year-old ex-amateur boxer; a heavyweight gone downhill. He still had the thick muscles in his upper body and arms, but also a gut to match, and his pale blue shirt was stretched tight all over. His dark hair had turned mostly grey in the last few years and his preferred hairstyle was a military crew cut. It made him look like the hardest bastard on the force. Which he probably was.

'How you doing, Becky?'

'Tired, you know?'

'Uh-huh. Long day for everybody.'

He closed the notebook on the desk, put his hands behind his head and leaned back in the chair. It creaked ominously under his bulk and Irvine had to curb her maternal instincts to pull him forward and tell him to sit up straight or there would be no dinner for you tonight, mister.

'You look pretty whacked,' he said. 'How are you holding up?'

It was the first time she could remember Moore asking anything remotely resembling a personal question and it surprised her. Her lips parted but at first only a silent breath escaped.

'It's been a tough first day,' she said finally.

Moore nodded. 'You'll get used to it,' he said. 'But it never gets any easier.'

Irvine couldn't tell whether that was supposed to be comforting or not.

'Tell me again about your man, the lawyer,' Moore said, changing the subject.

'Finch?'

He nodded slowly, an indication that his renowned lack of patience was already stretched thin.

'Um, well, not too much to say at this point. We found his card at the locus and he pretty much admitted that he had a relationship with her when they were at university. We checked the records and they both graduated in the same year, twelve years ago. They studied different subjects but we have a list of classmates for each of them that we're trying to chase down to see if they can tell us anything else.'

'And she's an only child with both parents dead?'

'Yes. We found an aunt on her mother's side in Pitlochry but no one was home when the local guys called today. We'll try her again later.'

'Otherwise, she's all alone in the world.' He didn't say it as if it was a question.

'Except for the daughter,' Irvine said, regretting the sharp way it came out before he'd even finished the sentence.

He looked up at her. His eyelids were heavy but his blue eyes were bright even in the gloomy office. 'Yes, except for Ellie.' He looked pensive for a moment. 'She's eleven, right?'

Irvine nodded.

'And the victim and Finch were together around twelve years ago, right? Could be she's his daughter.'

Irvine was sure her mouth must have dropped open in that instant. Stupid. Why hadn't she thought of it? Too caught up with Sharp and his bullshit and too scared trying to avoid making a mistake and not analysing the evidence.

'It would put Finch front and centre in the inquiry, sir,' she said.

She thought it was a good recovery.

'That it would. But let's not waste too much time on unsubstantiated guesswork. Do the legwork on the classmates, speak to the aunt and let's see what we come up with. Also, see if the girl was born in this country and get hold of a birth certificate if you can. Maybe Finch is listed as the father.'

He stood and stretched his six foot three frame, joints popping like gunshots in the quiet room.

'For what it's worth,' Irvine said, 'I didn't get the sense today that Finch is capable of anything like what happened at the house. He seemed a pretty straight guy to me.'

'Okay. Look, I'm running a press conference tomorrow before noon to catch the lunchtime news shows. We're going to get pictures of the daughter out there. Bring Finch in here tomorrow and we'll see him together and tell him about the wee girl before it's public and see how he reacts. See if we can't rattle his cage without that American being there.'

'Okay,' Irvine said. 'What's the plan for that? I mean, I assume you'll take the lead, sir.'

'Yes. We've not worked together before, Becky, so you need to be aware that I can seem like a pretty scary guy when I want to. But it's just an act, right. No matter how bad it might look, I'll be in control, so just work with me.'

Irvine tried not to look intimidated.

'Did we find out who he was, anyway?' Moore asked. 'The American.'

'No, sir.'

'Okay. You get going now and I'll see you back here at eight sharp tomorrow morning. We should be starting to get some lab results by then, and the post-mortem report. Work it the way you were trained, Becky. That's what we do.'

She nodded and he turned, cracking his knuckles one by one and sending shivers down her back. God, she hated that. He asked one more question before he left.

'Do you have children, Becky?'

'Yes, sir. One. A boy.'

'Uh-huh. I have two, both grown up with families of their own now. Don't take me for someone who doesn't care. We all have different ways of coping with these cases. Okay?'

'Yes, sir.'

Irvine was consumed by the thought that Finch was the girl's father as she drove home. She'd brought one of the photographs of the girl with her and had printed off a PR shot of Finch from his firm's website. They were lying on the passenger seat and she kept glancing down at them every time she stopped at a set of lights or at a junction.

She was almost home when she decided to turn round and head back to the house at May Terrace. Maybe something there would give her an answer, something the forensic team might not have thought significant enough to bag and tag for the evidence room.

She pulled up outside the house and saw the uniformed officer standing at the door start to walk down the path to head her off. She got out of the car and pulled her warrant card from her jacket pocket, holding it up for the young PC as they met at the gate. He opened the gate and told her to wait while he unlocked the door of the house.

Irvine shut him out and stood alone in the hall. The smell of blood was still strong and she flipped the switch to turn on the overhead light, thinking that things always seem worse when it's dark. It didn't help.

She went upstairs, figuring that the best place to look would be the girl's room, and pushed at the half-open door. The forensics had left it pretty much as it was, with the duvet still on the floor, but they had taken the fitted sheet from the bed to analyse the blood spatter there. Some blood remained on the wall behind the bed.

There was a little vanity unit under the window painted in a distressed, off-white colour to match the antique cream paint on the walls. Irvine thought it was a pretty sophisticated look for an eleven year old and clearly the mother's taste had prevailed here. She sifted through the drawers in the vanity unit but found nothing so she turned to the wardrobe. It was in the same style as the vanity unit.

Irvine pulled the girl's clothes along the rail to get a better look at each item, thinking maybe it would help if she got a feel for the girl's personality. If these were indicative of her style then it looked as if she was a bit of a tomboy. There were a lot of jeans, some printed T-shirts in various earth tones, one or two skirts and only one summer dress. There were also two light jackets not really suited to the Scottish climate and a couple of quite upmarket-looking tops. At the foot of the wardrobe she found a selection of (expensive) trainers and flat pumps. Okay, so maybe she was a stylish tomboy.

Hats and scarves were on a shelf above the clothes rail and Irvine found what she was looking for at the back, hidden under one of the scarves. It was a journal or diary of sorts, but the girl wasn't the kind to write something every day. It looked as if she only wrote when the mood struck her. Flipping through the book, Irvine got the impression of a pretty switched on girl – her vocabulary was excellent for her age. There were entries about piano lessons and little scribbled segments of music. Irvine didn't play and so couldn't tell if the girl had been copying something she was to learn or creating her own piece. Either way, it made Irvine feel inadequate.

She found a section for photos near the back of the book, but the plastic sleeve with *Dad* written beneath it was empty. She closed the book and as she stretched to put it back on the shelf something fell out of the back of it, fluttering to the floor. She kneeled down and picked it up, cradling it gently in both hands. It was a dried and pressed daisychain, the colours a little faded but still vibrant. As she turned it over, one of the flower heads fell off, breaking it. Irvine opened the book on the floor and carefully tried to put the daisychain back together inside the rear cover of the book. She could tell that was where it had been because there was a faint stain on the paper in the shape of a circle with 'Summer 2003' scrawled in a child's handwriting in the centre. She did the best she could to replace it, but it was broken for good now and she closed the book on it feeling a pang of regret. It clearly meant a lot to the girl for her to have kept it this long.

Irvine left the house and walked down the path to her car, hoping she'd get the chance to apologise to that little girl for breaking the chain, and wondering what happened in the summer of 2003 that was so significant.

When she got home, Irvine stayed in the car for a moment and switched on all the interior lights of her car. She held the pictures of Finch and the girl in front of her.

Maybe.

Tom was giving their son a bath when she went into the house. She shouted up to him that she was going to grab a sandwich and that she wanted to feed the baby his milk. She knew he wasn't really a baby any more, but it was how she still thought of him. She got a grunt in response from Tom.

She sat in the kitchen at an old pine table and chewed slowly on a Nutella sandwich. She liked the stuff better than the wee man did. The photographs were laid out side by side in front of her and she started to work through scenarios in her head as she stared at them.

She recalled Finch's reaction when he heard about Penny Grant's death and was certain it was not an act. And if he had no idea about the girl who might be his daughter he was in for a shock tomorrow when Moore planned to tell him about her. She felt a little anxious for Finch and hoped Moore would not be too rough on him.

She sipped at a glass of cold milk and listened to the two boys in her life splashing around in the bathroom above her, wondering how she would deal with it if something happened to one of them. The thought of not seeing Tom again did not engage any particular sadness in her.

How did it come to this?

15

8.00 p.m.

It was quiet now in the cabin. That was how Ellie had come to think of this place. Earlier, she couldn't tell how long ago, she'd heard a mobile phone ring tone through in the front. Some kind of old pop song that she recognised but couldn't quite remember. The leader, Drake, had answered the call. She recognised the sound of his voice but couldn't make out anything he said. Then she had heard the two men from the van and there was some shouting. After a while, she heard a car start up and drive away, its wheels spinning for a moment on what sounded like grass or mud.

She slept on and off after that, the drug Drake had given her making her drowsy. She didn't care about that because it also took the pain away. But it was dark now and the pain was starting to bite at her again. Thick waves of nausea rolled through her as the discomfort grew. It was worse in her sides, where her damaged ribs were. Her face was okay so long as she didn't move too much or touch it. One time, not long after the injection, she'd put a hand up to her eye socket to feel how swollen it was and a blinding bolt of pain had shot through her. She didn't do that again.

The fear returned with the dark and the pain. She held the picture of her dad and tilted it to find the best angle to see him by. Only very faint blue light from the weak moon drifted in and she could hardly make out anything of him.

She tried to trace the shape of his face in the picture, thinking it might somehow give her comfort, but all she could feel was the cold, dead surface of the glossy paper.

She cried then. For herself and for her mum. Her poor mum who was the best friend she had. She tried to block out the memory of the men this morning and what they did to her, but it was so vivid in sound and vision that it transported her back there.

They had sat together on the couch the night before, drinking hot chocolate and watching one of the Spiderman movies. She loved action movies, not frilly, giggly films about girls. She wanted good guys and bad guys and fighting. Except that in real life it wasn't like Spiderman. Not like that at all.

She'd gone to bed happy and her mum had sat on the bed beside her and pulled the covers up tight to her chin.

'Ellie,' she'd said. 'Do you still have that picture of your dad I gave you?'

Ellie nodded, excited at the mention of her dad and recalling the bright summer day in 2003 when her mum first told her about her dad and gave her the photograph. She knew he used to live here in Glasgow too. And now she was here in the same place.

Her mum looked strange, small lines bunching between her eyes.

'It's there,' Ellie said. 'In the drawer under the table.'

Her mum hesitated and then slid the drawer open in the small table beside the bed. She put her hand into the drawer and Ellie heard the sound of her fingers on the photograph. Her mum sat like that for a while, looking at the picture and moving her hand over it. It was like she had forgotten that Ellie was there.

'Mum. What is it?'

Her mum sniffed hard and wiped at her face. She looked at Ellie and her eyes shone wetly in the warm glow from the lamp on the table.

'How would you like it if we went to see your dad?'

Ellie couldn't speak. Her head felt light and her stomach fluttered and tingled. She sat upright and, without saying anything, hugged her mum as tight as she could.

'Can we? Please, Mum, please.'

'I need to try to speak to him first, okay, honey? 'Cause I haven't seen him for a while and, well, we can't just turn up. But I've been thinking about it a lot lately and it's kind of why I wanted us to come here, to Glasgow. It's why I bought this house. I want this to be a home for both of us.'

Ellie was crying now, salty water coursing down her face and her body spasming against her mum as she tried to breathe.

'Maybe we can be a family,' she said.

'I don't know, Ellie. Let's just see what happens, okay?'

'But,' she said, 'he will want to see me, won't he? He will. He has to.'

Ellie was aware of her mum's tears joining with her own as they sat on the bed on the last night of her mum's life.

Fast forward.

It's dark. She hears a bang and a scream. She's scared.

'Mum,' she calls.

No response.

'Mum!' This time a shout. 'Mum, where are you?'

Her door swings open hard, crashing into the wall and shaking the room. She screams at the sight of the man, shrinks into the corner and pulls the bedcovers up to her face.

More noise down the hall.

'Ellie!'

Her mum's voice, but not like she's ever heard it before.

Then a sickening sound, something no one her age should ever hear – skin and bone splintering together and hot, red life spilling out on to the floor.

Ellie's voice rises to a high-pitched utterance, more a sound than a word. Something ripped violently from her core.

'Muuuuummm.'

Then the man in her room is upon her and hitting her and hitting her.

Ellie sat bolt upright in the bed. She was crying uncontrollably and kicking her feet against the wall of the cabin.

Drake came into the room and pinned her down on the bed, holding her arms tight.

'You must be quiet or I will no longer be nice to you.'

She knew that she should do what he said, but her fear and anger overwhelmed her.

'You killed my mum,' she screamed at him, her saliva spraying his face. 'You killed her.'

Drake reached down to her right side and pressed gently on her ruined ribs. The jolt of pain silenced her immediately and her breath rasped into her lungs through gritted teeth. He sat there, pressing on her, for a full minute.

Ellie closed her eyes and tried to find an image of her mum to cling to, to give her life. But there was none. Then, as she sank into the embrace of black unconsciousness, another image burned bright for an instant. She shouted a word and then was lost to the pain.

Drake released her and stood when he was certain she was out. He checked her pulse. It was not strong, but steady – good. She was all they had now the woman was dead and that meant she had to be looked after while they still needed her.

He left the room and locked the door.

The woman who had cooked Ellie's lunch asked if everything was okay and he said yes.

'She asked for him,' he told her.

'Who?'

'She said dad.'

'I hate this,' the woman said. 'Why did that idiot Vasiliy

have to kill the woman? No one said we'd have to do this to a child.'

Drake sat beside her on the couch, lifted her chin up and kissed her on the mouth.

'It'll be done soon, Katrina,' he said. 'So long as those two can do what's necessary tonight and get the message through to Finch that he needs to co-operate. After that it's up to Finch to do his part. *Whatever* happens next is up to him.'

'What about Gabriel?' Katrina asked. 'Have you spoken to him about it?'

Drake stood and walked to the food counter where he filled the kettle in silence and switched it on. Katrina watched him, unsure if he was angry with her for asking about Gabriel.

'Fucking Sergei wants to take my place,' he said, turning to face her. 'He always resented me when we were running things in Russia, always thought he should be the boss. It's just gotten worse since we joined Gabriel and I got sent to start up the network in the States for those two years. He thinks he can usurp me and this is just the kind of thing he's been waiting for. I mean, maybe he told Vasiliy to kill the woman on purpose just to fuck me with Gabriel. I wonder if he'll wait until I'm asleep and then slide a knife into me.'

Katrina stood and walked to him, placing her hands on his cheeks.

'Then kill the fat bastard,' she said. 'Why take the risk?'

Drake laughed and kissed her. 'You're an evil bitch, you know.'

'What's your point, Yuri?'

He let her use of his old name go. He so rarely used it now that it sounded alien to him.

'Let's get this done and get the money to Gabriel,' he said. 'Then who do you think will be in his crosshairs – me, or the idiot fucks that put this whole operation at risk by killing the woman?'

'You'd best make sure Gabriel finds out about that from you first,' she said. 'It's his twenty-five million and he won't listen to any excuses. We were both there in Paris when he killed the American over that fifty thousand.'

Drake recalled the hot spurt of arterial blood when Gabriel cut the American's throat, and how he had marvelled at the steam rising from the expanding pool of blood on the cold ground as the American gagged his last breath.

'I will,' Drake told her, moving away and lifting his mobile phone from the window sill as the kettle boiled behind him. He punched in a speed-dial number and waited while it rang.

'Hello,' the voice answered in a cultured English brogue.

'Gabriel, it's Mr Drake. We have a problem.'

He looked at Katrina and she smiled nervously back.

16

11.45 p.m.

Logan was drunk – room spinning, grab the sides of the bed drunk. He went straight back to Frankenstein's after the fight with Crawford, stayed there drinking until after ten and then grabbed a Big Mac at the McDonald's on Sauchiehall Street. He wandered up the street a bit and then, after negotiating a surrender of his fries to a couple of neds outside M&S in return for not getting his head stamped on, went on to the Living Room on St Vincent Street for three more beers. Now he was on his way back to his flat. His empty flat.

Except for Stella.

He had a habit of talking to himself when any more than two sheets to the wind.

'Fucking loser, Logan. Fucking all alone with that cat.

Crying over some girlfriend from back when you still had a life.'

A young couple crossed the road to avoid him on the way along Bothwell Street. He was talking pretty loud.

'LOSER!'

He fumbled with his keys and took four attempts to open the main foyer door to his building, not noticing the two big men who stepped in behind him before the door swung shut.

He thought about trying the fourteen flights of stairs to walk off some of the booze, but decided that the lift was the smarter option after all.

'Fall down and break your neck, loser.'

He stood unsteadily in front of the lift doors and the two men leaned back against the wall behind him. It was a modern building with tiled floors and walls, making every sound echo hollow and cold.

'Fuckinglosercat,' one of the men said.

The other one laughed.

Logan turned and looked at them, staring blankly in that drunken way while the brain tries to work out exactly what it is seeing. The two men stared back at him, smirking. One was well over six foot with broad shoulders and thick arms and legs, like a slightly stretched bodybuilder early in his career before the muscles get grotesquely large. The other was much shorter and wider still. They both had longish dark hair that was kind of greasy. Their faces looked like mid-career boxers', doughy and scarred around the eyes.

Jesus Christ.

Logan turned back round and pretended to be immensely

interested in the green light that glowed round the up button.

'Bad day, mate?' one of them asked. He had a thick accent – eastern European, Logan thought, trying to ignore the question.

'Hey, you, I ask if you had bad day.'

Logan turned, figuring it was better to humour them than to ignore them. The questioner seemed insistent. The lift seemed permanently stuck on the ninth floor and Logan was sobering up fast.

'You could say that, yes,' he answered.

'How so bad?'

It was the tall one speaking. The short one just stared at Logan with a fixed smirk, though his eyes showed no sign of mirth. Logan could smell some pretty heavy body odour wafting across the foyer.

'Somebody I know – used to know – died. I'm upset.'

Logan was surprised at how angry he felt now. His fear was fast dissipating and he didn't much like getting intimidated by these two clowns. Of course, the alcohol flooding his system had a lot to do with the rapid shifts in his mood.

'Sad when that happens,' the tall one said. 'How did she die?'

Logan's brain registered something just off about the question, but the booze fog was still screwing with his senses.

'What? I don't know. She just died.'

'Sad.' The short one this time, still smirking.

'How's work?' The tall one again.

Logan just looked at him. The short one moved off the wall and took a couple of paces towards Logan.

Not good.

Logan twisted and looked up at the lift display above the doors.

8

7

6

5

It stuck on five.

He looked back to the main entrance doors and to the street outside. A woman ran past, pulling an umbrella down over her head. He realised for the first time that his suit was soaked and he started to shiver.

'Work,' the short one said. 'How's the deal going?'

She.

That was it. 'How did *she* die?' was what he had asked. Logan never said it was a woman.

He looked back at the lift display.

5

Should have taken the stairs.

The tall one walked slowly towards him, past the short one. He stopped right in front of Logan, who had to look up to see his face. Six five easy, he thought. Maybe more.

'It's sad when someone dies,' the tall one said.

The short one nodded. 'Sad,' he said.

Oh, Jesus.

The tall one brushed at the lapels of Logan's suit jacket with his hands. This time Logan realised that he no longer had his overcoat – must have left it in one of the bars. It's funny the details that seem important in the face of a potentially life-threatening situation.

'I don't know what you want,' he said.

'We want nothing,' the short one said.

'I don't understand.'

'If business is good, we want nothing. You understand?'

Logan didn't. His head felt as if it was filled with jelly and the cold rain penetrated to his bones. He shook even more.

The tall man leaned down until his nose was almost touching Logan's.

'Business was not good today, no?'

Logan wasn't even sure the man was speaking English. He stepped back until his head bumped against the wall. The tall man straightened up.

'Business is going to be better tomorrow,' he told Logan. 'So we hope no one else dies. No one you know. Understand?'

'No.'

The short man stepped up and the stench hit Logan like a fist. His head swam and he bent over with his hands braced on his knees, hoping he wasn't going to throw up or pass out. Something – two things – fluttered down past him and landed on the floor. The short man grabbed his jacket collar and pulled him upright.

'You miss no more meetings, okay? You get the deal done.'

Logan felt that the best course of action was to agree. He nodded, still barely able to breathe, never mind speak.

'Good. Then we are done.'

The two men walked towards the main doors and out into

the night. The lift doors slid open and Logan grabbed the bits of paper that the men had dropped, stuffed them in his trouser pocket and shouldered his way into the car past the departing occupants.

Up in his flat, Logan brewed the foulest coffee the world had ever known and quickly chugged down two steaming cups. Then he stepped into the shower and set it all the way to the hot side. He lasted about a minute and then got out, breathing in short, shallow gasps.

He turned all the lights on in the flat, closed the curtains and turned the heating up full. Even in a fleece-lined sweatshirt, thermal socks and a pair of jeans he sat on his couch shivering uncontrollably for five minutes. Then he remembered that he'd put something in his pocket and searched through his suit jacket before realising it was in his trousers. He pulled out two creased photographs. One was a Polaroid, a kind of arty-looking shot of a near naked woman curled up in a foetal position on a floor. He peered closer to try to make out her face, but red hair hung down obscuring her features. She seemed oddly familiar to Logan but the harder he looked at it, the more distant his thoughts became. He set the picture down and looked at the second photograph.

This one was of a little girl, maybe five or six years old. He was good at guessing kids' ages because his brother had four at various stages of development. In fact, the girl in the shot looked kind of like his youngest niece, Ashley – same eyes. It was a close-up of the girl's face, beaming a gap-toothed smile against the background of a grass field leading to the edge of a small beach. Her hands were held up in front of her face and there was something entwined in her fingers. He held the photo close, and saw that it was a daisychain. Logan couldn't remember the last time he'd seen one, but it evoked old memories of summertime on the estate where he was brought up – playing football using jackets for goalposts, riding his brand new racer bike (a big blue Raleigh Arena) and climbing the trees in the woods to get the best conkers to put string through for playground challenges.

He held the photograph further away again and felt sure it was Ashley.

He grabbed his phone from the table beside the couch and hit the memory button for his brother Craig. His sister-in-law answered.

'Logan,' she said. 'What time is it? Craig's not here just now. He's—'

Logan clicked 'end' and cut her off. He realised it wasn't Ashley, but she looked so familiar. He couldn't stop staring at her wide brown eyes and slightly lopsided grin but put it down to the booze.

He had another cup of coffee standing at the breakfast counter in the kitchen and tried to remember what the two men in the foyer had said. The volume of alcohol consumed and his confusion combined to screw up his memory. He squeezed his eyes shut tight.

Something about a meeting. And about business not being good. Beyond that, he couldn't remember much. He sat on a high stool and drained the last few drops from his mug.

His head started to clear and that finally triggered something for him. They were trying to intimidate him. About a deal? He thought that made sense but wasn't sure he was remembering it right.

Okay, what happened at work today? The Cahill deal with the big man and the hair and dodging Crawford's wide boys. The big man. That must have been it. He wasn't happy about the deal and sent his boys round for a bit of intimidation. Must be. What the hell had Cahill got him into?

He went back to his couch and dialled the number for Cahill's home office; he had a separate line connected to his study. It was after midnight but Cahill picked up on the first ring.

'CPO security.'

It was the name of Cahill's company. Logan lost some of his anger on hearing Alex's voice.

'Logan, I've got caller ID, you stupid fuck, so I know it's you. What's up?'

Busted.

'Um. Nothing. Sorry, I'm just drunk.'

'You want me to come over there? I don't want you taking a dive off that balcony of yours.'

'No. I'm fine.'

He picked up and fingered the edge of the Polaroid photograph of the woman. He noticed that she mostly had brown hair, different from the strands on her face. 'Why were you so aggressive with the cops today, Alex?'

'I was trying to protect you until I knew what it was all about. They probably went away remembering me being an asshole and not much about you. It was a bit of misdirection.'

'Do you think I did something?'

Pause.

'Did you?' Cahill asked.

'That's not an answer, Alex.'

'Let me tell you something, nobody knows anybody. In my business—'

'There's a thing,' Logan interrupted him. 'Just what is your business? What is it that you do?'

'You know. I run security for construction sites and stuff like that.'

'No. That's what the businesses you buy do. I'm asking what is it that you do. You said some things today when you were talking about your kids . . .'

Logan closed his eyes and tried to remember the conversation. Cahill stayed silent.

'Something about being overseas and about it being what you do – looking for people. Wasn't it?'

'I don't remember. We were just talking, Logan.' Cahill's voice had gone flat.

'Just talking,' Logan repeated. 'Right.'

'Why did you call?'

Logan almost couldn't remember. 'Two thugs came by my building tonight and tried to intimidate me into settling your new deal on more advantageous terms.'

'What?' Cahill sounded more surprised than angry. 'No way. You got it wrong, Logan. Must have.'

Logan wasn't so sure any more about anything that had happened in the last twenty-four hours.

'I can't be part of anything illegal, Alex, or it's my career. I'll have my practising certificate suspended and then what am I going to do?'

'It's not about my deal. You're drunk and you're upset. That's all.'

Logan stared at the Polaroid again, pulling it closer to try to make out the woman's features. He wanted to reach into the photo and pull the hair back off her face.

Red hair.

Not brown.

Cahill was talking but Logan wasn't listening.

Logan said goodbye to Cahill and clicked the phone off. He dropped it on the couch and stared at the Polaroid still in his hand. The room appeared to tilt and it wasn't the alcohol doing it. He was suddenly more sober than at any point in his life.

A voice in his head screamed at him to just drop the photo and run.

Slowly, he raised the Polaroid to eye level and then the freight train hit him full on at over a hundred miles an hour, tearing through his body and ripping his soul out as it thundered through the flat and out and up into the night. He didn't want to look at the photo but his mind had become detached from his body and was no longer in control. He pulled it close again and saw now what he had always known, what his mind in its fragile state had tried to block out. It was blood soaking the hair over the woman's face, thick and crimson. And he saw also the dark pool of liquid round her head and the misshapen facial features.

But through all of this, he saw that it was Penny.

Logan dropped to his knees. He opened his mouth but no sound came out. His head filled with noise, like the sound of surging waves. He felt certain that they would crash against the dam of his sanity and that his rational mind would be washed away in the torrential current.

Behind Logan, on the couch, the girl with the lopsided smile and his brown eyes played in the sunshine with her daisychain as he curled up and passed into unconsciousness.

Day Two

1

Tuesday, 6.00 a.m.

The Barrowland Ballroom, summer 1994. Legendary concert venue where, the story goes, the floor is sprung – how else to account for the endless bouncing of the crowd? It's one of those almost unbearably muggy days, when the threat of rain hangs in the air but almost never amounts to anything and your clothes stick to you, glued to your skin with sweat.

Logan is nineteen and single, eyeing up the 'talent' in the queue outside while shuffling forward to go through the security check for the gig. Bob Crawford and two of Crawford's pals are with them, ready for several pints of generic lager in plastic cups to get them oiled for the frenzy that is the front of the 'Barras' crowd. When you're nineteen, you think that the band members are gods and salute their every move. Tonight it's Oasis. Crawford's got their first album and swears they're the best fucking band in the world, man.

Logan's only heard one track — 'Cigarettes and Alcohol' — but thinks it's what Marc Bolan would be writing if he was still alive.

Rock 'n' roll.

They drink at the bar to the side of the stage while the support band, who aren't half bad, get pelted with half full cups of yellow liquid. Logan hopes for their sake that it's lager, but with this crowd you never really know.

Then they're gone and the roadies start getting the stage ready for the headliners. Crawford's big pal takes the lead and they barrel their way to the middle of the crowd, about six feet back from the stage.

The house lights go out and the band swagger on to the stage with a sense of entitlement not seen since . . . ever, actually. The singer's microphone is set high, at a downward angle and he takes up his position under it. Some dry ice curls in from the machines either side of the stage and the opening riff of 'Cigarettes and Alcohol' takes the top layer of skin off those in the front row. Crawford's big pal puts his arms round the other three and they start to jump. Logan thinks, *I fucking love this!*

Five songs in and Logan is drenched. It's the loudest gig he's ever been to and the crowd is packed tight. He's already seen two guys fall down and get pulled up before disappearing under the mob.

'Columbia,' the singer says, announcing the next song.

There's a surge from the right of the crowd and Logan gets forced away from the other three. He feels himself about to fall as the legs of the person next to him give way, but he grabs the shirt of the guy in front and just manages to stay on his feet. He looks round and sees a girl on the floor beside him. She takes an *unintentional kick to the ribs and doesn't look as if she can get up. Instinctively, Logan bends and grabs her around the waist, pulling her upright.*

The stage lights flash white, illuminating the crowd. The girl looks up at him and he's lost. She's small, no more than five three, with a narrow nose and shortish brown hair tied up in bunches at the back. There's a smattering of freckles across the bridge of her nose and her blue eyes are tinged green. She screams thanks in his ear as the crowd surges again. Pushed against her, he feels the soft pressure of her breasts on his abdomen and she puts her arms round him to steady herself.

When the surge recedes, they look at each other and laugh. Then she puts her arm tight round his waist and they bounce together with the rest of the crowd until the last power chord fades from the PA system and the house lights go on.

Logan's hearing is completely gone — like listening underwater to constant feedback from an electric guitar. He still has his arm round the girl and shouts at her if she wants to go for a drink.

'Yeah, sure,' she screams back and he just about hears her.

Logan can't see Crawford and the others and isn't too bothered. She looks for her friends, but it appears likewise half-hearted.

They get outside and start walking towards the centre of the city, away from the pretty rough pubs around the Barras. They talk about the gig and music as they walk and then the first peal of thunder rumbles overhead and the rain comes down in sheets. She grabs his hand and runs, pulling him along and laughing when he trips and almost falls, his arms windmilling as he frantically tries to stop himself from taking the pavement on face first.

They turn a corner and lightning jags down in the west. Logan has no idea where they are 'cause he still lives at home in Ayrshire and doesn't know Glasgow too well, other than the area around the uni.

The girl seems to know where they are and pulls him down a side street and round behind some derelict-looking shops. She leans up against the wall, her clothes soaked against her body, and pulls his mouth down on to hers.

Logan's had a few girlfriends but he's never felt a kiss like this one and he presses up against the girl. Her hands go round his back and pull his T-shirt up and it feels to him like electricity when her fingers touch his skin.

She pushes him back and lifts his T-shirt up over his head, and as he leans towards her she presses gently on his chest.

'This isn't me,' she says, her face serious. 'You understand what I'm telling you?'

Logan leans in until his face is inches from hers.

'I understand,' he tells her. 'It's us.'

He kisses her this time, his hands sliding up under her T-shirt and his fingers brushing gently over her breasts. The kiss lasts for ever and when they break the thunder roars and the rain drenches them.

He starts to pull at the buttons of her jeans and she does the same with his. She looks up at his face and he sees those eyes again before she pushes her hand down inside his jeans and rises up on her toes to kiss him again.

People run past the front of the shops screeching at the rain, but neither of them hears anything as the rainwater courses down their faces. They work as one, sliding their jeans and underwear down, and then Logan turns her to the wall and moves inside her.

After, they go back to the flat she shares with two friends. She leads him by the hand through the hall, past the wide stares from the living room and into her bedroom. She gets towels from the bathroom and they shed their clothes and rub dry with no feeling of embarrassment. They stand together in the galley kitchen waiting for the kettle to boil, wrapped in towels and talking about the exams they've just finished at the end of the university term. Moving back to her room, they sit on the bed watching a portable TV and sipping at the hot tea.

Logan grabs the remote control for the TV and flips through the channels, finding the Hitchcock movie Rebecca *on a late night slot on BBC2. He absently puts the remote down, not even checking to see if she likes the movie.*

'You're not telling me you like this film?' she asks.

He looks at her and sees she's smiling.

'No,' he tells her. 'I love it. It's my favourite Hitchcock.'

She kisses him gently on the lips. 'I'm Penny.'

'Logan.'

'How do you do,' she says, and they both laugh.

Logan woke in the dark lying on the couch. He sat up and saw the Polaroid of Penny lying on the wooden floor and felt numb. Then the hangover drums started in his head and his tongue clicked drily against the roof of his mouth.

He sat up and felt something under his leg. He reached down and pulled out the photograph of the little girl, and

111

stuffed it carelessly into one of the pockets of his jeans.

He picked up the remote control for the flat and fiddled with it to open the curtains. He gave up eventually, went to one of the glass panels, pulled the curtain and the panel back and stepped out on to the decked balcony. It was just above zero and the cold was like a physical force, knocking his breath out in a thick white cloud. He looked down and watched the cars stop and start at the traffic lights along Bothwell Street, glad of the opportunity to empty his mind of substantial thoughts and concentrate on trivia. He stood leaning on the balcony rail for ten minutes watching life pass by, then went inside to the kitchen and gulped down a half-litre bottle of water from the fridge without pausing. He filled the coffee machine with water, put a fresh filter in it and went for a hot shower.

Sitting in what he called his movie chair, a battered old leather recliner, he sipped at his black coffee thinking about watching a retrospective of Hitchcock movies in the dark of the Glasgow Film Theatre with Penny. The best of times.

A red light was flashing on his telephone indicating he had several messages. The first one was from his brother, asking what the hell was so important he had to phone so late last night. All but one of the rest were all from Cahill timed at various times through the night and once this morning. Finally one of his pals had called to confirm a game of football that night. He had forgotten about the game but in the middle of all this madness the idea of playing football and then having a few beers sounded like the best, most normal thing in the world.

He was in the process of deleting the messages when the buzzer from the main entrance sounded, making him start.

He went to the door and pressed the button to activate the video phone on the wall next to the door. It connected to the main door of the building, at street level, and he saw Cahill standing there in a camouflage jacket, one of those Desert Storm affairs in beige and brown, with a black woollen hat pulled down over his ears.

'What?' Logan said into the intercom.

'Don't fucking "what" me, Logan. Buzz me in, it's freezing.'

Logan pressed the button to release the lock on the door and watched Cahill disappear from the screen. He pulled the door to the flat open, then sat in the movie chair and swivelled it round to face the entrance. He had dressed in navy suit trousers and a pale blue checked shirt open at the neck. Getting ready for the work day ahead. Nothing better to do.

Cahill walked out of the lift and across the hall into the flat, closing the door gently as he came in. He pulled off the hat and coat, revealing jeans and an olive green T-shirt underneath. He ignored Logan and went to pour himself a coffee.

The flat was largely open-plan with the living area immediately inside the door and the kitchen at the far end. Logan's bed was in the farthest corner from the front door, screened off from the rest of the flat by large wooden panels, not quite ceiling high. The only separate room was the bathroom, behind the kitchen area. The place was huge, with the bed over fifty feet from the entrance. It was on a corner site on the top floor with glass panels on two of the four sides and a deck on the outside along the longest wall.

Cahill leaned on the breakfast counter and stared at Logan through the steam rising from his coffee.

'Not taking my calls any more, Logan?'

'I was drunk. I slept through all of them.'

'Uh-huh. Why did you hang up on me?'

Logan stood, walked over to where the Polaroid of Penny was lying on the floor and picked it up. He didn't want to look at it but couldn't help himself. His stomach flip-flopped and he held his hand to his mouth. After taking a couple of breaths, he walked to the breakfast counter and placed the photo in front of Cahill and sat on one of the high stools.

Cahill lifted the photo and looked at it for a minute without saying anything. Then he placed it face down on the counter.

'Is it real?' Logan asked him.

Cahill looked at him and decided to hell with the implications of answering the question.

'It's real,' he said. 'Where did you get it?'

They both recognised what had passed between them in the exchange – Cahill's acknowledgement of the things he knew.

'Those guys from last night left it for me.'

He'd put any thoughts about the picture of the little girl out of his head, figuring it was some kind of mistake and it just got mixed up with the other one – the one he was supposed to see. Otherwise it made no sense to him. He didn't know the girl; didn't recognise her at all after mistaking her for Ashley.

'Do you know who it is?' Cahill asked.

'It's her. It's Penny.'

'How do you know? I mean, it's difficult to make out her face.'

'It's her. I know.'

Cahill walked out of the kitchen area and stood at one of the glass panels looking out over the city.

'It doesn't make any sense,' he said, still looking out of the window. 'You know? Why kill her and then do what they did last night?'

'To intimidate me into doing something?'

'I don't buy that. How would it work?' Cahill turned and leaned back against the glass. 'It would make more sense to take her and then use the threat of doing her harm as leverage. That's a much more effective tool than just killing her as some sort of proof that they're willing to go that far.'

'Because most people would sacrifice themselves but not someone they loved?'

'Correct.'

Logan stood, anger now beginning to course darkly through his veins, replacing the shock and fear.

'What the fuck is it that they want? Why not just tell me?'

'Because they think they're clever and that by talking in riddles they protect themselves if one of them gets caught. Think about what they actually said. Was any of it explicit?'

Logan squeezed his eyes shut and tried to remember, visualising the scene in the foyer and recreating the encounter in his mind. It was still just a scramble of images and words, nothing coherent.

'I can't remember,' he said. 'Something about a meeting and how I wouldn't want someone I know to die.'

'What about the deal with Bob?' Cahill asked. 'There's enough money riding on that to make this kind of thing worthwhile.'

'Yeah, maybe. Bob told me he knew Penny was back in town.'

'I don't believe in coincidences,' Cahill said. 'Bob might have been the one to tip them off about Penny.'

'But it's just a software firm run with money from two Weegie suits. What's the connection with the thugs? I just don't see it.'

Cahill was looking at him blankly. 'What's a Weegie?' he asked.

'It's slang for someone from Glasgow. A Glas*wegian*, a Weegie. You never heard me say that before?'

'Not that I recall, but I like it.'

They both smiled for the first time that morning.

'Okay, let's leave Bob out of it for a second. Any other deals – maybe something you're not really fronting? Are you helping anyone else out?'

Logan ran through the deals he was working on in his head. There was nothing else that could possibly be a prospect and he said so to Cahill.

'Then it must be Bob's deal,' Cahill said.

'But it's all legit so far as I can tell.'

'Where's the funding coming from?'

'It changed after I got involved in the deal,' Logan recalled. 'They switched from one of the banks in London to some French private equity outfit I've never dealt with before.'

'What does that mean, private equity?'

'Okay, equity really just means that cash is provided to fund the purchase and in return the investors take a stake in the business. And it's private because there are no national banks involved. The money comes from cash-rich private vultures looking to invest in new ventures and make a killing by selling at a profit if it becomes a success later.'

'Right, I get it. So if it's not a national bank, it's more of a possibility the money could be dirty?'

'Yeah. I mean, it's more likely that a money-laundering deal could come via foreign private equity than a recognised bank. I made some noise about the funding switch at the time because we need to know where the money comes from and even if we just think it's dodgy, we have to report it to the police.'

'But that's been sorted now?' Cahill asked.

'Well, not totally. I've asked Bob about it a few times and he says he'll take care of it.'

'That could be it,' Cahill said. 'They might think you need to be pressured into forgetting about it.'

'But I've not made a big deal of it, really. I just told Bob we both need to have it signed off before the deal gets completed.'

'It could be a big deal to them. Think about it. If the money is dirty they'll never be able to give you what you need, you won't complete the deal and they won't get to wash their money through it.'

'I hadn't thought about it like that,' Logan said. 'But why would Bob involve me in it if he knew it was dirty? It would be smarter just to do it alone and he could have done that.'

'Maybe getting you in it gives him a layer of deniability.'

'I can see that.'

'You and Bob used to be big pals?' Cahill asked.

'Not really. Like I said before, I knew him from university. Penny knew him too.'

'Now it gets interesting.'

'But he's on the up, you know. He doesn't need the money from a dirty deal.'

'How much does a partner make at your firm?'

'Top profit share? Maybe three hundred grand.'

'And Bob?'

'He'll be making that in three years' time. He probably takes home over two hundred now.'

'So why do the dodgy stuff?'

'Right,' Logan said.

Cahill raised his eyebrows and gave a big, theatrical sigh. 'I was being ironic. Some of us Americans do know how to do that. Listen, when it comes to money, too much is never enough. Someone making two hundred grand a year knows the kind of life that can bring. And also knows the life half a million or a million brings with it because he deals with guys that make that much. The more you make the more you want.'

'I don't see Bob like that. He's got Rachel and the two girls. He wouldn't put them at risk.'

'Someone put *your* neck on the line and from what you've told me it's likely that money is the determining factor.'

Logan got up and paced the floor as the sun started to bleed light into the sky. 'So what do I do?'

'Go see Bob and tell him what happened here last night. If he knows something, he'll give himself away. It'll be a small thing, like he won't be able to look you in the eye for an instant, or his response will be too quick. Like he rehearsed it before because he knew what was going to happen.'

'You coming with me?'

'No. He doesn't like me and he'll be on guard. You'll have to do it. Today.'

'What if he doesn't give anything away and we need to progress the deal?'

'Then you have to keep it going but don't commit to completing it.'

'I could lose my job,' Logan said. 'And my career.'

'Would that be so bad?' Cahill asked. 'You don't love it, do you?'

'No, but what else would I do?'

'You could always come work for me,' Cahill said with a wink.

He went and picked up his jacket and hat, pulling the latter down over his head. Logan saw him silhouetted in black against the red sky.

'Anyway, I need to get back home,' he said. 'Call me and let me know how it goes, Logan.'

'I will.'

Another thought struck Cahill. 'This building has CCTV, right?'

'Yes. I mean I think so. Why?'

'I'll get the recording from last night in the lobby.'

'How? Why?'

'That's two questions. I'll answer one of them. Because it's better if we know what they look like. It would be more than we have right now.'

'Why don't we just give it to the police?'

Cahill paused. 'What we spoke about just now will change our relationship – how you see me. I know about things like this, Logan, and maybe having an edge over these guys, whoever they are, is what will end this particular thing right for you. We keep it for now. Trust me, okay?'

Logan nodded and Cahill walked to the door.

'Alex,' Logan said. 'I never saw you wear that jacket before. Is it yours? I mean, is it real army issue?'

Cahill looked down at his camo parka and grabbed both lapels with his hands.

'This old thing,' he said, smiling. 'Sure it is. And I didn't get it at no army surplus store either.'

2

7.00 a.m.

Ellie had heard the men arrive back late. She had no sense of time, really, other than knowing it was night and had been for a while. They were big and noisy and the drugs in the injection the man called Drake had given her were all the way gone now. Pain throbbed through her constantly.

She strained hard to hear what was being said, but it was muffled and indistinct apart from one time when one of the big men laughed loudly.

'I don't think Finch will be giving us any more trouble,' Sergei had said as he and Vasiliy took their coats off.

'Why is that?' Drake asked.

'Because he's a pussy,' Vasiliy said. 'I thought he was going to wet himself when he saw us.'

Sergei smiled.

'You didn't say anything too obvious?' Drake asked.

'I know you think we're idiots,' Sergei said. 'But give us some credit.'

'We all need to be sure this time that he got the message.'

'Well, he did. So stop whining at us.'

Katrina watched Drake, seeing the anger in his eyes as Sergei challenged him again. She knew Drake would only be pushed so far and he was nearing his breaking point now.

Drake did not react to Sergei but knew that a reckoning was coming between them. He would do it on his own terms, when it suited him, and would not let Sergei goad him into it. He waited before speaking again, to maintain his voice at a level pitch.

'Good. I'll go to the meeting today at Finch's office and everything will work out. Right, Sergei?'

Sergei nodded. 'I need to take a piss,' he said, turning and walking to the bathroom.

Ellie sat up in her bed when Drake came into her room and asked how she was. She said she wanted the pain to go away again and could he give her more medicine.

'It's too soon. You'll get sick.'

'But I need it. Please.'

She hated to sound so weak in front of him but it was how she felt.

'I can't,' he said.

He stood then and hesitated, looking down at her. 'I have

to go out later, but someone will give you medicine. Understand?'

Ellie nodded that she did.

'Good.'

He turned and opened the door. Then he hesitated again and looked round at her, his eyes reflecting the pale morning light.

'I'm going to a meeting today, to see someone who can help you. Maybe someone who can get you out of here if he does what I tell him to do.'

Ellie said nothing. Her mind emptied of all thought.

'Does that make you happy?'

'Should it?' she asked.

The man stiffened at the attitude in her voice, the hint of defiance.

'You would rather stay here for ever?'

Anger flashed in her again. 'Where else am I going to go?' she asked.

'I don't understand.'

'My mum is dead. You killed her and now she's dead. Where am I going to go now? Can you tell me?'

He stood for a moment and then came back into the room and sat on the bed beside her. She smelled soap and expensive aftershave on his skin.

'Little girl,' he said. 'You would rather be dead?' His voice was light. He knew he had won this small battle. 'Like your mum?'

Ellie felt tears slip down her cheeks and she wiped quickly at them. He leaned in close and she expected his breath to stink. But it didn't. It smelled of mint toothpaste and sweet tea.

'I'm not your friend, little Ellie. Understand me, okay.'

She looked down and away from the light shining in his eyes. He pinched her chin between his thumb and forefinger and lifted her face up so that she had to look at him.

'You want to be dead?'

Ellie shook her head violently, oblivious now of the pain it caused. Salty tears flew off her cheeks.

'Then be happy,' he told her. 'I will go see someone and then maybe we can all go home.'

Ellie wanted to scream at him that she had no home and it was all his fault. She wanted to scratch at the light in his eyes and feel them burst under her nails. He must have seen the violence in her face.

'I have no mother,' he said. 'No father. They too were killed. Look how it made me, little Ellie. Stay in your world, not mine.'

Ellie stayed awake after he left and after a while heard him go outside and drive off in another vehicle. Not the same as the others used — it sounded quieter but more powerful.

When he was gone, she slept.

3

9.30 a.m.

Logan left his building late. He'd lost track of time, sitting thinking everything through and reaching the conclusion that he had no fucking idea what was going on. But he was determined to find out and Bob Crawford was first on his agenda.

He walked briskly out of the lift and through the foyer, shivering involuntarily at the memory of the previous night and not really seeing the man fiddling with his key at the mail boxes near the front entrance. The guy was nondescript anyway; no taller than five ten and of medium build. As soon as Logan was out of sight, the man pocketed his key and followed him.

On the way up the hill towards Blythswood Square, Logan switched his mobile on and it beeped immediately, telling him he had new voicemail messages. He dialled into his mailbox and found three messages from Crawford.

'Fuck you, Bob,' he muttered, switching the phone off again.

He breezed into the office, ignoring the two men on the couch in the reception area and Megan's subtle attempts to catch his attention. In his office, he closed the door and buzzed Crawford's extension. No answer. He phoned down to Megan.

'Where's Bob?' he asked. 'He's not in his room.'

'If you hadn't ignored me on the way in, Logan, you would have found out that he's in the boardroom and that the two men who were in reception are here to see both of you. Bob's been looking for you for ages.'

'Those guys are not there now?'

'No, they just went in to join him in the boardroom. My guess is that you should do the same.'

'Will do. Thanks.'

Shit. He'd wanted to catch Crawford on his own. Never mind.

He mouthed 'sorry' at Megan on the way past her desk to the boardroom door before opening it and striding confidently in. Crawford's face was pinched and pale.

'Morning, Bob,' he said, wearing his best smile. 'Gentlemen, I'm Logan Finch.'

He shook hands with both the men and sat next to Crawford on the opposite side of the table. The two strangers looked expectantly at Crawford.

'Logan,' Crawford started. 'This is the main investor for GeneTech.'

One of the men nodded. He was around Logan's height with sculpted cheekbones and pale blue eyes. His skin was lightly tanned and stretched tight over his face. Logan sometimes liked to imagine a new acquaintance as a professional sports player; an easy shorthand to remember them by. This one was a professional tennis player; European. Slavic, maybe.

'And,' Crawford went on, 'this is one of his legal team.'

Logan just nodded at the lawyer. He was more interested in the tennis pro. 'I didn't catch your name,' he said.

'John Drake.'

Weird accent – vaguely American, but Logan doubted that English was his first language.

Crawford spoke again. 'Logan, they wanted to get together with us today because—'

'We're, frankly, a little pissed off at the attitude you guys are displaying towards this deal,' the lawyer said. 'We spoke to your clients and they told us about missed meetings and phone calls being ignored. So we thought—'

'Hold it,' Logan said, lifting a hand to stop the speech in mid-flow. 'What do you mean "we spoke to your clients"?'

Drake looked at the lawyer and then stared back at Logan.

'Because,' Logan continued, 'as you well know, it would be improper if not a flagrant breach of professional ethics for you to speak to our clients direct. Is that what happened?'

He hadn't intended to sound so aggressive but felt that if Cahill was right and the deal was dirty they would suspect something was wrong if he acted too placidly. He turned to Crawford with an exaggerated look of disgust on his face.

Crawford didn't meet his eye. He looked a little paler than usual today, Logan thought.

'Logan,' he started. 'I think all they're trying to say is that they're keen to see this deal put to bed. We all are. There's money to be made for everyone in this.'

'Thanks, Bob,' the lawyer said. 'And yes, that's about the size of it.'

Drake continued looking at Logan and he began to feel a bit like the outsider in the meeting.

'Our clients are happy with everything so why don't we just get the thing rolling downhill?' Crawford went on.

Now clearly was not the time to bring up the funding issues and Logan felt excluded. He stood and walked to the table under the window to pour a glass of water and gather his thoughts. He looked out of the window and saw a guy sitting on the low wall that went round the park. The guy was smoking and trying to look nonchalant. Logan thought he just looked cold. And out of place. A small part of his mind tugged at him, telling him there was something he should remember about the guy; was he the one in the foyer of his building this morning?

'Logan?' Crawford asked. 'Everything okay?'

The guy on the wall looked over at their building and met Logan's gaze for a moment. Then he stood slowly and walked off.

Logan wondered how it was that his perfectly ordered life had just gone down the pan in the space of two days. The photo of Penny flashed in his head. It occurred to him that if the men behind Penny's death were in this room, who was the man out there on the wall? He felt as if he no longer knew what was going on and the last thing he wanted to do right now was allow this deal to race towards completion. He needed to play for more time.

'Bob,' he said, turning back to face the table. 'The price is good and our guys are up for it, right?'

The lawyer smiled. Tennis pro didn't.

'Except,' Logan went on, 'these guys here seem way too keen to me and even a little intimidating and it makes me nervous.'

Crawford went from pale to almost translucent and Logan thought he would throw up right there, all over the table – which might be quite an effective negotiating ploy.

'That's not what we wanted to hear.' Drake spoke at length for the first time. 'I find that a very disquieting attitude, Mr Finch.'

'Logan didn't mean anything—' Bob started.

'No, Bob,' Logan cut him off. 'I did.'

The lawyer leaned forward and clasped his hands on the table in front of him. 'Why don't we get your clients on the phone, now?' he said. 'Clear it all right up.'

A light rain began to patter against the windows.

'Sounds like a good—' Crawford again.

'It's not good,' Logan said, cutting across him again. 'Not good at all.'

There was definitely something off about Crawford's desire to placate these guys and Logan's anger at the situation he found himself in was starting to take over. He wanted to push these guys and see where it would lead.

'I think we can safely say that this meeting is over,' he told them.

'Is that really what you want to do, Mr Finch?' Drake asked.

'It is.'

Drake stood and left quietly, which was much more effective than shouting and slamming doors. The lawyer sat in the eerie silence for a beat before grabbing his leather briefcase and shuffling out after him.

'Logan, what the fuck are you playing at? I mean, really?' Crawford bawled.

Logan went to the window again to cool his rising anger. Crawford was the one screwing the best deal for their clients. The smoking guy was back on the wall. This time he had his hands in his pockets and was watching Drake and the lawyer walking away from the building.

Crawford was still on the rampage.

'This is it for you. This is the one that might push you on to the partnership track. Why are you messing with it?'

Logan turned to face him, leaning back against the coffee table.

'What I really want to know is why you're so keen to bend over and take what these guys want to give you. We don't even know those two; never met them before on this deal. What happened to the other lawyer?'

Crawford looked away.

'What's the story, Bob, really?'

Logan was into it now. He still found it hard to believe that Crawford was really mixed up in a deal that had resulted in Penny's death. He couldn't comprehend that Bob would do that deliberately. But Crawford was one of the few people in the world who knew of his connection to Penny and he was the only one who had known she was back in the country.

He felt a thick knot rise in his throat and tasted bile at the back of his tongue. Did Crawford really sell Penny out to these guys?

But why? It would be easier for Crawford to just take him out of the deal team and finish it himself. It made no sense.

But he couldn't get the connections out of his head. He felt as if he needed fresh air and walked to the door leading out to reception, Crawford's voice rising close to falsetto behind him. He opened the door and saw DC Irvine turn to face him, with a tall uniformed cop standing behind her.

'Mr Finch,' Irvine said. 'Just the man I was looking for.'

4

11.00 a.m.

Logan had never been in the back of a police car before. It was an odd experience. First, the big uniform put a meaty hand on top of his head and gently guided him into the car with his other hand gripping Logan's upper arm. The door was closed quietly and Irvine sat in the front passenger seat waiting for the big one to drive. Logan's curiosity got the better of him and he pulled at the interior door handle.

'It's like a childproof lock, Mr Finch,' Irvine told him, still looking through the windscreen. 'We can't have criminals escaping from custody that easily now, can we?'

'Makes sense,' Logan said.

The big cop climbed in and pulled smoothly away from the kerb outside the Kennedy Boyd office building. The car crossed over West Regent Street at the corner of the square and then indicated left to turn on to Bath Street. The lights turned red as they approached the junction and the car stopped behind a dark blue Mercedes saloon. Logan leaned over so he could see through the windscreen between the seats. He wondered if Drake and his lawyer were in the car. It seemed just like the kind either of them might own.

He didn't want to be the first one to talk again and so sat there in silence as they turned on to Bath Street and then quickly left again on to Pitt Street. They slowed and stopped in front of the police headquarters building. If they'd walked from the office to here it might have taken about thirty seconds. They were fucking with him. He sat and waited while Irvine and the uniform got out. Irvine walked to the entrance and stood holding the glass door open while the uniform opened his door.

Logan stepped out and stretched in the light drizzle. He made a snap decision to test the water with them, because it was clear that he wasn't under arrest at this point.

'Thanks for the ride, guys,' he said to Irvine across the roof of the car. 'I needed the fresh air.'

He turned and started to walk across the road to the opposite pavement.

'Mr Finch,' she shouted after him.

He ignored her until he reached the pavement and then turned round. She had walked to the kerb and stood dwarfed by the big cop.

'What?' Logan shouted over at her.

She seemed lost for words for a moment.

'We'd like to ask you some more questions,' she said eventually. 'About Miss Grant.'

He watched her for a moment, wondering what her place was in all of this. Not lead investigator, he didn't think. But she seemed smart and probably trustworthy.

'Please,' she said.

Well, okay then.

The big uniformed cop took him to the back of the ground floor and then through a door and down a flight of stairs. The décor changed from functional office space to sterile stairway and then to institutional dungeon in the basement. The walls and floor were the same sickly grey, with strong fluorescent overhead lighting. A series of steel doors stretched along each wall at regular intervals.

'I thought I wasn't under arrest?' he asked his guide.

'You're no'. So just shut it.'

Logan felt it was best not to mess any more with this one.

They stopped outside the third door on the right. The cop fiddled with a set of keys attached to his belt, picked one out and opened the door. He ushered Logan in and then closed the door with a hollow thunk. Logan figured it was either a holding cell, an interview room or both. He reckoned that not many ordinary citizens saw the inside of one of these rooms. He'd seen a few like it early in his career when visiting one of the many violent young men he'd had the misfortune to represent before he decided that criminal work was not for him. These kinds of places were one of the motivating factors in the career switch.

The interior design scheme was the same as the hallway

and there was a Formica-topped table with three folding plastic chairs set up in the centre of the room. They must have been taken from the canteen this morning because furniture wasn't usually allowed in these rooms. Not the kind you can lift and swing over your head anyway.

Somebody wanted to intimidate him – that much was becoming obvious. It wasn't Irvine because she'd been too polite out on the street. If she was going to strong-arm him the big guy wouldn't have let him get even halfway across the road. So it had to be someone new. The lock in the door clicked again and the door swung out.

This guy was much bigger than the uniform and Irvine was all but hidden behind his massive torso. Logan's shock must have shown on his face because the man smiled broadly. He then waited for Irvine to come in through the door before closing it hard, the sound bouncing around the walls and in Logan's head. Okay, Logan thought, this is the intimidator. No question.

Irvine pulled one of the chairs round and sat opposite Logan. The bear crossed his huge arms across his chest and leaned back into the corner of the room. He still seemed to fill it and Logan could not take his eyes off the man's forearms.

Irvine spoke first.

'Mr Finch,' she said, 'this is Detective Superintendent Liam Moore. He's in charge of the inquiry into the murder of Penelope Grant.'

Inquiry seemed like such a sterile word to use, given the image of Penny in the photo. Logan cleared his throat and tried to swallow, but his mouth had dried up. Moore nodded at him, but said nothing. Irvine sat quietly watching Logan. Logan knew the interview technique: get the subject to talk first and openly without limiting his answers with closed questions – or any questions. He'd spoken to enough cops in his time as a criminal lawyer. He felt he had little to lose by playing along.

'Okay,' he said. 'What do you want to ask me?'

'You have any kids, Mr Finch?' Moore asked, his eyes hot and dark underneath a grey crew cut.

Logan felt himself frown. Caught off guard by that one. Just as they wanted.

'Well?' Moore again.

Logan had hesitated long enough for the man to ask again and he sensed a shift in the room's atmosphere – not for the better.

'Um, no. No, I don't.'

'Sure about that? Young man like you sowing your seeds, eh?'

'You have me confused with someone else,' Logan told him. 'That's not my style.'

'What is your style, Mr Finch?' Moore asked.

Logan looked at Irvine and thought that she appeared uncomfortable with Moore's approach.

'I don't know where this is going or what you want. I'm not gay, if that's what you're asking.'

'So, you like girls then?' Moore back on point again.

'Yes.'

'You liked Miss Grant?'

'Yes. We were together back at uni. You know that already.'

'We do,' Moore said. 'But otherwise you have not been particularly open with us. Why did you feel the need to hide behind your pal last time, Mr Finch?'

'I was in a bit of shock and it just happened that way.'

'The American saw to that, didn't he?'

'I apologise for that. It wasn't my intention to appear evasive. I've got nothing to hide.'

'That's all we're trying to establish here,' Irvine said.

Logan was getting an increasingly bad feeling about Moore. The superintendent continued to lean in the corner with his arms crossed and his gaze seeking to burn Logan's face off. Logan sensed they were holding something back; something they thought made him look like a suspect in Penny's death. He knew they wanted him to keep talking and he couldn't help but oblige. He needed to know where all of this was going. The more information he had from all sources, the better.

'Look, I want to help. I really do. Penny and me, well, I cared about her a lot. I still do.'

'Did,' Moore said, moving forward and letting his hands fall to his sides.

Logan held his stare.

'Do, Mr Moore. Just because she's . . .'

He felt his grief bubble up suddenly from within. He blinked hard and breathed in through his nose, smelling the rank odour of the room: dried piss and blood behind industrial-strength disinfectant. He looked at Irvine. She was watching him closely and it looked to him as if she was increasingly unhappy at the direction this interview was taking. But Moore was her boss.

'She's what?' the superintendent asked. 'Been beaten to death? Choked on her own blood and vomit?'

Logan stood abruptly, knocking his chair over. It was more violent than he had intended.

Irvine pushed her chair back and Moore came round the table much faster than Logan would have guessed he could move. Logan stepped back and found himself hard up against the wall.

'Sir,' Irvine said sharply, standing quickly.

Moore stopped, his fists clenched at his sides. He was no more than three feet from Logan, who could smell the incongruously light fragrance of his aftershave. If he was meant to be intimidated, they'd succeeded. He felt blood rushing in his ears and heat rising in him as adrenalin started to pump through his veins. He moved forward off the wall towards Moore.

'Step back, sir,' Irvine said to the superintendent.

Moore didn't move.

'Sir.'

It looked to Logan as if Moore couldn't hear her. He glanced at Irvine and saw genuine concern in her eyes. It didn't feel like just a game.

'Ask him about her,' Moore said to Irvine.

Irvine looked at Logan.

'Ellie,' Moore said.

'I will if you step back, sir.'

Moore was still for what seemed like an age to Logan. Then

he backed up, turned Logan's chair round and sat in it. 'Good enough?' he asked, though there was no hint that he was expecting any answer.

Irvine sat again and looked at Logan.

'Do you have any knowledge of the whereabouts of Ellie Grant, Mr Finch?'

Logan's mind was blank. 'Who?'

Moore was up again, ignoring Irvine's shout.

'Don't fuck with us on this, Finch,' he roared, 'or I'll take your head off. There's no CCTV in this room.'

'Sir,' Irvine said. 'You're forgetting about me.'

Moore turned and stared at Irvine. There was a long pause before he sat back down again, looking away from Logan as if he couldn't bear to be in the same room with him.

Logan's heart was beating somewhere north of his throat, but he kept outwardly calm.

'Mr Finch,' Irvine went on, 'Miss Grant had an eleven-year-old daughter, Ellie. She is missing and we are focusing our efforts in this inquiry on finding her. You understand?'

Logan nodded, not really in answer to the question.

Penny had a little girl.

'And we need to know if you have any idea where she is.'

Logan stared at Irvine, a storm raging in his head, and knew that she was watching him closely. The room started to shudder and the walls warped in and out of focus. Logan tried to maintain eye contact with Irvine as the room shook violently around them. He was glad of the wall at his back, otherwise he was sure he would have collapsed.

Irvine stood and walked towards him.

'Are you all right, Mr Finch?' she asked.

'I don't think so,' he told her.

She took hold of his left elbow and guided him round the table to Moore's empty chair. Then she reached into her jacket pocket and placed a photograph of Ellie on the table in front of Logan.

'That's her – Ellie Grant. Have you seen her?'

He looked at the picture and saw again the girl with the brown eyes. This time, he knew they were *his* brown eyes.

5

1.00 p.m.

Ellie had heard one of the big men speak on his phone about an hour ago. He got angrier as the call went on and there was a sound like he threw the phone down on the floor when he was finished. He went outside after that and Ellie had heard him shouting to no one out there. Then lighter footsteps – the woman, maybe – went out after him.

Sergei sat on the couch as Katrina went outside to calm Vasiliy after the call from Drake. He didn't know why Drake had brought the whore with them, but she had a way with Vasiliy and if she calmed him down then maybe she would have paid her way.

Finch had screwed up at the meeting with Drake this morning, but still Drake didn't want to kill him and he was to get one last chance to do his part – once Drake decided how to send the message this time. Sergei felt that Drake was getting soft in his desire to appease Gabriel. If it was up to Sergei, he'd personally take pleasure in killing the girl right now and then Finch.

Sergei resented being an errand boy for Gabriel, even if Drake didn't. No matter how much money was involved, that's how he thought of this piece of shit job. Not like back in the old days, where they all grew up on the streets together and made their own way in life and *everybody* answered to them. He'd bought Drake's sales pitch – that they would all make more money this way – but he boiled with anger every time he had to yield to that English prick Gabriel.

Sure, they would make a lot more money. But now he knew it was the power he craved, or more precisely the power of fear – of life and death – they held over their towns back in Russia. No amount of money or drugs could replace that rush.

Still, he knew he had to bide his time to see off Drake. Maybe then he would be able to stop running these shit jobs and take his place at the top table with Gabriel. Then he would wield real power. The kind of power that Gabriel exercised in Paris over the American. Till then, fuck them all.

Katrina came back without Vasiliy, who was still outside in the cold.

'He'll be fine,' she said.

Sergei looked at Katrina, aware of how uncomfortable he made her now that he was alone with her.

'Don't worry,' he said. 'You're not my type.'

He turned and headed for the girl's room, and behind him Katrina rubbed at her arms as if feeling a chill.

Ellie heard heavy footsteps approach her room and shrank back against the wall, knowing she could not hide but wanting to try anyway.

It was the shorter of the men who came into the room. He kneeled down and peered at her in the gloom.

'What you do back there, girl? You hiding?'

Ellie stayed quiet, watching him.

'Huh? You no talk now. Fine, I tell you what the story is for now and then maybe you cry, eh?'

He started to laugh but it caught in his throat and he choked out a short cough.

'Things did not go so well today for you and for him, you know. If we do not get what we want, then things will go worse. He will only have one more warning.'

Ellie had no idea who or what he was talking about.

The man shuffled forward in a crouch and sat on the edge of the bed. He slid his hand along the top sheet until his fingers touched Ellie's foot. She gasped involuntarily and pulled her knees tight to her chest. He laughed/choked again and Ellie felt some of his spit on her arms. Up close, he smelled really bad and it made her feel sick. She pinched her nostrils with the fingers of one hand.

The man smiled and eased himself fully on to the bed. He propped his hands either side of her legs and leaned in until his nose almost touched hers. Ellie found herself unable to look away from his eyes.

'You don't like me, eh, girl?'

She nodded and this made him laugh again. A single fleck of spit landed on her right cheek, just below her eye, and she flinched.

'I will make sure when it all goes bad – and it will, I know – that I am the last one to come in here to see you. How you like that, eh? Tuck you up in this bed all nice and cosy. Just you and me.'

He leaned in as if to kiss her and then licked his own saliva from her cheek. It was all Ellie could do to keep from throwing up all over his face.

'Taste nice. More to come later, girl – you and me. Maybe even if things go well, we can still have fun, eh?'

Ellie looked into his eyes and saw nothing there.

He pulled back from her, stood and left the room. After he was gone, Ellie heard the woman say something to him and he shouted at her in response. Then it went quiet.

Ellie was not a stupid girl. She realised that these people were probably going to kill her. Maybe they brought the woman with them to make her think they wouldn't do it, but she knew that was just a trick. She did not know why they had done this to her and her mum or who this man was that they talked about – the one who was supposed to do something to save her – but she did not think she would ever be saved now. She would not let herself cry. She sucked in all her fear and grief and turned it to anger against these people who had done her harm.

Ellie pulled herself to the edge of the bed and tried to stand. Her head swam and her ribs throbbed. She thought she would fall and reached out to steady herself on the frame of the bed. She stood like that for a few minutes, breathing shallowly and waiting for her head to clear.

After a while she felt able to try to move again, but was careful to do so as quietly as possible so as not to attract any attention from the others in the cabin. She gingerly stepped round the bottom of the bed and traced her hand over the window. Except she could not, and realised that the boards blocking the window were fixed to the inside of the window frame, not the outside. Steadying herself with one hand against the wall, she felt along one of the boards until she found the end. Then she ran her hand up over the ends of all of the boards and found one nail head slightly proud of the surface of the wood on the bottom board.

Ellie got the nails of her forefinger and thumb under the nail head and pulled and wiggled at it with all her strength. It didn't move. She tried again with the same result and a tear born of frustration and fear slipped down one of her cheeks. She wiped it away angrily and told herself that if she was going to die here, she was at least going to try to help herself; one nail at a time, one board at a time. If she could just get outside when it was dark, maybe she could hide. And then they would leave and someone would find her.

She tugged at the nail again and felt sick from the physical effort. A metallic throb started up behind her damaged eye and more tears slipped down her face.

One more try, she told herself. She braced her hand against the wall and pulled as hard as her damaged body would allow.

The nail moved. Or at least she thought it had. She was sure it had.

That was enough.

For now.

6

1.39 p.m.

Logan was alone in the interview room, picking at the loose Elastoplast on his right index finger and staring at the photograph of Ellie Grant still sitting on the table. He couldn't remember where he'd put the other photo of her; the one that the two thugs had dropped on the foyer floor.

I have a daughter.

He rolled the word around on his tongue – *daughter* – until it wasn't a word at all any more, just a couple of sounds with no meaning.

The lock in the heavy door clunked and the door swung inwards. It was Irvine.

'So,' Logan said. 'How long till we get the test results back and find out for sure?'

After going over the history of his relationship with Penny

he had volunteered to give a blood sample for DNA paternity testing. They had samples of the girl's blood from the house. He still couldn't bring himself to use her name, even when he was just thinking about her.

'These things usually take a couple of days,' Irvine told him.

'Can't they do it any faster in situations like these?'

Irvine sighed and sat in the chair across the table from him. 'I know this must be tough,' she said. 'But we're here to help.'

'I'm not sure your boss shares that view.'

'He did what he thought he had to do to get to the truth.'

'You think it was too much?'

She paused for a moment. 'We all do things differently,' she said.

'Very diplomatic, detective,' Logan said.

Irvine smiled and Logan felt oddly better.

He had given Irvine and Moore an edited version of events since Monday morning, omitting the guys in the foyer of his building, and his suspicion that the whole thing was connected to one of his deals back at the office. He could tell Irvine wasn't really convinced that he was being open with her.

'Shouldn't there be two of you in here?' Logan asked. 'I didn't think you were allowed to spend time alone with me.'

'You're not a suspect, Logan. You're just assisting us with our inquiries, that's all. You are assisting us all you can, right?'

He noticed she had switched to using his first name, although she seemed unaware of having done it.

'I am,' he said, holding her stare.

'Okay, then. I guess you can get back to your office now and we'll be in touch when we have the test results.'

Irvine walked him back up to the building entrance and out on to the street. She held out a hand and he shook it. She gripped his hand firmly and talked to him, her voice low.

'I know that you're not being up front with me. There's nothing I can do about that right now but I do want to help you. We both want the same thing, to get Ellie Grant back alive.'

Logan said nothing.

'It's not your place to go running around looking for her.'

He nodded because he couldn't think of anything sensible to say.

'Let me do my job. I know it's scary and frustrating and you're a guy who's used to being in control of situations, but this is not something that you can do. So if there's anything else you need to tell me, just tell me, okay?'

Logan pulled his hand from her grip and shoved it in his trouser pocket. He almost told her then – about the photos and the threats and the deals. About everything. He couldn't work out in his head why he didn't. Maybe after all these years he felt a responsibility to the girl and to Penny that transcended rational thought. Maybe the primordial, macho, bullshit part of his being that is part of every man was taking over; protecting him from the grief and terror that bubbled just below the surface.

Or maybe it was something to do with Irvine. He hadn't known her long but he felt she was someone he could make a connection with, someone he could trust; but maybe not quite yet. She was still a cop and it would be dangerous to confide in her before he was sure of her.

Irvine watched his face closely, no doubt seeing all of the conflicting emotions playing out in his eyes. Finally, she reached in her jacket and took out a business card and a pen. She started scribbling on the back of the card.

'I'm giving you my mobile and home numbers, Logan. I want you to call me if anything comes up that might help, okay? I mean, even if it's something that's happened already and it just comes back to you as maybe being important now.'

He realised she was trying to give him a way out and was almost tempted to tell her everything.

'Thanks,' he said, taking the card and closing his fingers round it. 'I'll do that.'

The muscles in her face tightened and then sagged in disappointment. She decided that she had one last card to play.

'I have a son, you know. He's just a baby really, but he's my whole world. They do that to you, grab you from the first second they explode into the world, screaming and crapping and crying. Needy little bastards; totally vulnerable and alone until they get cleaned and wrapped up and put in your arms. And they sense it straight away. I mean, that they'll be safe with you; that you'll be the one to look after them. So I know how you feel right now.'

Logan had not been involved with police investigations so closely before, but he sensed that she was not talking to him as she would normally to someone involved in a murder inquiry.

'How can you know?' he asked her. 'When I don't know how I feel myself. I see that little girl in the picture and I can see how she has my eyes and Penny's mouth and . . .'

Logan stopped and drew a long, cold breath into his lungs.

'I see that,' he said. 'I really do. But I have no idea how I feel about it – about her. I didn't get the chance to make any connection with her. Penny took that away from me. She was the one who decided I should never know that I had a daughter. My brother has four kids and I love them all. But I've seen them grow from babies to become real people. How can you expect me to look at an eleven-year-old girl I never met before and know how I should feel when I'm told she's mine? How should I feel?'

She reached out and touched his hand for a second before pulling back from him. They stood awkwardly for a moment, unsure of how to end the conversation.

'You're right,' Irvine said finally. 'No one can tell you that; it's something *you* have to work out. But you should give yourself that chance and tell us everything you know so we can find her for you. Give you the opportunity to understand your feelings for each other, Logan.'

'I'll call you if anything turns up,' he said, moving away from her.

'Logan,' she said, almost pleading with him now.

He stepped off the kerb and walked over the road, heading up the hill and back towards his office. Irvine watched him for a moment and then turned to go back into the building, resolving to help him even if he wouldn't help himself.

*   *   *

She found Moore back in his office, sifting through a bundle of files sitting on his desk. He stopped what he was doing when she came in and closed the door behind her.

'What's on your mind, Becky?'

'Finch, sir. I think he needs our help.'

Moore leaned back in his chair and crossed his arms over his broad chest.

'Uh-huh,' he said. 'In what way does he need *our* help?'

Irvine was starting to regret this already. Judging by Moore's body language he'd had enough of Finch after today.

'Well, I mean I think there's more going on with him than he's willing to let on. I think he might be keeping information from us.'

'I have absolutely no doubt about that, Becky,' Moore said. 'I just don't know if what he's got is going to help us find the little girl. He seems like a pretty confused young man to me, you know.'

'Who wouldn't be, right?'

Moore nodded and glanced at his computer screen as an e-mail notification message popped up on it.

'I just think it's worth doing more,' Irvine said.

Moore kept his focus on the screen and placed a hand over the mouse on his desk, manoeuvring the pointer on screen to open the e-mail. He scanned what was there for a moment, some internal bulletin, and then looked at Irvine again.

'What do you have in mind?' he asked her.

Irvine thought she was losing ground but persevered anyway.

'I think we should allocate some resources to following him, sir.'

Moore sighed. 'Becky . . .'

'No, sir, let me say what—'

'Becky,' he said, his voice increasing in volume and cutting her off. 'I have just about reached the limit on authorised overtime for the department already this month and I can't justify surveillance on Finch.'

Irvine knew he was waiting for her to argue, but she was losing faith in the argument herself now.

'Look, I can see that you like the guy as a human being. He's a likeable sort even if he's got a stubborn streak that does him no favours. And even *I* kind of liked the way he managed to stand up to me just a little bit, but that doesn't mean I can spend money in the budget that I don't have.'

Irvine nodded. 'I understand, sir. I do.'

'Okay, then.'

Irvine turned to leave.

'Listen, if you don't have anything else that needs following up on straight away, go home and get some rest. You'll be better for it.'

She looked back at Moore, wondering what he was trying to say. No one got any time off on a murder investigation. Ever. Moore put his hands above his head and stretched upwards.

'What you do on your own time – off the clock – is up to you,' he told her.

Now she got it.

'Thanks,' she said. Then a thought struck her. 'What about DS Sharp?'

Moore put his hands behind his head after finishing off his stretch. 'What about him?'

'Well, I mean, he's technically my superior on this case, so how's he going to react when I'm officially taking the afternoon off?'

'Technically,' Moore repeated with a smile. 'I like it. Listen, don't worry about Jack. I'll look after him for a while. I am *technically* his boss, you know.'

'Right,' Irvine said, somewhat redundantly.

Moore leaned back towards his computer screen and waved her out.

Irvine sat alone on a grey plastic chair in the canteen on the first floor, drinking a weak cup of tea and trying to work out where to start. She'd never been on a surveillance before and wasn't really in a position to ask anyone what to do. She had her notebook open on the table with the intention of writing out some kind of structured plan, but nothing came to mind.

She eyed a pile of used magazines on the table in front of her and guessed that she might need something to read to pass the time. Picking up an old issue of *Cosmopolitan*, she flicked to an article enticingly titled 'Ten ways to drive a man wild in bed'. Somebody had been there before her and had crossed out all the entries with a blue biro, writing 'blowjob' ten times instead. She decided maybe she'd pick up something new at a petrol station instead. She needed to fill the tank up anyway.

7

3.30 p.m.

Irvine decided on the drive home that the best place to start her surveillance was at Logan's flat. She calculated that he would go back to his office and work as usual, or as best he could, to avoid any problems at work. Most lawyers in the big commercial firms didn't finish work at five, so if she got to his flat by then she thought she would definitely catch him coming home and take it from there.

Her house was empty at this time of day with Tom at work and the wee man at the childminder's until six. She went straight to her bedroom and opened the wardrobe, wondering what the well-dressed stakeout cop was wearing this season. Given it was winter in Glasgow she opted for a sensible ensemble of jeans, T-shirt and fleece accessorised with a Berghaus ski jacket (not that she was a skier), a hat, a scarf and gloves. She expected to be sitting in the car for a while and didn't want the engine running the whole time, so she had to be prepared for the cold.

The fridge was not well stocked, so she decided to buy some drinks and snacks at the petrol station on her way to Logan's. First, she went for a quick shower to freshen up and then drank a cup of hot coffee a little too quickly, feeling it burn all the way down into her stomach. Fortified for the night ahead, she went out to the car after leaving a brief note for Tom on the kitchen table. He was going to be (more) pissed off at her anyway so she didn't want to waste time with a long explanation. She did sign off with a single kiss, though she felt like a fraud for doing it.

She listened again to her old boyfriend's band on the drive to the petrol station, wondering whether she and Tom should sit down and have 'the talk'. She had pretty much resolved of late that the marriage was broken and not even No More Nails was going to fix it, no matter how good its bonding qualities were.

'When we get Ellie Grant back safe,' she said aloud, not wanting to contemplate the fact that the girl might already be dead.

Her brain flashed up a memory – reaching out to Logan earlier that afternoon – and she wondered where that came from. She wrote it off to her feelings of sympathy for him and for Ellie Grant, though that didn't sound totally convincing even in her own head.

*   *   *

Irvine filled the car with petrol, went into the shop and searched the shelves for crisps and sweets or something with some vague nutritional value. After a few long minutes of deliberation, she settled on a Snickers bar (peanuts have protein), a chocolate chip cereal bar ('cereal' equals healthy), a bag of pickled onion flavoured Monster Munch ('corn' snacks; corn is good) and a large bottle of Lucozade. Jesus, she thought, I'll be on a sugar high for days.

She cruised east towards town along the Clydeside Expressway, glad that it was still early enough in the afternoon for her to avoid rush-hour traffic. After ten minutes, she pulled on to the slip road marked 'City Centre' and was soon on Bothwell Street where Logan's flat was located at the top of the Pinnacle building.

In her mind, she had envisaged parking discreetly in the car park of the Holiday Inn City West directly opposite, but had forgotten that the hotel was in the middle of being demolished. She settled for an on street parking space beside the demolition site, feeding as much change into the ticket machine as she could. The last thing she wanted was to have to flash her warrant card at a traffic warden – nothing like drawing attention to yourself when you're trying to be subtle.

Irvine let the car engine run for a few minutes to build up some heat in the interior and then switched it off to settle in for a long night. She put the CD back in the stereo and kept it on for comfort.

After the second track, her favourite, her mobile phone rang. She checked the display and saw that the call was from Pitt Street.

'Irvine,' she answered, switching the stereo off.

'Thought I would check and see how you're getting on.' Moore's voice boomed out of the tinny speaker. Irvine held the phone away from her ear.

'Um, okay so far,' she said. 'I've got a Snickers and some Lucozade.'

'Doesn't get much better than that,' Moore said.

'No, sir, it doesn't.'

'Listen, just to let you know, I spoke to Jack. He came looking for you after our little chat.'

'What did you tell him?'

'I said that our interview with Finch went well and that I decided to let you follow a line of inquiry as a result. All of which is true. Sort of.'

'Thank you, sir. I appreciate it.'

'We're not colluding against anyone here, Becky,' Moore said. 'I mean, you are following a line of inquiry to do with Finch and it did come up after our interview.'

'Still, chain of command and all . . .'

'I'm the top of the chain so far as Jack is concerned and we both know he's not getting any further up before he retires. Don't worry about it. We're under control.'

Irvine wanted to say something constructive.

'Should I report in to you, sir?' she asked. 'As things progress tonight.'

'Well, if there is anything to report then sure, let me know. But don't feel that you need to check in with me on an hourly basis or anything. After all, you're on your own time, officially.'

'I know, but someone ought to know where I am all the same.'

She heard Moore's chair creaking as he leaned back in it.

'You're right, of course.'

'Okay, I'll let you know my movements if nothing else.'

'Be careful.'

8

4.00 p.m.

Logan passed time at the office checking his inbox and thinking about what to do with all the information clogging his head. He decided he needed to check what he could about the transaction with Crawford and see if he could confirm his suspicions about it. He called Josh Davey, one of the corporate trainees at Kennedy Boyd and the one Logan trusted most to do any job right. He was two floors up and all the way on the other side of the building. It was easier to phone.

'Josh, it's Logan Finch.'

'Hi, Logan, how you doing?'

'I'm good, Josh. Listen, I need you to run a Companies House search for me.'

He heard paper rustling on Josh's desk.

'Okay, Logan, what's the name?'

'Brinksman Scotland Limited. You need the company number and registered office too?'

'That's Bob's client, right? So we should have all that info already on the system. You could look it up yourself, you know.'

'I know that, Josh. But what I need right now is a complete history of the shareholding in the company from day one to now. We don't have that on file.'

'Okay. I can do that. You want me to run down any info on any companies or individuals that have held shares? I could do that for you.'

'Sounds good, thanks. Give me everything you can lay your hands on, okay?'

'Will do. What's the deadline?'

'Today.'

'I'll get back to you.'

Every UK company has to be registered at Companies House and basic information on all of them is available free online. But if you want to check every document ever filed by the company you have to pay for it. Kennedy Boyd had an online account with access to everything within a few minutes. All the accounts ever lodged could be downloaded in seconds, as well as every annual return with shareholders' names and addresses.

It was time to do a bit of digging on Bob's client to see just who was in control of the company. Logan realised he would eventually have to go to Irvine and tell her what he knew, but he wanted to do it on his terms and when he had all the information he needed. It was too important to screw around with.

Logan swivelled in his seat and looked out at the square. He thought about the girl – his little girl – and it was two or three minutes before he noticed the guy was back on the wall again, reading a magazine and looking bored. On impulse, Logan rapped his knuckles loudly on the window and waved when the guy looked up. The guy went back to his magazine and Logan turned back to his desk. He thought about going to see Bob but decided to wait until he heard from Josh. Best to have all the facts before reaching any conclusion. Then he thought about calling Cahill but he still wasn't certain about his friend's role in all of this. Instead, he went out into the hall and got a coffee from the machine and sat sipping it at his desk.

It took Josh almost an hour to call back. Logan ignored any calls that came in until he saw Josh's name flash up on the caller ID screen.

'How long does it take, Josh?'

'Sorry, Logan. Been busy. Look, can I come down to go over this with you? I got lots of stuff.'

'Sure. Can you come now?'

'Absolutely. See you in two minutes.'

Josh Davey was twenty-three and tall with curly brown hair. He looked older than he was, which would probably help him in a corporate career where experience counted for a lot. He set a large pile of papers down on Logan's desk. He did it hard so that it made a loud thump – as if he was saying 'Look at the great job I did for you'.

'So, Josh, what's the story?'

'Before I tell you, the reason I wanted to come down was just to ask what this was all about. I mean, is someone in trouble or something? Is there a problem with this?'

Logan was part intrigued and part pissed off.

'Just tell me, Josh.'

'Okay, okay. Well, this Brinksman weaves a tangled web, as they say.' Josh looked over at Logan and smiled. Logan gave him a blank get-on-with-it look in return. He got the message.

'It's part of a group structure. All of the Brinksman shares are held by another of the group companies, called . . .' He flicked through his pile of papers. 'Here it is – Alter Ego Limited. Great name. And the Alter Ego shares are all held by the ultimate parent company.'

'Okay,' Logan said. 'Pretty unremarkable stuff. Why all the fuss, Josh?'

'I'm getting there. Like I said, it's pretty tangled so bear with me for now. Okay, so the parent company has some of its shares owned by an English registered company and there's only one private individual who's a shareholder of that company. See how it starts to get complicated? Turns out this shareholder is a lawyer, an English lawyer.'

'Okay. More interesting now. Where does it lead?'

'I knew I'd get you. So I thought I'd check out this guy's history with other companies. We can't do a search of shareholdings but we can check what companies he's a director of.'

'And I'm guessing you did that and it gets even more interesting?' Logan said, sitting forward now.

'Correct. This lawyer is in business with five other individuals who all hold directorships with him in a number of other English-based companies. And in one Dubai-registered company.'

'Now we're getting somewhere,' Logan said.

Dubai jealously guards information on companies registered there. Which usually means that anyone in the UK with a company interest over there has something to hide. Not necessarily something illegal. But something.

'Right,' Josh went on. 'Trouble is, we can't really get anything out of Dubai except the address of the company. But I know a guy works for a law firm out there so I called him and he did some quick checking on the address. The company shares its office with a law firm – the Dubai office of the firm this English lawyer works for.'

'I'm starting to get a headache,' Logan said. 'But finish it for me anyway.'

'We're on the final stretch. There's also a French company at the same address, some kind of accounting or freight forwarding operation or something. And the good news is that France is more open about info on its companies than Dubai. So I got the names of the shareholders.'

'And this took you just an hour? I'm impressed.'

'Tell the partners that when they review my salary this year.'

Logan would have laughed in other circumstances. 'Take it all the way home for me,' he said instead.

'These French directors have some directorships in Scotland. One of them is the company that's supposed to be buying Brinksman.'

Logan waited for Josh to go on.

'That's it, boss,' Josh said.

Logan sat back and tried to think it through. It sounded as though there was something bad going on but he couldn't visualise it after that briefing.

'I can spell it out for you, if you want?' Josh asked.

'Go for it, Josh.'

'Near as I can tell, and it's guesswork at this point, you and Bob might be tied up in a flip.'

'Shit.'

'It's a con, right?' Josh asked.

'Sure, if it's true,' Logan said, wanting to keep Josh at arm's length.

'So,' Josh went on, undaunted, 'on the face of it, two unrelated companies enter into a deal where one buys out the other. In reality, the companies are effectively owned by the same people. It's a simple money-laundering exercise. Dirty money is transferred from company A, the buyers, to its lawyers. They then pay that out to the lawyers of company B, the sellers. Finally, the money is sent by the lawyers to company B – which is owned by the same guys behind company A.'

What he didn't say, Logan thought, was that the way to avoid alarm bells ringing with the lawyers was for company A to hire a crooked lawyer and take the chance that the lawyer on the other side never saw the deal for what it really was – or pay him off as well.

Logan was acutely aware that as a lawyer he was subject to strict money-laundering regulations, meaning if he even just suspected a laundering deal he had to report it confidentially to NCIS – the National Criminal Intelligence Service.

'I mean, there's no direct link between the two companies,' Josh told him. 'But you can follow a long chain tying them together. It doesn't look good.'

'It's bad, Josh. You're right.'

'Does Bob know?'

'He will shortly.'

'We've got to report it, right? To NCIS, I mean.'

'We have,' Logan said, with no intention of doing any such thing.

After Josh left, Logan sat brooding at his desk until it turned five o'clock and then he went to the window and watched as the secretaries and other support staff headed out of the office and home. Even if there wasn't enough work to hold the lawyers there long past five, they stayed just to show their commitment to the firm because everyone wanted the trappings of success: the big house, the plasma TVs and the fast cars. Logan had done it for years to try to make his mark and show his worth. And Bob Crawford had done the same.

Logan wondered now what else Crawford had done to broker this deal, the biggest one of his career. Was Crawford really dirty or just a victim? And just how much did Crawford know about Penny's death and Ellie's abduction?

The pavements around the square started to fill up with the mass of workers leaving their offices. Logan searched for his shadow and eventually found him sitting on one of the benches inside the park. He was sipping from a bottle of water and staring up at Logan's building.

Logan figured that they would keep tabs on him twenty-four/seven now until either he started to play ball and help Crawford put the deal to bed or they decided it wasn't worth the effort and killed him instead.

Time to call out Crawford.

'Crawford,' came the usual terse response when Logan phoned.

'Bob, it's Logan. Can we talk?'

Silence for a beat.

Then another.

Too long.

'Sure. I mean, I'm busy now but I'll have a window tomorrow.'

Something was up. Logan heard it in his voice straight away.

'No,' Logan told him. 'It has to be today. We need to talk about the Brinksman deal.' He wanted Bob to know that he was not going to back down on this. He heard Crawford sigh.

'Let me check then and I can maybe move some things around tonight. I can't promise, though.'

'Listen, I know I was stupid at the meeting this morning and I'm sorry. Let's work to get it back on track, okay?' He did his best to put conviction into the delivery. Crawford mumbled something about its not being a problem and hung up.

Things would have to move fast from here and Logan didn't expect a return call tonight. He guessed that if

Crawford was in on the scam he would be making some calls to tell the bad guys that he (Logan) was saying all the right things now. He knew that Crawford would try to sell it, even if he had not been convinced by Logan's performance.

And that was when it hit him that they might actually kill him, and not just the girl. It was a business decision for these guys, nothing more. He represented an obstacle to the deal and they would do what was necessary to remove that obstacle. He felt oddly calm in that moment of realisation; and also utterly alone. He picked up his mobile and dialled the only person he thought might be able to keep him alive if it all went to shit – if he could be trusted.

Cahill picked up after the second ring. 'Logan.'

'Alex, I think I may be at the point of no return with this thing.'

'Why?'

'I called Bob and told him I wanted to get the deal back on and—'

'So you're convinced now that it is Bob's deal?'

'Pretty much, yes.'

'What did he say?'

'Well, I didn't ask him straight out if he was laundering money on the back of murder, kidnapping and extortion, you know? But I told him I was back on my game and ready to move it forward. I don't know if he believed me. I kind of got this feeling from him that it had gone too far now, that I had blown it. I think he'll try to get these guys to hold off from going nuclear on me, but he's not really functioning at his best. I don't know if he can sell it.'

'You need to come see me, Logan. Right now. You're at risk.'

'Maybe it's too late already.'

'Why?' Logan heard the tightness in Cahill's voice.

'I've had a guy following me around all day. He was in my building this morning.'

Silence for a beat. Just like with Crawford. Logan began to wonder if everyone he knew (thought he knew) was tied up in this. He decided not to say anything about Ellie to Cahill, at least for now.

'Is he still there now, the guy following you?' Cahill asked.

Logan craned round in his seat and looked out at the park. He couldn't see the guy any more.

'I don't see him,' he said to Cahill.

'Right, I'm coming over there now. And we're leaving together.'

Logan wondered if this was how the end game was going to play out, killed by the man he thought would protect him. He felt sick and pressed the button to end the call without saying anything else.

He watched Crawford skip down the front steps of the building below his window and then run round the corner, heading for the firm's car park at the back.

'Running out on me, Bob?' he asked no one. 'The fuck you are.'

He grabbed his suit jacket and went to confront the man he thought might have killed Penny. Maybe not with his own hands, but he had killed her all the same.

9

5.06 p.m.

Ellie had succeeded in working the first nail all the way out of the board. She fingered it in the gloom of her room, feeling the dull point and realising that the boards had been in place for a long time. She wondered if that was because no one used the old cabin any more or because this was where these bad men brought people to be killed.

How many other people had died here, she wondered.

Pushing the ugly thought from her mind, she pressed and wiggled the nail in and out of its hole a few times to make sure that she could put it back in place and they would think nothing was wrong with it. But also so she could get it out again without much effort.

When she was satisfied with her work, she used the old nail to try to get under the second nail at the same end of the board. There were five boards in all and they were all held in place by two nails at either end. She guessed that she would only need to remove the bottom three to squeeze out of the window.

No matter how hard she tried, she couldn't get any movement on the second nail. She sucked at the raw, red tips of her fingers. They were cut to the quick by the constant effort of pulling and twisting at the nail heads. She was used to the taste of her own blood now and it didn't faze her.

She stared at the board and then an idea hit her – if one nail was out, then that end of the board would not be as secure as before. She put both sets of fingers on the edge of the board and tried as hard as she could to pull it from the window. The effort sent a fresh bolt of pain through her and she had to double over and take a deep breath to stop the nausea roiling around her stomach. After that passed, she tried pulling again at the board. This time it did move a little. But the wood squeaked and creaked against the nail holding it in place. It sounded to Ellie as loud as an explosion. She stopped and listened for any sound from the front of the cabin.

Nothing.

She realised she had stopped breathing and sucked some air into her lungs before pulling again at the board. It moved some more. This time she saw that the nails at the opposite end also moved. She would have to be very careful, but she thought she would be able to get the whole board off pretty soon.

She was tired from the pain and the physical effort and

decided to rest. She was pushing the first nail back into place when she heard the familiar ring tone through the walls. She moved quickly to get the board secure and then shuffled back to bed.

She strained to hear what was being said. It sounded like the man who had last been in her room answering the phone. Maybe he was talking to Drake. The man started to shout, and then he laughed, but it didn't sound as if he was happy. Then she heard footsteps heading back her way. She closed her eyes when the door started to swing open.

'I know you awake, girl,' he said. 'I hear you move around.'

Ellie opened her eyes and stared at him soundlessly.

'It all be over soon now for everyone and I get to go home. But we have our fun first, you and I. Like I told you earlier, girl. Something for you to look forward to.'

Ellie tried to hold his gaze but could not. She bit her bottom lip to stop herself from crying.

'But first my tall friend goes to see your daddy, eh? Make sure he understands what happens if he doesn't help us any more.'

He gave a low chuckle and left the room, gently closing the door.

Ellie sat silently in the deepening dark of her room and listened to the tall man walk outside, start up the van and drive off. She had never met her dad, had never even spoken to him, but the absolute certainty she felt that this man would kill him filled her with a dread so immense, she feared it would overwhelm her.

*   *   *

Sergei had gone back to the main living area of the cabin, where Vasiliy was getting ready to leave for Glasgow.

'Vasiliy, my old friend,' he said, 'if you fuck this up and something bad happens again, don't bother to come back, okay. I will end you myself.' He smiled as he said it and clasped his hands on the tall man's arms.

'I'll do it right,' Vasiliy told him. 'He'll come round this time, and if you'd let me do it in the first place we wouldn't be in this fucking mess anyway. Sneaking around and threatening women and little girls is not how we used to do it, Sergei. We'd go straight to the lawyer, cut his thumb off and tell him next time it'd be his dick.'

'I know, Vasiliy. Believe me, I know. But this is the new world order, where we can wear made-to-measure suits, socialise with real people and pretend to be normal. We only cut off their dicks if we really have to.'

'But you still need men like me, eh?' Vasiliy asked, aware that he would always be the muscle, and no more.

'That we do, yes. So go do your job, right?'

Vasiliy nodded and left.

10

6.05 p.m.

It took Logan nearly forty minutes to make it through the rush-hour traffic to Pollokshields and the street full of big sandstone houses where Crawford lived. He saw all of the city's eclectic architecture on the way – from the Victorian town houses round the square and down West George Street to the modern glass and steel offices and penthouses along Bothwell Street and then back to the glorious big houses on the south of the city in Pollokshields.

Logan wasn't a native of Glasgow and had seen the place change enormously in the twelve years and more he had been studying and working there. The city centre was now a vibrant, cosmopolitan hub of trendy shops in classic buildings along Buchanan Street, abundant bars and restaurants throughout the centre and into the Merchant City area, and new glass-fronted high-rises (well, high by Scottish standards at eight or nine storeys) springing up at regular intervals. His own modern block of apartments (no longer 'flats') was right beside the newest and shiniest example of the office block, the Aurora.

Logan had tried both old and new now, from his flat on Byres Road to the new one in the Pinnacle building, and he liked both in different ways.

There were still tough areas of town, council estates you wouldn't go to without an armed guard where poverty bred crime and drug abuse and gangs of youths hunted in packs. But as he drove through the streets with big houses hidden behind tall hedges and walls, he wondered if this was where the real criminals went about their work. Because for the affluent it was a choice, a career move, rather than something done out of ignorance, necessity or hardship.

Crawford's house was one of the more modest examples in the area: a four-bedroom semi-detached villa with a grey slate roof and red sandstone walls. There were full, double-height rooms on both floors and a dormer window jutted out of the roofline where they had extended into the attic space too. Logan had been here many times before and knew that inside was a beautifully realised blend of the old and new – original polished floorboards with contemporary abstract art on the walls; luxurious, floor to ceiling curtains beside wall-mounted plasma screens. He guessed it took a lot of cash to maintain that lifestyle. Maybe the temptation ultimately proved too great.

Logan pulled into the driveway, stone chips crunching

under his wheels. Outside, it was almost fully dark now and the rain flurried off and on. Rachel Crawford answered the door. She was quite tall at five eight, with short bobbed auburn hair and wide brown eyes. Logan had always thought Crawford had done well in marrying her.

Rachel stepped back to let him into the hall and closed the door. She leaned up and kissed Logan's cheek, smiled and said hi.

'What brings you here?' she asked.

'Got some business I need to talk to Bob about, Rachel. Sorry to bring it back with me.'

Her smile faltered a little and Logan thought he saw something hollow flicker across her face, as if she knew (or at least suspected) that something wasn't right with her husband.

'I get used to it,' she told him, the smile back in place.

She crossed the big hallway to the bottom of the stairs and shouted Bob's name. Logan heard footsteps echo on the wooden floors above and then Crawford looked down at him from the half-landing. Logan couldn't read the blank expression on his face.

'Come on up, Logan,' he said, turning to go back up the stairs and out of sight. 'I'm in the study.'

Logan gave Rachel a half-smile as he passed her and went up the stairs. He sensed her still standing down in the hall watching him, but did not look back.

The stairs doubled back after the half-landing heading towards the front of the house, and Logan passed one of the girls' rooms on his way to the study. He saw a quick flash of pink and white wallpaper and a bed loaded with furry animals. He wondered what kind of room Ellie Grant had, before the men took her from it and killed her mother.

Crawford's study wasn't large: big enough only for a wide mahogany desk, a couple of grey filing cabinets and some bookshelves. The laptop on the desk had its screensaver on, reflective 3D text spinning and tumbling all over the screen. Logan thought it looked like it said 'The Boss'. Typical Crawford.

Crawford was sitting behind the desk, creaking back and forward in a worn leather chair. The only light came from a desktop lamp and it highlighted the weariness in his face and the dark circles under his eyes. Logan figured he probably looked just as bad. He sat in the chair on the other side of the desk and watched Crawford without saying anything for a moment. He got the impression that Crawford knew why he was here. He had a good idea how Crawford might have come to know.

'You speak to Josh Davey?' he asked.

Crawford nodded slowly. Logan laughed, a harsh bark of a sound.

'I should have known. He's a proper little bastard.'

'He'll go far,' Crawford said, smiling emptily.

Logan suddenly felt all the pain and exhaustion of the last couple of days settle into his muscles and he sank back into the chair.

'It's not the money,' Crawford said. 'I want you to know that. It wasn't about the money.'

'It's about something.'

Crawford maintained his empty smile and nodded.

'You think you're the only one who lost something, don't you, Logan? You always were a self-righteous prick.'

'You're in no position to criticise,' Logan said, leaning forward and feeling the ashes of his anger start to smoulder again. 'You got Penny killed.'

Crawford rubbed his hands over his face and up into his hair, where he clasped them on top of his head. He put a foot on the edge of the desk and leaned back in his chair. Logan smelled the musty, old house aroma of the room.

'Just what was it with you and her, Logan? I mean, I'd really like to know how she had this hold over you after what she did to you. Is she what kept you single all these years?'

'You trying to embarrass me?'

'No. I really want to know. She was a good-looking girl, I grant you that. But she wasn't spectacular.'

'I don't know what it was. We just had something.'

Logan was quiet and Crawford turned his face to the ceiling. They both heard the old stairs creaking and someone walk along the hall to the study. Rachel came into the room.

'You boys want a drink or something? A beer, or some coffee?'

Her voice sounded strained to Logan. He wondered just how much she knew.

'Coffees would be good, hon,' Crawford said.

Logan didn't want anything but said nothing to contradict Crawford. After Rachel was gone he tried to articulate his feelings. He didn't do it for Crawford, but for himself — to rationalise in his own mind how he felt.

'I read this book a few years ago; it was a regular American crime novel, nothing too literary or pretentious. The author was a guy called Jefferson Parker. I remember his name 'cause I thought it was kind of cool, in an American preppy sort of way.'

Crawford looked at him with a frown, totally confused about where this was going.

'Anyway,' Logan went on, 'there's this one idea in the book that I thought was just so right. I've still got the book somewhere in the flat, I think. One of the characters is a bit of a dark horse. He's married to this incredible woman and yet he still has a roving eye and he gets tied up in a lot of criminal stuff. But he tells his adopted son what it is that draws him to his wife. He calls it TUT – That Unknown Thing. You know, it's about how he can't explain with words in any meaningful way how he feels. There's just something about her, something . . .'

Logan tailed off, unable to finish the thought. Crawford watched him and then sat forward again.

'That's the best I can do,' Logan finished.

'We were into the deal before I got suspicious,' Crawford said without any preamble. 'Otherwise I never would have involved you or anyone else at the firm. But once we were both in it there was nothing I could do about it; I couldn't get you out.'

Logan couldn't work out whether that was supposed to be some sort of apology. He decided to say nothing.

'I got the referral from some lawyer in London I met at a party down there. You know how it is, you shake hands and exchange business cards with so many people that you forget who half of them are. So he phoned out of the blue and I pretended I remembered him. Said he had a contact looking for some help with a deal in Scotland. He gave me the identification verification and it all looked above board, you know? But I was as nervous as you about the switch of funding. You remember, when they switched it to that French private equity fund?'

Logan nodded.

'Anyway, I didn't tell you but I grilled them hard about it for a few days. Then one night I get this urgent call to go and meet the buyer and his lawyer at a restaurant. It's an upmarket place so I figure it's just the way they want to do business. You know it, the one on West Regent Street that you like – has the private rooms down in the basement.'

Logan knew it. He often took contacts and potential clients there if he wanted to impress them.

'So I get there and they have a private room booked. We have a nice meal and they bring in the coffee and then close and lock the door. I'd had some wine so I didn't think it was all that weird. Then the buyer, the guy you met this morning, comes and sits beside me.'

'The tennis pro?'

'What?'

'Drake,' Logan explained. 'Looked like a tennis player to me.'

'I guess he does a little bit, yeah,' Crawford said. 'He puts this envelope in front of me and then sits back and says nothing. I'm game for some intrigue and open it up.'

Crawford stopped and took a deep breath.

'There're some photographs in there. The girls in the school playground – my girls. And one of Rachel through the window of our bedroom here getting undressed. That kind of thing. I stood up and knocked my chair over, spilling red wine all over the white tablecloth. This guy Drake is up like lightning, I mean he was so fast, Logan.' Crawford shook his head. 'He grabs my neck and forces me back down into my chair. The scumbag lawyer sits there across the table smirking the whole time like he's seen this all before and it's just so fucking funny. Then this guy leans in and tells me that if I don't see this deal through he stands to lose a lot of money. That's not something he's prepared to accept. So either I play along and be a nice little money-launderer or he kills my family.'

'But you let me keep going on about the funding change, Bob. Why?'

'I couldn't tell you about it, could I? I hoped it would just go away. I know it sounds stupid now, but you have to understand the pressure I was under.'

Logan remembered something else Crawford had said, and he wasn't going to let him off that easily.

'You said it wasn't about the money.'

Crawford blanched.

'What money?' Logan asked.

Crawford looked blankly at him across the desk. Logan stood, his arms hanging down at his sides.

'What fucking money, Bob?'

Crawford sat back in his chair. 'It was the carrot and the

stick, Logan,' he said. 'What was I supposed to do, eh? Either they killed the girls or I did the deal and got a brown envelope.'

'With how much in it?'

Crawford looked away and sighed. 'What does it matter how much,' he said. 'I mean really, Logan, what the fuck does it matter?'

His voice started to rise in anger and frustration but Logan felt that he had no right to those emotions. Not now.

'It matters because there's blood on it,' he shouted, feeling his own blood swell the veins in his face. 'Penny's and maybe Ellie's too. How about that? Save your girls and sacrifice mine, was that the deal?'

Crawford looked up at Logan with a frown. Logan's voice rose to a scream.

'You were the only one who knew she was back in town. You were the one who told them how to get leverage on me by doing this to Penny – and to Ellie.'

He walked round the desk, clenching his fists and for the first time feeling real emotion run through him when he said her name – Ellie. Crawford pushed out of his chair and stepped back.

'I don't know any Ellie, Logan. What are you talking about?'

'You gave them up to your guys. Sold them out to those murderers.'

Crawford backed up until he bumped into a bookcase and could go no further. He held his hands out, palms up, and shook his head. His voice rose to meet Logan's.

'What was I supposed to do? It was my family or some old girlfriend of yours, you stupid fuck. You'd have done the same. Can't you see that? How was I supposed to know they would kill her? What purpose would that serve?'

'Fuck you,' Logan screamed, tears filling his eyes and raw emotion giving his voice a ragged edge. 'You told them about her and they killed her.'

Logan moved forward and swung an arm round, twisting his body at the last moment and slamming his fist down on to the desk with a roar. Pain bolted up his arm, jagged shards of it shooting into his brain.

'You want to hit me?' Crawford shouted. 'Go ahead then. But if you hadn't been so fucking obsessed with her it never would have happened. Why couldn't you let her go? Why? Twelve fucking years, man.'

Logan squeezed his eyes tight and tried to shut out all of it. But one image was a constant – Ellie staring out at him from the photo dropped at his feet by the two Neanderthals.

'What about Ellie?' he asked in a whisper.

'I don't know who that is, I told you. For Christ's sake, Logan, it's—'

Logan was on Crawford faster than he knew he was capable of moving. He swung a short, hard punch at Crawford's head and felt it connect with his chin. Crawford's knees buckled, but Logan grabbed him by the shoulders and stopped him from falling.

'Logan!'

He turned and saw Rachel standing in the doorway with

two big mugs of coffee. They'd been so busy screaming at each other that they hadn't heard her come up the stairs. Her eyes were difficult to read.

'How much do you know?' he asked her, dropping his hands and stepping back from Crawford.

'All of it,' she said, unable to maintain eye contact with him.

He snorted out a breath and wiped at his wet face with the sleeve of his jacket. 'All of it?' he repeated.

Rachel nodded.

'About Ellie too? You could sit back as a mother and let that happen, Rachel? Like some kind of monster?'

Rachel looked up at him this time, and then at Crawford.

'I don't know what he's talking about either,' Crawford told her.

Logan looked at Crawford and then back at Rachel and it suddenly hit him what had happened: Penny had told Crawford she was back but not mentioned her daughter, wanting to maintain the secrecy until she had spoken to Logan. The guys who had taken Ellie probably hadn't even known she existed until they got to Penny's house.

Logan had nothing left. He felt utterly drained and sick to his core, and he wanted to make sure that he shared that with the Crawfords. Let them see just what they had done. He walked to the door of the study and Rachel stepped away from him, letting him pass. He paused with one hand on the door and looked directly at Crawford.

'Penny had a daughter, Bob. My daughter. Her name is Ellie, she's eleven years old and those fuckers took her. For all I know they tortured and killed her just for fun. Maybe even . . .'

He couldn't articulate that final awful thought as his whole body heaved and shook.

'Why didn't you just call the police and let them handle it, Bob? Why?'

Rachel dropped the mugs, spilling coffee all over the floor as she raised her hand to her mouth. Crawford looked as if someone had hit a switch in his brain and turned all the lights off. Logan left them there like that and walked down and out to his car.

11

9.00 p.m.

Logan felt emotionally numb and wanted to feel the same way all over. He decided upon the traditional Scottish remedy of drinking until he was out of his face. Not the most mature approach to the situation, but at least it would dull the pain.

He left his car in the office car park as usual because he could park there for free and it was just a short walk from his apartment. He stood for a moment in Blythswood Square, trying to figure out the best place to get drunk. He settled on Vroni, a tight little wine bar down the hill on West Nile Street, mainly because it was usually packed and the music turned up loud enough to obliterate any kind of rational thought. He didn't notice the old van rattle to a stop across the road and the big man within watch him amble down towards the centre of town.

Logan dug in his jacket pocket for his mobile. He found it and then started a fresh search for Irvine's business card, thinking that he didn't really see the harm any more in telling her all about the sad story of his life. He turned the phone on and after a few moments it beeped to tell him he had voicemail messages. He dialled in and found three messages from Cahill, all asking where the fuck he was and telling him that he should call right fucking now. Logan thought Cahill sounded slightly panicky, which was unusual for him. He deleted the messages and decided not to call back, still unsure if he could trust him.

He got to the corner of West Nile Street and stood for a long few seconds looking up and down, totally unable to recall where Vroni was. He saw a place across the road called the Bar Room and decided it was probably as good as anywhere, though he'd never been in it before. He crossed over to the bar and stood outside to call Irvine.

The big man from the van loitered behind him at the traffic lights on the opposite side of the road. Logan stared right through him, oblivious of the fact that it was the taller of the two men he had encountered once before in the lobby of his own building.

He called Irvine's mobile and she answered after two rings.

'Irvine,' she said, sounding tense.

'It's Logan Finch.'

There was a pause on the other end of the line.

'I didn't expect to hear from you,' she said eventually. 'Not so soon, anyway.'

'Can you talk?'

187

She said yes, but hesitated before answering and Logan sensed she wanted to say something more to him. He let the silence drag on and spoke again when it was clear the moment had passed.

'Sorry. I shouldn't have bothered, it's just . . .'

'What?'

'I guess I just want to come clean, you know.'

'Okay.' Logan heard anticipation in her voice this time.

'Look, it's not as if I know anything that will help you find her any sooner.'

'Ellie?'

This time the sound of her name was like a hammer punched bluntly through his skull.

'Yes.'

'Why don't you let me decide what might help or not. I mean, that's my job.'

'No.'

'You're a very frustrating person.'

'I get told that a lot.'

'Where are you?'

She sounded concerned and he felt glad that he had called her after all.

'I'm in town and I'm about to go into a bar and get very drunk. Consider it my last supper.'

Her voice took on a sharper edge. 'Are you in danger? Let me help, Logan. I can be there soon if you let me know where you are.'

'I'm okay. I just need some anaesthetic.'

'Alcohol isn't going to help, you know that, don't you?'

'Yeah, but it'll make me feel better for a while and right now I'm prepared to accept that because nothing else will do it.'

'I don't believe that's true,' Irvine said. 'You've got plenty of people to get you through this. What about your American friend?'

'I don't know what I think about him or anyone else,' Logan said.

'You can trust me, Logan.'

He believed she was sincere and he liked the sound of her voice, but he really just wanted to be alone at the moment.

'I'll call you again later,' he said.

He clicked a button to end the call and stuffed the phone back in his jacket. Rain started to drizzle and he wished he'd brought his overcoat. He turned and went into the bar.

Inside, there was a long counter on the left with the remaining space split on two levels and a small, square area at the back. A DJ was just finishing setting up some decks there and Logan figured it would end up an impromptu dance floor before long. The place was already busy and he had to weave through the traffic to the bar, where he found a free stool. He pulled himself on to the seat and waited to catch someone's eye to order a pint of Caffreys.

He chugged the first pint down quickly and ordered another, this time with a single malt to go with it. Best to get started early, he thought. He looked in the mirror, marvelled at his rumpled appearance and then downed the whisky.

Halfway through the second pint, he began to feel a pleasurable buzz. It was about nine thirty now and the place was really heaving, which was odd for a Tuesday night. Then he saw a poster on the wall advertising the DJ as some kind of local guy gone big time and guessed that he was the reason for the crowd. The music started up at the back at incredible volume and the little dance floor started to pulse with human life. The heavy bass line shuddered along the floor and up through the stool and embedded itself in Logan's belly. It was not unpleasant as he finished off the second pint.

After a while, each beat of the concussive bass started to feel like an explosion, thudding up into his gut now that the track (you couldn't call it a song) was in full flow.

Boom-Boom

Boom-Boom

Christ, it was loud.

He was looking along the bar to find someone to pull him another pint when his eye caught something in the mirror. He squinted in the low light and saw a familiar face. It was the guy from the park wall, sitting up on the raised level almost directly behind him. The guy sipped from what looked like a glass of iced water and casually looked away from Logan.

Boom-Boom

Boom-Boom

Not good. Not fucking good at all. Place as crowded as this, you could get knifed fast and left bleeding on the floor before anyone knew there was a problem. And being half cut wasn't exactly the best condition for a bar fight.

Logan wasn't small and worked out regularly at the gym, but he'd only ever been in three fights in his whole life, one of which happened when he was sixteen. The last one was about two years ago when he accidentally bumped into a particularly aggressive teenager in a club and spilled his beer all over the place. Logan was fortunate in that his dad had been a bit of a brawler in his youth, growing up on a tough council estate in the west of Scotland, and had imparted many words of wisdom on the fine art of avoiding getting your head kicked in. His motto went something like hit first and keep on hitting. Not subtle, but effective.

The teenager had advanced on Logan with the pint glass still in his hand, looking to shatter it on Logan's face. But Logan saw it coming because the boy wasn't particularly fast or skilled and was swinging his arm round in a wide arc like an old-fashioned haymaker. Logan stepped in, butted him in the face and punched him fast, twice, as he reeled back. It was instinctive and he hadn't realised he had it in him until it happened. The old man's genes kicking in.

The door staff had bundled him quickly out into the street, where adrenalin had pumped through his veins and made him shake all over and then vomit on the pavement.

Still, if this was a serious bad guy he knew he'd have no chance, sober or otherwise. His dad had told him you never beat a real fighter because they don't know how to give up until either you or they are out. Or dead.

Logan reached for his phone again and scrolled through his contacts until he found Cahill's number. He stared at it, wondering if calling him was the right move.

Boom-Boom
Boom-Boom

Logan thought he felt the stool actually vibrate with the bass. Fucking DJ must have amped it up again.

He dialled Cahill's number and tried to watch the guy behind him in the mirror without seeming obvious. It looked as if he was watching something further along the bar. As Cahill's phone rang in Logan's ear and the bass –

Boom-Boom

Boom-Boom

– shook his fillings loose, he leaned forward and looked along the line of punters at the bar. The place was dark now, with light pulsating at the back, silhouetting those in front. He couldn't see the big man staring back at him from just ten feet away.

Boom-Boom

Boom-Boom

He sat back on the stool and heard the familiar message on Cahill's answerphone. He waited for the beep at the end and tried to shout a message over the din.

'ALEX, IT'S LOGAN.'

Boom-Boom

Boom-Boom

'LOOK, I'M SORRY I'VE BEEN PISSED OFF AT YOU.'

Boom-Boom

Boom-Boom

'I THINK I MIGHT BE IN TROUBLE. BAD TROUBLE. THIS GUY –'

Boom-Boom

Boom-Boom

'– THAT'S BEEN FOLLOWING ME. HE'S HERE.'

BOOM

BOOM

BOOM

The fucking noise went past twelve on the volume control and didn't stop until it hit somewhere around thirty. Logan shouted for Cahill to call him and then pressed the button to end the call.

The crowd down on the dance floor was jumping now with the bass line and the whole building seemed to shake.

BOOM BOOM BOOM **BOOM** *BOOM BOOM BOOM* **BOOM**

It was next to intolerable, but Logan knew the track from MTV and thought he would just ride it out until it finished. But the fucking DJ just mixed it in with the next track – a chunky, hip-hop swagger of a beast – and as the bass from that kicked in even the crowd in the front part of the bar started to move.

Logan looked again in the mirror for his shadow and saw that some girl was trying to flirt pretty heavily with him, and she wasn't half bad looking. Logan found himself comparing her looks unfavourably to Irvine's.

The shadow pretended to be interested in the girl but Logan could tell he wasn't; he was too busy sneaking glances back up the bar to the spot he'd been looking at before.

Ten feet away, the big man decided to make his move and stepped back from the bar as the thudding bass sent a wave of movement through the crowd.

12

9.50 p.m.

Irvine was seriously worried about Logan. She wasn't an expert, but he had sounded pretty low when he called and she wondered whether he might be suicidal. He'd certainly had a pretty big shock over the last couple of days, but he seemed robust enough when she'd left him this afternoon.

She knew that he was somewhere nearby – in town was what he had said – and she thought about driving around to see if she could find him. Glasgow wasn't the biggest city centre, but even so she knew the chances of finding him at random were negligible – particularly if he was going to be stuck in a bar all night.

She unscrewed the cap on her Lucozade and took a couple of big mouthfuls before setting it back down on the passenger seat. She'd been sitting there for more than five hours now and was getting frustrated. Logan had not come home from work and now she knew she was going to have to wait for a while yet before he showed up. She slapped at the steering wheel with one hand and accidentally set off the horn. She jumped at the sharp noise and then looked sheepishly around to see if anyone had heard her, glad to see that this far along Bothwell Street was empty at this time of night.

She picked up her mobile phone and called the incident room at Pitt Street, hoping to catch Moore still at his desk.

'DS Sharp,' the voice answered.

Shit. She thought about hanging up and decided against it.

'Jack, it's DC Irvine,' she said, keeping it formal.

'Nice to hear from you, Becky,' Irvine said, the sarcasm obvious in his voice. 'How's Mr Finch been this afternoon?'

'You spoke to the boss, then?'

'I did. We had a long chat, in fact. I think he likes you, Becky.'

Irvine recalled the stories she'd heard about Sharp – that he was a misogynist and a dick – and found herself agreeing. *Screw it.*

'It was all cleared, Jack, so you can cut the sarcasm.'

So much for formality and the chain of command. Sharp had nothing to say and she took it for a small victory.

'Put me through to the gaffer.'

The line hummed quietly as Sharp put her on hold. Clearly Moore had not been as gentle with Sharp this afternoon as his earlier conversation with her had implied. Irvine was glad. Sharp was a dinosaur.

'Becky.' Moore's voice sounded. 'Did you not play nice with DS Sharp?'

'Nope.'

Moore laughed. 'I think you'll go far in this job, DC Irvine. Glad to see that you're finding your feet this early in your CID career.'

'I haven't been able to find Logan yet,' she told Moore, immediately regretting the use of his first name.

'Uh-huh.'

'But I got a call from him just now and I think he's at risk, sir.'

'At risk how?' Moore asked, all trace of humour gone from his voice.

'I mean, he's had a rough couple of days and he was talking about getting drunk tonight.'

'Okay. I'm not sure I see the need to be concerned at that.'

'It was just, you know, how he sounded. Not so much what he said.'

There was silence on the line for a few beats.

'Becky, you're not starting to get too close to this case, are you? Because if you are . . .'

That image again in her head – reaching out and touching his hand.

'No, sir,' she said, trying to sound pissed off. 'He's a key witness and I'm concerned he might self-harm.'

'Well, unless you can find him I'm not sure there's much I can do. I already explained that I'm at the limit on my budget. Now, if this was a fresh line of inquiry or something like that, I could find the money. Otherwise . . .'

She noticed his habit of tailing off, which she didn't take as a good sign.

'Fine, sir,' she said. 'You're right. Leave it with me.'

She hung up sharply and regretted it. Alienating Sharp was one thing; Moore was a whole different beast altogether.

Irvine looked along Bothwell Street and started the car up. She turned the ignition off again after a few seconds and slumped back in her seat, grabbing the Snickers bar from the dashboard and tearing at the wrapper.

13

10.00 p.m.

Logan was oblivious of the big man moving towards him and not so much heard as felt the second track the DJ had mixed in. It was much slower than the first one, with an irregular, staccato beat.

BOOM BOOM boom-boom BOOM-BOOM
BOOM BOOM boom-boom BOOM-BOOM

Logan watched in the mirror as his shadow moved behind him. He was silky smooth and fast as he went past the girl and headed along the barrier of the upper tier towards the stairs. He'd be at Logan's position in a few seconds. Logan stepped sideways off the stool and moved into the crowd, shouldering hard through the steamy mass of bodies.

Boom Boom boom-boom Boom-Boom
Boom Boom boom-boom Boom-Boom

He got lucky and passed unnoticed by the big man, about three bodies further from the bar. He didn't see the carnage that the wide-bodied thug was leaving in his wake as he smashed his way through the crowd. Logan kept moving forward and craned his neck, looking for his shadow. He saw the man glide down the steps and start towards his stool, and realised he'd made a mistake by heading deeper into the bar. He didn't like his chances of trying to slip past the shadow, so his way out to the front entrance was blocked.

Shit.

There was nothing to do other than keep going towards the rear, and maybe getting lost in the bear pit that was the dance floor.

Boom Boom boom-boom Boom-Boom
Boom Boom boom-boom Boom-Boom

The big man reached the stool a fraction after the shadow and saw that it was empty. He paid no attention to the shadow, who was leaning over the bar and looking along it to the rear, but turned, almost bowling two young girls over, and started clawing his way towards the back. The shadow stayed still, his eyes searching the strobing nightmare of the place until he caught sight of Logan's head moving slowly through the crowd. He set off after him, some way behind the big man, whose strength and bulk propelled him more quickly through masses.

Boom Boom boom-boom Boom-Boom
Boom Boom boom-boom Boom-Boom

Logan had almost reached the edge of the dance floor when he saw the sign for the lavatories off to his left, past the end of the bar. He changed direction, hoping that he might be able to hide out in one of the stalls until the shadow lost interest. He wasn't thinking particularly clearly at that point, with the trauma of the day and the alcohol in his bloodstream creating a dizzying cocktail in his head. He went through the door into the relative calm of the corridor and then pushed into the Gents, not hearing the big man grunting heavily as he followed eight feet behind.

Here the sound of the music was little more than a muffled, underwater kind of beat, but Logan could still feel the floor vibrate as he walked along the line of stalls until he found a vacant one. The floor was slick with a mix of piss and water and the air reeked, as if the place hadn't been cleaned for a while. Behind him, the door banged open. Logan turned his head at the sound, and locked eyes with the big man.

'Business is still not so good, eh?' the big man said in his thick accent.

Logan froze, recognising him now from the foyer of his building last night.

The big man moved towards Logan.

Logan backed up with nowhere to go.

His dad's voice cut through the crap in his head and, just as the big man got to within six feet of him, Logan took one stride forward and swung his foot as hard as he could up into the big man's balls. He felt it connect pretty solidly.

The big man's eyes opened wide and he staggered back a step or two, his hands clutching at his crotch.

Logan did what he was taught and went forward, buoyed by his early success. He swung two hard punches at the big man's head, catching him on the cheekbone with the first one and grazing his chin with the second as the big man moved to avoid the attack.

Logan moved to butt him but the big man saw it coming, ducked his head, and thrust it forward to meet Logan's.

Logan felt the sickening impact as his forehead caught the top of the big man's head and he went down, slipping on the wet floor. He put a hand to his head and it came back bloody. A blade of pain ripped through his skull and he blinked hard to ward it off.

The big man had a thick skull and recovered far more quickly. He kicked out at Logan and connected with his chest, sending him sliding back against the far wall. Logan felt as if his chest had collapsed and fought for breath.

The big man moved forward again, a trail of blood starting to run down his face from his hairline; an unstoppable thing from some evil creator's worst nightmare. Logan tried to stand but his head felt light and his legs were incapable of bearing his weight.

He looked up and saw the big man reach into his coat and pull out what looked like a big butcher's knife.

I'm gone.

14

10.05 p.m.

Logan tried to push himself up again and then the door to the Gents crashed back against the wall, sending plaster dust spraying into the air.

Logan looked past the big man and saw the shadow glide in with something big and black in his hands.

A flare went off and the air exploded with an incredible noise, ringing off the tiled walls.

The big man lurched forward suddenly, slipped on the wet floor and fell sideways against one of the stall doors, pulling it partially off its hinges.

The shadow walked forward coolly and stopped in front of the big man with his knees slightly bent and his arms stretched out in front of him. Logan saw that he held a gun in his hands.

The big man looked at the shadow as the weapon flared to life again and the sound erupted in the tight space.

The big man's head jerked back. Blood sprayed out and misted pink from where the back of his head used to be and Logan turned his face as he felt some of the blood land on his cheek. The big man dropped straight to the floor and his head hit with a wet thud. Blood pooled quickly around it. It looked black in the weak, artificial light.

The shadow walked towards Logan, smoothly sliding the gun into a holster inside his jacket. Logan wiped the blood from his cheek with his sleeve. The shadow stopped and held out a hand.

'Cahill sent me,' he said. 'Let's go.'

The shadow pulled Logan along the wet pavement and down to the corner where West Nile Street met St Vincent Street and from there along towards number 123 where Cahill's office was. The shadow looked back a couple of times to check they were not being followed and then pulled a mobile phone out of his trouser pocket with his free hand. He turned Logan and shoved him into the recessed doorway of a hairdressing salon and then stood out in the rain, flipping the phone open and dialling in a number.

Logan noticed then how young he looked, no older than in his late twenties. He was slightly shorter than Logan at around five eleven, but the hard muscles in his arms and chest could be seen through the loose-fitting blue windcheater he was wearing over plain black trousers. His cheeks were flushed with colour as he put the phone to his ear and stared back to the corner of West Nile Street.

'Alex, it's me,' he said into the phone.

He shook his head while listening to Cahill's voice.

'No, it was a complete cluster fuck. I had to get your man out of there and someone got in my way.'

He listened to Cahill again and this time gave an affirmative nod.

'I took him out.'

The shadow pulled the phone from his ear and Logan heard the volume of Cahill's voice shoot up.

'No . . . let me explain it to you . . .'

He was clearly having a hard time getting past Cahill's anger.

'Alex, shut the fuck up, okay. Listen to me. He had bad intentions in mind and I had to make a decision . . .'

He got cut off again.

'If you let me finish.'

Cahill's voice rose again and the shadow decided he'd had enough.

'We're coming up now.'

He flipped the phone shut, grabbed Logan again and pulled him across the street. On the other side, they broke into a fast jog until they reached the entrance to Cahill's building. The shadow turned to face Logan, rain dripping from his hair and running in thin rivulets down his face.

'Does it ever not rain in this goddamn country?' he asked.

The temperature had dropped a couple of degrees since

Logan had gone into the bar and the shadow's breath puffed out as he spoke.

'Not usually,' Logan told him.

The shadow ran his hands up through his hair, pulling it back from his face.

'Okay,' he said. 'You're not going to bolt if I let you go, are you?'

Logan shook his head. 'I don't want to get shot,' he said.

The shadow smiled and nodded. 'Let's go, then. The elevators are at the back of the lobby, past the security desk on the left. Once we're in, move smooth and easy and say something to me so that it looks casual. I'll laugh even if it's not funny.'

Logan was suddenly aware that he had an American accent – east coast somewhere. Maybe Boston or Maine where the vowel sounds got elongated.

They went through the main revolving door and into the marble-tiled lobby. While the outside of the building was still the original red sandstone shell, the inside had been demolished and rebuilt. It was redeveloped about six years ago and Logan remembered walking past it many times. It had looked weird after they ripped the old inside down and left only the exterior walls intact, supported by a complex arrangement of steel girders.

The lobby formed a central atrium stretching up to the third floor, and their wet shoes squeaked as they moved to the rear. The shadow elbowed Logan.

'You're a fucking nut-job,' Logan said.

The shadow laughed and it sounded genuine. 'Bet you're glad I am?'

'Too fucking right.'

They got to the bank of five lifts as one of them pinged and the doors opened. A bunch of young guys got out with an impressive array of tattoos and facial piercings. They were all holding cigarette packets and lighters.

'Twenty-four-hour call centre on floors two through five,' the shadow explained when they were in the lift.

'I know,' Logan said. 'I've been here before with Alex.'

The lift rose smoothly to the third floor and the doors opened out on to the low key reception area for CPO Security. The reception desk faced the lift with a large 'CPO' sign above it. The O was a series of concentric circles. This was Logan's third time in the offices and for the first time it struck him that the O maybe looked like a stylised target.

The reception area was empty at this time of night but it backed on to a glass wall that looked out into the building's atrium. Through it, Logan could see lights on further back in the CPO office.

'Wait here,' the shadow said and then went round a corner and disappeared.

Logan stood where he was told, smelling the fresh carpet aroma in the still relatively new offices. One of the property partners at Kennedy Boyd had done the deal on the lease for Cahill and the first time Logan had been here was for the opening party. It was a casual affair with very few people and he was the only lawyer there.

The place was set up to look like a respectable professional services firm with dark carpeting, light-coloured paint and appropriately conservative artwork on the walls, although Logan had never been into the heart of the place – just the reception and the suite of meeting rooms off to the right. He ran a hand over his damp skull and tried to shake his wet clothes till they hung comfortably. He failed. He was cold, wet, hungry and still shaking from the encounter at the bar. He'd never seen a gun before, let alone heard it used in anger.

The shadow came back and handed Logan a soft white towel and some clothes – plain black combat trousers and a black polo shirt with the CPO logo on both sleeves. He put a bottle of water on the reception desk, rested a hand on Logan's shoulder and leaned in to look at his eyes. Then he stepped back, apparently satisfied by what he saw.

'You're doing fine,' he told Logan. 'I've seen plenty of guys go into shock in situations like that. Back at the bar, I mean.'

Logan nodded. The shadow smiled.

'I'm Bailey Judd,' he said, holding his hand out to Logan.

Logan shook it firmly the way his dad taught him and nodded, his mouth a tight line in his face.

'You can dry off and change into those things in the boardroom. You know where that is, right? Alex said you would.'

'I know where it is, thanks.'

'And drink that water – you need to get rehydrated after the booze.'

'Okay, I will.'

Judd watched him for a moment, then turned and walked

through a door into the main part of the office without saying anything more.

Logan was sitting at the boardroom table dressed in the fresh clothes and sipping from the bottle of water when Judd came back. He had changed into a similar set of clothes and his hair looked recently rubbed dry.

'Where's Alex?' Logan asked.

'He'll be here soon.'

'Did he send you here to keep an eye on me, to keep me away from any sharp implements?'

Judd tried to smile, but it looked forced to Logan.

'Have you done that before?' Logan asked him. 'I mean, killed anyone?'

Judd turned and went to a cabinet just inside the door, opening it to reveal a small fridge. He took a bottle of chilled water and gulped down half of the contents without pausing. He came back to the table and sat beside Logan, screwing the cap back on to the bottle.

'First time it's been that intimate,' he said, keeping his eyes on the bottle of water and turning it with his fingers.

It was an odd word to use in the circumstances and Logan wanted to ask more, but he let the silence grow, hoping that Judd would fill it without prompting. He looked as if he wanted to talk about it.

'I was in Afghanistan after nine eleven,' Judd said finally. 'Signed up after watching Bush pump up the crowd at Ground Zero.' He looked at Logan now. 'Did you guys see that over here?'

'I think the whole world saw it,' Logan said.

Judd smiled without humour and went back to turning the bottle.

'I was just out of college and working in Boston when it happened. The twin towers, I mean. My grandpa was killed at Pearl Harbor when my dad was just a baby and there was always military stuff around the house, framed medals and photographs and the like. My dad never went into the service – he owned a car dealership – but his mom always made sure he remembered his dad and I was just like any kid and loved her stories and the medals.' He took a sip of water. 'So I went to Ranger school at Fort Benning and then off to war full of all the patriotic shit that the government could muster.'

'You came back safe, though,' Logan said, trying to sound positive.

'*I* did, but I knew plenty of guys that didn't. Guys who lost legs or arms or both, and guys that got brought home in boxes too.'

Logan was fascinated by Judd's story, but he was starting to feel some regret for having brought the subject up – clearly it was a source of some pain to Judd.

'So how did you end up here with Alex?' he said, trying to refocus the conversation.

Judd stood and walked to the window looking down on to St Vincent Street. He was quiet for a moment and Logan said nothing.

'I lost my dad not long after I came home,' he said. 'Cancer.'

'I'm sorry,' Logan said.

'I was just bumming around without a job and wrapped

up in my own misery and I tried not to let his death affect me. Trouble was, I didn't realise how hard it had hit my mom. I mean, I was an only child and I was all that was left after Dad was gone. She died six months after him.'

Judd didn't volunteer how his mother had died and he came back and sat at the table, taking another sip of water.

'Then Chris Washington, one of my buddies from Afghanistan, called me up while I was wallowing in booze and self-pity and said he'd heard about my parents and wondered if I wanted a change of scenery. He was working for Alex over here and they were looking for another guy with combat experience, you know? What we do here is not really like what happened tonight. I mean, we're not mercenaries or anything. I had nothing really to stay in the States for and flew over here on Alex's dime with a duffel bag of clothes and not much more.'

'And are you glad you came?'

Judd paused for a moment, screwing the cap back on the bottle.

'Yeah, I am.'

The door opened and Cahill came in alone. He sat beside Logan and checked him out just as Judd had.

'What am I?' Logan asked. 'An exhibit in a zoo or something?'

Cahill sat back in his chair and rubbed his face. He looked older tonight, and Logan told him so.

'Fuck you,' Cahill replied. 'You look like shit, Logan.'

'I know.'

They fell into an awkward silence. Logan broke it.

'Thanks,' he said.

'No problem.'

'I mean it, Alex,' Logan said, leaning forward. 'You saved my life tonight.'

'Bails did, not me,' Cahill said, nodding in Judd's direction.

'You sent him after me,' Logan said with force, his voice wavering. 'You did that.'

Cahill nodded, and then stood. 'Come on,' he said, gesturing with his head for Logan to follow.

Judd got up but Logan remained in his chair and sipped again at his water before setting it down. He wiped a trickle of condensation that ran down the outside of the cold bottle and then watched as another followed it and pooled on the table. Cahill and Judd watched him without speaking.

'I got another photo from those two guys,' Logan said, looking up at Cahill. 'A little girl. She's Penny's daughter.'

'Go find the guys,' Cahill said to Judd. 'They're in the War Room and we'll be there in a minute.'

Judd nodded and left.

'She's my daughter too, Alex,' Logan said after Judd was gone. 'The police are checking DNA from blood they found at the house, but I know she is. I know it for sure. She's missing and I think those guys must have her. That's the leverage they're going to use, not that they might kill me.'

Cahill's eyes appeared to darken and his breathing sounded shallow.

'I told you that story, about the time I lost one of my girls on holiday – and how it made me feel?'

Logan said he remembered.

'This is the same, Logan. Let's go and talk with my boys.'

Day Three

1

Wednesday, 12.01 a.m.

'You know, Alex, until now I thought maybe you were somehow part of all of this,' Logan said as they walked along a wide corridor deeper into the CPO office complex.

Cahill kept on walking. 'I guessed as much,' he said. 'So what?'

'I just wanted to tell you that I feel pretty bad about it, you know?'

'No reason to feel bad. We're friends, but my business requires a high degree of privacy; secrecy, you might say. So I can see how that might have seemed suspicious. Plus, you've really been put through the wringer in the last couple of days, Logan. Any of us would be fucked up after that.'

Logan saw that two of the doors they passed in the corridor did not have any handles but small electronic keypads instead, flush mounted in the wall to the side of the doors. The signs on the doors read 'A1' and 'A2'. Cahill saw Logan checking them out.

'Armouries,' he told him, matter-of-factly.

Logan stopped but Cahill kept walking, gesturing with his hand for Logan to follow. Logan jogged to keep up.

'This isn't America, Alex. I mean you know that, right?'

'Sure I do. You think I'm stupid or something?'

'You know what I mean.'

'Look, I'm kidding,' Cahill said. 'We keep that stuff at a different site.'

They turned a corner and reached a set of heavy wooden doors at the end of the corridor with another keypad in the wall.

'Is this where you keep the nukes?' Logan asked.

Cahill laughed and keyed in his pass code. There was an audible click and he pushed the doors open.

'This is what we call the War Room,' he said and then turned to walk inside.

The room was about twenty-five feet square with a large, wall-mounted flat screen TV at one end and what looked like a regular schoolroom whiteboard at the other. There were no windows, internal or external, and light was provided by recessed spots in the ceiling. The wall opposite the doors looked as if it had a series of built-in cupboards, maybe five or six in total, and a small conference table: sat in the middle of the floor with most of the surface taken up by laptop computers and scattered pieces of paper. Three men sat at the table: Bailey Judd and two others. They were all dressed in blue jeans and black CPO polo shirts and turned to look as Cahill entered.

'These are some of my boys,' Cahill said, pushing the doors shut. 'You already know Bails.'

Judd nodded and raised a hand.

'The other two are Tom Hardy and Chris Washington.'

Hardy was the tallest man in the room at around six four – a lean, ropy Texan with receding sandy hair and distinctive, pale blue eyes. He stood and shook Logan's hand, though 'crushed' might have been a better description.

'Hi,' he said.

Logan nodded.

Washington stayed where he was and nodded his head once as a greeting. He was about Logan's height, black with an impressively blunt-looking shaven head and a goatee beard. Logan recognised his name from his talk with Judd.

'Don't mind him,' Cahill said. 'He doesn't like anybody.'

'Especially you,' Washington shot back.

Logan walked round the table with Cahill and sat next to him, facing the other three. Cahill punched a series of four digits into a phone on the table and after two short rings a voice came over the speaker.

'Bruce.'

'Yeah, Bruce, it's Alex. We're ready for you now.'

'Okay. Be there in a sec.'

Cahill tapped on the keyboard of the laptop in front of him, picked up a long remote control and pointed it at the TV. Logan watched as the screen came to life, showing what looked like the standard CPO website, although it seemed different from how Logan remembered it. He said nothing, assuming there was some significance in what Cahill was doing.

The door to the War Room opened and a short, muscular man walked in. He had long hair and wore jeans and a faded black Rolling Stones T-shirt. Logan guessed he was in his late thirties.

'Hey, Bruce,' Cahill said. 'It's all yours.'

He stood and allowed Bruce to sit at the laptop, where he immediately went to work. Logan watched as his hands danced over the keyboard.

'Bruce is our ethical hacker,' Cahill told Logan. 'Just look at this.'

Logan thought Cahill sounded almost like a proud parent. He watched the images on the large screen on the wall change as Bruce did his thing.

'What's ethical about it?' he asked.

'We go in, get what we need and get out again,' Bruce said in a strong Glasgow accent. 'We don't go looking for secrets or money or anything else that might benefit us. It's just about information to do our job. We leave the system we go into entirely intact and don't screw around with viruses or the like.'

He continued to work as he spoke.

Logan watched fascinated as the site for a CCTV company came up on screen. It looked like an internal network screen and not a website. After a couple of minutes Bruce appeared satisfied that he had what he was looking for and sat back in his chair. A still from a surveillance camera was displayed on the screen. It looked familiar to Logan but he couldn't immediately place it.

'Is that it?' Cahill asked.

'Yeah,' Bruce said. 'You want me to play it?'

'Go ahead.'

The picture on the screen started to move and Logan saw himself walk into what he now recognised as the lobby of his building, followed by two big men. The scene from the other night played out on the screen and Logan shifted uncomfortably in his seat. He remembered being drunk, but not as bad as he looked on the screen, wobbling through the lobby to the bank of lifts. Bruce let it play for a while and then paused it as the two big men came into view more clearly.

'This is the best shot we have of them,' Bruce said.

He turned to look across the table at Judd.

'Was he one of them?' Cahill asked. 'The guy tonight.'

Judd sat forward with his elbows on the table and studied the screen for a while.

'Let it play a bit more,' he told Bruce.

They watched for another minute or so before Judd spoke again.

'Not sure,' he said, leaning back in his chair. 'I didn't really see his face, but he kinda moves the same way; light on his feet for a tall guy.'

Logan had been captivated by the images playing out on the screen and was still staring up at it as Judd talked. He finally noticed that the room had gone quiet.

'What do you think, Logan?' Cahill asked.

'It was him. No question.'

Cahill stretched his arms up and let out a long breath. 'That's a problem,' he said.

'Am I done now?' Bruce asked.

'Yeah, Bruce, you can go now, thanks,' Cahill said.

'So what do we do now?' Judd asked after Bruce had left the room.

Cahill shifted his seat back from the table and laced his hands behind his head.

'You sure it's Bob's deal that's behind all of this?' he asked Logan.

'Yes. I went to see him and he told me everything.'

'Okay, then I need to speak to Bob tonight. We can't waste any time. That guy came for you tonight for a reason, Logan. My guess is that they finally reached the conclusion that you're too stubborn to play their game so the next best option was just to take you out. And that means the little girl—'

'Ellie,' Logan said firmly.

Cahill looked at him. 'That means Ellie's usefulness has, or is about to, come to an end. So we need to go get her back now.'

Logan sat quietly for a few seconds, trying to think it through.

'I'm not sure that's right, Alex,' he said finally. 'I mean if they take me out – kill me – then that's just going to intensify the police scrutiny of my life. Including what was going on at work. They wouldn't want that kind of pressure this close to the end of the deal.'

Judd spoke first.

'Logan, that guy was coming at you with a knife, man. The decision has been made.'

'Maybe not. He only pulled the knife after I got into it with him. It could have been an attempt to subdue me and end the fight. Maybe all he wanted was one last shot to get me on side.'

'I wouldn't bet on it,' Judd said.

Cahill stood and leaned on the table. 'It doesn't matter, really,' he said. 'Either way there's no time left to waste. We need to get in touch with these guys and Bob's the best option for that scenario.'

'Why do we want to talk to them?' Logan asked.

'Because they'll know pretty soon that their man is not coming back to wherever they are and no matter where their heads are at now, that will be the end of it. So we need to reassure them that the deal is still on and that what happened tonight was a mistake.'

'Some mistake,' Logan said loudly. 'He got shot in the head, Alex. That's not going to look like a mistake, is it?'

'That's not what I mean. Look, they won't know what happened to him; not specifically, anyway. We need to get in touch and explain that he got killed in a fight with you, and that you want to bring all of this shit to an end. You're willing to co-operate now to do that.'

'What good does that do?'

'You have to be convinced that you and Ellie will both get out of this if you co-operate.'

'How do we do that?'

'You ask to meet the boss, so that he can be convinced by you.'

Logan laughed involuntarily. 'These guys scare the shit

out of me so how exactly is it that I convince him without him knowing it's a lie?

'He'll expect you to be scared. You let him be in control and you let him scare you.'

'I could probably do that.'

The others smiled at him.

'You do everything you can to make sure Ellie stays alive until we can get to her.'

'You're going to watch us and then follow him?' Logan asked.

'Correct.'

'And how do you get Ellie out?'

Cahill looked at him without speaking, letting Logan work it out for himself. Logan looked round the table at the four very serious individuals there in the room with him. He turned back to Cahill.

'This is Scotland,' he said. 'You can't just go around with guns shooting people.'

'The fuck we can't,' Cahill told him.

Logan looked over at Judd who shrugged back at him.

'Now,' Cahill said. 'Let's go wake up fucking Bob and have a chat with him.'

2

12.30 a.m.

Irvine switched off the car radio and rubbed at her eyes as a black cab drove past the entrance to Logan's building. It was the only car she'd seen in the last half-hour or so. Her mobile rang and Liam Moore sounded ultra-serious when she answered. His first question cleared any lingering drowsiness from her head.

'Did Finch tell you where he was going when he called you earlier?'

She tried to recall the conversation and couldn't recall him mentioning any place in particular. Moore's tone was setting her on edge, as though he was leading to some bad news. She felt emotion rising in her, but was unable to decipher what the feeling was or what it meant.

'No, not that I can remember. Why?'

'There was an incident earlier tonight at a pub in town.'

Irvine knew the cop parlance – an 'incident' could be anything from a minor altercation to a murder and Moore's tone indicated to her that this was likely to be closer to the latter. She wanted to ask if it was Logan, but settled for something more neutral.

'What happened?'

'A man got shot at the Bar Room on West Nile Street. Place was packed and a DJ was playing a set so no one heard anything.'

'Any CCTV coverage?'

'Yes, but only at the door. Nothing inside.'

Irvine thought Moore was deliberately dragging this out, testing her to see if she was too close to the case now.

'Was it him?'

'The description doesn't match, no. Guy has no ID on him, just a lot of cash held in a silver money clip. Oh, and a fucking big knife as well.'

'Sounds like maybe he got into a fight with the wrong man.'

'Knives I can understand, Becky, especially in this town. But we don't get too many guns and this guy has a bullet in his head, execution style. I want you to get down there and see if this might be connected to Finch. Trouble has a way of following that guy around and it's leaving a trail of bodies in its wake.'

'Of course, sir.'

'Becky,' Moore said, 'this is not your case, okay? It's already assigned to the duty officers and they are at the locus now.

Unless we can make a connection with Penelope Grant's murder you are strictly there as an observer. I've briefed the duty officers so they'll be waiting for you.'

'Who's on tonight?' Irvine asked.

'Ewen Cameron's the DS and Sandy Alexander is with him.'

Irvine was glad. She'd come up through the ranks with Alexander and they'd been in the same training class at Tulliallan. Cameron was old school like Jack Sharp, except he wasn't a dick and treated women cops with proper respect.

'I'll be there in a couple of minutes,' she told Moore. 'I'm not far away.'

'Okay. Let me know as soon as you have anything. And Becky . . .'

'Yes?'

'I'm trusting you on this case more than I should. I want you to understand that and to make sure you don't make me sorry for it, okay?'

'I appreciate it, sir.'

Irvine strapped her seat belt on and pulled out into the road. She raced along a deserted Bothwell Street and after a sharp left and then a right she was at West Nile Street. She immediately saw the place as there was still a big crowd outside, spilling on to the road and causing a headache for the four uniformed officers trying to protect the entrance and keep the largely drunk crowd from fighting with each other.

Irvine parked quickly and crookedly on a double yellow line, and when she got out of the car one of the uniforms, a tall woman in her early twenties, was already moving towards her to get the car shifted. Irvine pulled her ID from her jacket pocket and asked the PC to get her through the crowd and into the bar.

The place reeked of alcohol when Irvine got inside, and the wooden floor was sticky from spilled drinks. There were two more PCs inside and she could see the scenes of crime team getting organised at the back of the pub on what looked like a small dance floor.

Sandy Alexander nodded at her from the upper part of the bar where he was speaking to a witness, an affluent-looking older man in a black suit who she assumed owned the place. She nodded back and then walked towards the dance floor looking for DS Ewen Cameron. He was a small, wiry man with thick grey hair and an old school moustache. She saw him coming out of the corridor marked 'Toilets' as she reached the dance floor. He was talking intently to the scenes of crime team leader, who was dressed in a white overall. Irvine waited for them to finish and then went over to speak to Cameron.

'DC Irvine,' he said. 'I spoke to the super, but there's not much I can tell you at this point that I haven't already told him.'

'I understand,' Irvine said. 'Can I see the body?'

Notwithstanding Moore's confirmation that it wasn't Logan, she wanted to see for herself.

Cameron nodded and turned back down the corridor, motioning for Irvine to follow. It was a tight space and Irvine had to follow behind Cameron in single file. The door to the men's lavatories was fixed in an open position. Another PC was standing outside with an entry log, and as Irvine approached she could see the large pool of drying blood on the tiled floor. Cameron walked past the door and stood outside, preserving the scene for the forensic examination about to get under way.

'Just look from here,' he told Irvine. 'There've been enough people already trailing in and out of there before we arrived. The fewer people we have in the log, the better it will be if this thing goes to trial.'

Irvine nodded and looked in through the doorway. The body of a large man lay slumped on the floor with blood pooled around him and a knife with a serrated blade close by. She saw immediately that it wasn't Logan and felt tension ease in her neck and shoulders, unaware that it had been building in her.

'Anybody you know?' Cameron asked, watching her reaction closely. 'From your case, I mean.'

Irvine told him no and they went back out to the front part of the bar, where Alexander had finished speaking with his witness.

'Owner knows nothing,' Sandy said. 'But I spoke to the door staff and they remember two guys coming out together and heading down on to St Vincent Street not too long before the body was discovered. We should get CCTV film later and we can maybe get a shot of them off that.'

'Good,' Cameron said.

'Could they give you a description?' Irvine asked.

'Nah, not really. Both of them were pretty average-looking, nothing memorable.'

'Ages?'

'Twenty-five to forty was the best they could do.'

'Could be anybody,' Cameron said.

Alexander nodded and said he was going to speak to the bar staff now, pointing at two young men and a woman sitting drinking coffee on the upper section.

'Sound like anyone that might be connected to yours?' Cameron asked Irvine.

'Could be, I suppose,' Irvine said, thinking the age was certainly right for Finch, although she hadn't expected him to be with anyone else. That was a new twist on things, if it was him.

'Thanks, guys,' she told them. 'I need to get going so I'll leave you to it.'

Irvine got back in her car and drove slowly past the crowd still spilling on to the road. There were a lot of twenty-something men and women and some of the women were in pretty short skirts and flimsy tops. They appeared immune to the Glasgow winter and Irvine assumed it was a mixture of adrenalin, from being in close proximity to the murder, and alcohol dampening their senses.

She continued down to the junction with St Vincent Street, looked left for a moment, saw nothing, and then turned right on to the one way street. She drove along slowly, not really sure what she was looking for, but looking anyway. She saw lights on in the building at 123 St Vincent Street but thought nothing of it. She knew it was full of bankers, lawyers and twenty-four-hour telephone workers so seeing lights on at this time was nothing out of the ordinary.

She continued west, eventually going back to her vantage point opposite Logan's building at the edge of the city centre. She called Moore and told him what she'd found. He agreed it might be nothing, might be something and hung up. Irvine settled back in her seat to continue her wait, finding it difficult to concentrate as her mind filled with images of bloodstained floors and dead bodies. She closed her eyes to try to clear her mind, but instead saw the body in the bar, only this time he was not an unidentified man, but Logan – his dead eyes staring at her.

3

12.53 a.m.

Logan sat in the back of the silver BMW X5 with Cahill while Judd drove. They pulled slowly up the steep ramp out of the garage in the basement of the building into the rear lane and then along on to Renfield Street.

'Go through town,' Cahill said to Judd. 'This time of the week there will mostly be police foot patrols in the centre. More chance of the cop cars being out on the motorway.'

'I thought you called them freeways,' Logan said.

'I'm an honorary Scot now. Plus Sam hates it when I go Yank on her.' Cahill raised his hands and indicated quotation marks when he said 'go Yank'.

'You're whipped,' Judd called back.

'I know,' Cahill said.

The streets were empty and Judd drove carefully within the speed limit, which was no mean feat with their four-litre engine. They went south over the river and past a drive-thru McDonald's before they were stopped by a red light at Shawlands Cross.

'You're kinda quiet back there,' Judd said.

'Lots to think about,' Logan replied.

'I guess.'

Logan pressed a button on the door and his window slid down, letting cool air into the car. He closed his eyes and took in a long breath. When he breathed out again, a thin stream of white plumed out of the window and he buzzed it shut again.

'Going to be cold over the next few days,' he said, turning to Cahill.

'Snow, according to the weather forecast.'

'Does that make it better or worse?'

Cahill looked at him. 'Depends on where they are and what the terrain is like. But if it's going to lie on the ground it makes it worse because we'll make a noise going through it. Plus, you can't tell what's under the snow so you might step on a branch or hit a hole and lose your footing.'

'But you guys are professionals, right? I mean, you were a soldier, weren't you?'

Cahill sighed and looked out of the window as they got the green light and pulled through the cross.

'We all were,' he said finally.

Logan looked at Judd's eyes in the rear-view mirror. They flicked up and back down quickly.

'Does Sam know?' Logan asked Cahill. 'About what you really do, I mean.'

'Of course.'

'And?'

Cahill pulled at his seat belt to find some give in it and then shifted round in his seat to face Logan.

'This isn't really what we do,' he told Logan. 'We're not assassins, you know.'

Logan nodded.

'CPO stands for Close Protection Operative. We're bodyguards and we look after some pretty important people – heads of state, politicians, corporate types who have reason to need protection. That kind of thing.'

'Movie stars?'

'Sometimes.'

'The pay must be good, then.'

'People will pay to get the best in any walk of life and there's nothing more precious than your own life.'

'And you're the best?'

'Absolutely.'

Logan looked out of the vehicle and realised they were turning on to Crawford's street, although he had not been conscious of the time passing. Judd slowed and pulled up two houses down from Crawford's.

'We all going?' Logan asked.

'No,' Cahill said. 'Bails, you stay put and keep the engine running.'

'So we can get away fast if we need to?' Logan asked.

'No,' Cahill said. 'Because it's fucking freezing out there

and I want to get back into a warm car. I mean, did you think we were going to "take him out" right here?' He did the quotation marks thing again with his hands.

'Don't do that again,' Judd said, turning in his seat. 'It makes you look like a jerk.'

Cahill stood in front of Logan and pushed the button for the bell at Crawford's house. They both heard the loud ring of the old-fashioned bell in the hallway – an original one dating back over a hundred years. Cahill gave it three long rings before they saw a light go on inside.

Crawford opened the door on a security chain and squinted outside, still half asleep. His eyes were red-rimmed and he sighed when he saw Cahill in front of him.

'We need to talk,' Cahill told him.

'No we don't,' Crawford said. 'Get lost.'

He tried to push the door shut but Cahill was faster and lodged his foot in the gap. It just made Crawford push harder. Logan thought that he looked demented, straining pointlessly and then putting his shoulder into it to no effect.

Cahill unzipped his jacket, slipped his hand inside and pulled out a handgun. He stuck it through the gap and pressed it hard into Crawford's forehead. Crawford's eyes widened and he stepped back, raising a hand to his head where a red welt stood out. Cahill leaned back and gave the door two kicks. The first one buckled the screws holding the chain in place and the second one burst the whole device, sending the door crashing back against the wall.

Cahill put the gun away and went inside with Logan

following closely. Logan pushed the door shut and turned to see Crawford scrambling up the stairs shouting for his wife.

'Fucking guy,' Cahill said, exasperated, then took off after Crawford, taking the stairs three at a time. He caught him in the top hall, putting him down on the floor with a quick leg sweep. Crawford's chin thumped heavily into the carpet and when he looked up he saw his two daughters standing in their nightgowns. The youngest one began to cry.

Logan came up behind them and told Crawford to get the girls back in bed and calm them down.

'We're not here to do anyone any harm, Bob,' he said. 'But we need your attention, so get your act together.' He was surprised at how in control he felt.

Rachel Crawford came out of her room pulling a robe closed over her silk pyjamas.

'What the hell are you doing, Logan? And who is this man?'

'We need some information from Bob,' Logan said. 'To save my daughter's life.'

Rachel Crawford's face blanched.

'That good enough for you, Rachel?' Logan said, staring hard at her.

She nodded slowly and backed into her room with the two girls, closing the door softly behind her.

'Let's go downstairs, Bob,' Logan said.

4

2.10 a.m.

Logan switched the coffee machine on and sat at the breakfast bar next to Cahill. The kitchen was part of a modern extension at the rear of the property, with a glass roof sloping away to a decked patio area. The black granite breakfast bar separated the kitchen from an open-plan dining area. It was all beautifully finished with solid maple units and oak flooring.

'Nice place,' Cahill said. 'Must have cost a few bucks.'

'Let's just do this, okay,' Logan said, looking sideways at him. 'We don't need to get into it with him on why he's involved. I mean, I've done that already and what good will it do us? Or Ellie?'

'You're right.'

Crawford came into the dining area and walked past them to the fridge, where he got a bottle of water. He leaned back against the door of the fridge and took a long pull from the bottle.

'Coffee would be good,' Cahill said to him. 'We might have a long night ahead of us, Bob.'

Crawford lowered the bottle and stared at Cahill. 'Where do you get off sticking a gun in my face and kicking my door down in the middle of the night? And just who the fuck are you anyway?'

Cahill stood and took his jacket off, revealing the holster rigged to his belt. He put the jacket over the back of his stool and sat down.

'Bob, don't fuck with me. You think the guys you're dealing with are bad, but I haven't even started yet, okay? Pour the coffee, sit the fuck down and do what I say.'

Logan saw in Crawford's face that he wanted to say more, but Cahill stared him down. Crawford went across the kitchen, opened a cupboard and came back with three white espresso cups that he half filled from the hissing coffee machine. He set two of the cups down on the breakfast bar and leaned back against the big fridge again, sipping at his own brew.

'We need a phone number,' Cahill said.

'I don't know how to get in touch with them,' Crawford told him.

'Bullshit,' Cahill spat back.

'Look, let me explain, okay? I do everything through a lawyer, the one in England. He's my contact. He told me it was better for me to have him as a buffer between them. Suits me.'

'We need the number,' Logan told him. 'Tonight.'

Crawford's gaze shifted quickly between Cahill and Logan. 'Why?'

'Because Logan wants to get the deal done and get his little girl back before they kill her, fuckwit,' Cahill said.

Crawford sighed. 'I get that,' he said. 'I mean, I'm not totally stupid. What I meant to say was that they won't be intimidated by you. You'll need more than that.'

'Bob,' Logan said, fixing his eyes on Crawford, 'the deal's back on. Didn't you hear what Alex just said?'

Crawford's brow creased in a frown and the coffee cup stopped halfway to his mouth. He looked at Cahill, who nodded, and then back at Logan.

'I don't believe you,' he said finally.

'I don't care,' Logan told him. 'It's true. We can't take these guys head on because whoever they are, they're serious fuckers. I just want . . .' He paused and swallowed, trying to find the right word. 'I just want *her* back.'

It was still difficult to think of her as his daughter or say her name without its feeling out of place in his mouth.

Crawford looked down at his coffee and swirled the dark liquid around his cup. 'The lawyer told me they were from Russia,' he said, looking at Cahill.

Logan supposed this was meant to have some great import because Crawford had lowered his voice to a whisper.

'Fucking Russian mafia bullshit,' Cahill said, putting his cup down on the granite with a bang.

Crawford jumped. 'Some bullshit,' he said. 'They killed Penny, or did you forget that? These guys aren't playing around and they are not amateurs. There's a lot of money at stake for them and they're not afraid of using violence, against anyone.'

'The lawyer told you that to scare you – the big, bad Russian mafia. And you took the bait and the hook and swallowed that fucker whole. Listen, it's not like *The Godfather*, okay? There's no countrywide network of Russian hoodlums all operating under the umbrella of one head man. The Russian mafia was just a sound bite dreamed up by the media as a cheap shorthand to avoid having to do any real journalism.'

'What do you mean?' Logan asked.

'It's like this. There are hundreds and maybe even thousands of organised criminal gangs in Russia, but only a few have any kind of serious numbers. The biggest ones hail from Moscow and maybe have a couple thousand members. They deal in drugs and gun-running and extortion rackets to squeeze money out of foreign businesses in Russia. Over the years they've spread out across the world as the Russian borders opened up after the fall of the old Soviet Union and they've gotten some decent footholds in the States. If the guys you're dealing with really are Russians, they're just small time in the big scheme of things. Probably looking to launder money from drug or prostitution operations.'

'So what?' Crawford said, his voice rising. 'They're still prepared to kill. What's your point?'

'My point is it's not like we all have to worry about some worldwide network of Russian hoodlums coming after us. We won't have to check around every corner for the rest of our lives, no matter what happens.'

'If the deal's back on, why would we have any worries at all?' Crawford asked, the sarcasm heavy in his voice.

'Don't be a child, Bob. Doing their bidding doesn't mean that they'll just walk away and let you live happily ever after with your blood money safe in a bank somewhere.'

Crawford started to speak again but got cut off by the wave of a hand.

'Bob,' Cahill said, rising from his stool, 'just give me the fucking number for the lawyer and we'll take it from there.'

Logan could see the wheels turn in Crawford's head as he tried to think it through.

'But what if they call me here and they want to know what's going on?'

'You tell them the truth,' Logan said. 'That I came to see you to get the number because I wanted to get things back on track before it went too far. They'll buy it.'

Crawford stared into his coffee some more, then quickly swallowed what was left in the cup and walked past them into the front of the house. He came back after a few moments with his mobile phone, his thumb working the number pad rapidly. He got what he was looking for and read out the number for them. Cahill scribbled it on the back of an envelope he pulled from a magnetic noticeboard on the wall next to him. Then he stood to leave and Logan followed him. Crawford stayed put in the kitchen, letting them find their own way out. Cahill stopped at the door leading from the extension to the front of the house. He turned to Crawford.

'What's the lawyer's name, Bob?' he asked.

Crawford looked down at his phone again. 'Gabriel,' he said. 'Gabriel Weiss.'

Cahill nodded. 'If they call here, Bob,' he said, 'let us know, okay? Or you'll have to deal with me again.'

Back in the car, Judd asked them how it went before they even had the doors closed.

'We got the number; now it's up to Logan,' Cahill told him.

He turned to Logan, who looked pale and drawn as the interior lights faded out and only the watery yellow street lighting illuminated the vehicle's interior.

'How you feeling?' Cahill asked.

'Like I want to throw up.'

'Good. We want you to sound scared – that way they'll believe you. Let's get back to the office and make the call.'

Logan stared straight ahead as a fox ran out from behind a hedge on the opposite side of the road. Judd switched on the headlights and the fox stopped, frozen in the blue-white glare of the xenon bulbs. Logan saw pinpricks of light reflected in its eyes as it stared fearfully at the huge metal beast. The fox pressed its body low to the road, then quickly darted into the front garden of one of the houses and disappeared.

5

3.30 a.m.

Ellie had dozed on and off for a while, drowsy from the last dose of painkillers the woman had given her with her meal around seven that evening.

The front door of the cabin slammed shut, pulling her out of the doze and wide awake. She heard one of the men shouting. It sounded like the leader – and he was angry. She listened while he shouted and then heard the woman's voice, much softer, trying to calm him. It didn't seem to work because his voice just got louder and then she heard what she thought sounded like him kicking something and knocking it over. She felt the terror rise in her again and squeezed her eyes tight shut, pushing out salty tears.

Things seemed to go quiet after a bit so she risked sitting up and looking over at the window. She wanted to make sure that they wouldn't be able to see what she had been doing to the boards, especially now that she had the bottom one completely loose and the first nail out of the second one. She didn't want to get caught now, when it was going so well.

But she was also scared that she wouldn't have enough time to finish the job and try to get away before they decided to kill her. And she was certain that time was drawing closer because of what the other man had said to her earlier and now the leader's angry return to the cabin.

Ellie lay on her back on the bed and pulled a stray hair away from her mouth. She had thick, brown hair just like her mum's. It used to be long, cascading halfway down her back, but she had had it cut much shorter for the trip to Scotland. She had cried when she saw the result of the hairdresser's work and had not really been able to stop until they had got home that night, about an hour later. But now she was glad she had done it because all that hair would just have got in the way now. And it would probably have been sticky and hard with the blood she had lost. She looked more grown up with the new hairstyle. That's what her mum had told her, anyway, and she believed her mum.

'This is what happens,' Sergei said to Drake. 'This is what happens when you work for someone else. Do you see now why I said this was a mistake right from the beginning?'

Drake stood looking out of the window, moonlight reflecting off the dark surface of the loch. Behind him, Sergei continued to rant.

'And now look what's happened, eh? Vas is dead and all

because fucking Gabriel wanted to wash our money here in this shithole country. It'll be much easier, he says, because it's so small and the dirty lawyers will be *so* desperate for our cash they'll fall over themselves to help us.'

Drake turned to Sergei and put a finger to his lips – shush. 'We need to tell Gabriel what happened.'

'Great idea, just great. Why don't we slit our own throats right now and be done with it.'

'Shut up, Sergei, and stop crying like a woman for fuck's sake.'

Drake took his mobile from his back pocket and dialled Gabriel's number. While the phone rang he motioned with his head for Katrina to leave the room. She got up from the couch and went down the hall to her room.

Gabriel answered the phone sounding bright and alert.

'Not asleep at this time of night?' Drake asked.

'I'm not in the mood, Mr Drake,' Gabriel told him. 'Are we back on track with this thing yet?'

'No. In fact things took a turn for the worse tonight.'

'How so?'

'Vas is dead.'

Gabriel said nothing and Drake knew that silence was usually a bad sign where Gabriel was concerned.

'I don't exactly know what happened,' Drake went on. 'He went to see the lawyer, Finch, to make sure he knew what was at stake. Now he's dead. Beyond that I don't know any more.'

'This deal is at risk of blowing up in my face, Mr Drake, and in yours. You told me it was going to go through and that you'd make sure Finch was not going to be a further problem. Now Vas is dead and it looks increasingly like I'm not going to get my money washed.'

'I know it's not ideal—' Drake started.

Gabriel cut him off with a sharp laugh. 'It's very fucking far from ideal, Mr Drake.'

It was the first time Drake had heard Gabriel use profanity and he guessed it was not a good sign. The man was usually cool no matter what. Drake stayed quiet, waiting for Gabriel to speak.

'Listen,' Gabriel said finally. 'Much as I'd rather just kill the girl and get out of this mess, I need that twenty-five million cleaned. You need to get me that money. Am I clear on that?'

'Yes,' Drake said, knowing that now was not the time to argue with him.

'So how do you propose going about it?'

Drake looked at Sergei, who met his gaze with a blank stare. Sergei wants to kill me, Drake thought. He's probably thinking about it right now – about how Gabriel would react if he killed me while I'm still on this call. Gabriel has no soul, but he believes in order, in the hierarchy of the organisation. Sergei knows that. Otherwise he'd make his move.

Sergei sat down on the couch, keeping his eyes fixed on Drake. The petty power games he plays, Drake thought, turning again to look out at the loch and wondering what it would feel like to watch Sergei slip motionless below the dark water, where the fish would feed on his flesh until he was nothing but bone.

'I need to think about it,' he told Gabriel.

'You do that. And while you're thinking, I'm going to send some support up there for you so that there are no more mistakes.'

The line went dead and Drake pushed the end call button.

'He's sending someone up here, isn't he?' Sergei asked.

Drake nodded.

'We'll not get out of this alive,' Sergei said.

'Don't make such a drama out of everything, Sergei,' Drake told him. 'We've been in this with Gabriel for a while now and he trusts us. We've made more money for him than anyone else these last two years, and he's not going to risk that just because Vas got himself killed.'

'So what do we do?'

Drake thought for a moment and then walked quickly past Sergei, heading for Ellie's room. 'We show Finch just how serious we are,' he said, motioning for Sergei to follow him.

Ellie was just starting to doze again when she heard footsteps coming towards her door – more than one of the men was coming. When the door opened she recognised the boots that the leader wore, and when he hunkered down next to the bed he looked angry and it frightened her. He crouched there by the bed without saying anything for what seemed like a long time, just staring at her. She saw the other man, the one that really scared her, standing behind him in the doorway staring at her in that way that made her feel sick.

'Why are you angry?' she asked Drake.

He was surprised to hear her speak and it seemed to catch

him off guard. He opened his mouth and closed it again. Ellie thought he looked like a fish and fought the urge to laugh. She drew herself up and back against the wall, deeper into the shadows thrown by the light from the open door.

'One of my men went to see your daddy tonight and he hasn't come back. I heard a story on the radio news that made me think maybe something bad happened to him and he's never coming back. That makes me angry.'

'Maybe he just got stuck somewhere?'

'No. He would still have phoned me. He knows to do that.'

Ellie felt a flutter in her stomach and a warm feeling rise up from her chest into her face. She pulled the bedcovers up to cover her mouth, frightened at what the man would do if he saw her smiling.

Dad got one of the bad men.

Drake watched her and Ellie held his gaze this time.

'You're a strong girl,' he said.

Drake reached out and rested the palm of his hand on Ellie's injured face. She mistook it at first for affection, but then he pressed hard, causing the pain to explode again. She instinctively pulled his hand away, surprising him with her strength. He stood up and she saw him clench his hands into fists and then release them again and she pulled her knees into her body and wrapped her arms around them, trying to make herself as small as she could.

The woman came into the room and said something in a foreign language. The man at the door turned his head and shouted at her. The woman left and Drake kneeled down again in front of Ellie and held out his hand.

'Come with me,' he said.

'Why?' Ellie asked, frightened by the anger she heard in his voice.

'Just do it, or maybe I'll leave you alone here with Sergei.'

Ellie saw the man called Sergei smile at her and she pushed the covers back and stepped out of the bed, putting her hand in Drake's. He led her past Sergei and along the hall to the front door. The woman was in the living area, watching but saying nothing.

Drake opened the door and pulled Ellie out into the cold night air, where her breath misted in front of her face. Sergei followed after them.

Drake turned at the corner of the cabin and pulled Ellie down a short slope to the top of a slightly steeper incline, leading down to the edge of the loch. She heard water gently lapping at the stone shore.

'Walk down there,' Drake told her.

Ellie was starting to shiver, with only her thin cotton pyjamas protecting her against the cold.

'I don't want to,' she said, feeling close to tears now.

'Move,' Drake said, pushing her in the back.

Ellie skidded on the wet grass of the slope and almost fell. She managed to steady herself and stumbled to the lochside, stubbing a toe on a large stone on the way.

She looked around for a place to run or hide, but there was nothing and the men would be too quick for her anyway, she knew.

'Why are you doing this?' she shouted at Drake.

Drake walked towards her, putting his hand behind his

back. When he brought it round to the front again Ellie saw that he was holding something but couldn't make out what it was. Behind Drake, Sergei struggled down the slope while the woman stood at the top watching them.

'What did I do wrong?' Ellie pleaded, shaking uncontrollably.

Drake stopped a few feet from her and raised his hand. She saw that the thing he was holding was a gun and she screamed, holding her hands out in front of her face to protect herself from the bullets.

The woman shouted something from behind Drake but he ignored her. Sergei came up beside him and stood watching Ellie scream.

Drake pulled the hammer back on the gun.

'Please don't,' Ellie screamed, falling to her knees with tears streaming from her eyes.

'You can tell your daddy it was his fault,' Drake said. 'When you see him in heaven.'

6

3.50 a.m.

'Why do I have to do it alone?' Logan asked Cahill as they sat together at the table in the War Room.

'Because if I'm here you'll look to me for help if it gets scary and if these guys are really as bad as they seem, they'll know it. And we can't risk that. It has to sound as if you killed their guy and that you are fucking terrified as a result.'

'Okay, but how do I explain where I got the number?'

'From Bob,' Cahill said, sounding confused. 'Your old pal and boss. Nothing sinister in that, right?'

'I guess.'

'Okay. Look, we'll be in the boardroom. You know, the place Bails put you last night when you first got here?'

Logan nodded.

'Come get me when you're done.'

'You sure you want the meet there, at Rouken Glen park?'

'Yes. Open and public. Less chance of you getting shot in the face.'

'I feel better already,' Logan said, smiling weakly at his own sarcasm.

'You'll do fine,' Cahill told him. 'You don't have any other choice.'

Logan sat and stared at his mobile, sitting there on the glossy surface of the table. He felt the way he used to before going into court, back when he was still just a newly qualified lawyer – his stomach in his mouth. He tried some deep, slow breathing but it didn't help so he picked up the phone and dialled the number from the back of the envelope from Crawford's house.

The phone rang at the other end five or six times and then switched to voicemail. Logan pressed the button to end the call and then redialled. Voicemail again. He wanted to throw up, but swallowed hard and redialled again. This time someone answered on the first ring.

'What?'

'This is . . . it's Logan Finch.'

Silence, not even the sound of breathing.

'Hello?' Logan said to prompt a response.

'How did you get my number?'

Logan thought the man had a slight northern twang, but tried to conceal it behind a reasonable facsimile of a cultured London accent.

'From Crawford.'

No response.

'Look, I need to speak to them.'

'To whom?'

'The men who have the girl. I need them to know that it's okay.'

'I don't know what you're talking about.'

The line went dead. He'd hung up. Logan felt more anger than fear and banged the phone down hard on the table, carving out a tiny chunk of the surface lacquer.

After a few long breaths, he picked the phone up and dialled again. It was answered on the third ring.

'Hello.'

'It's me again.'

'I've told you already, I don't know—'

Logan cut him off. 'This is Gabriel Weiss, right?'

No answer. He didn't hang up so Logan took it as an invitation to continue.

'Listen, I made a mistake last time, okay? I got confused and said some stuff that was out of line. Look, I didn't mean anything about the girl. It's just that it's late and I've been working hard recently and . . .'

He tailed off, exhausted and unable to think any further. He realised that the man had not hung up this time. He still had him.

'Okay, listen, all I meant to say was that the deal is still on. But there was a problem with something tonight and I need to sort it. It's just a negotiation, right?'

'Go on.'

Don't fuck it up this time, Logan.

'I need a number to call. To speak to someone.'

'That would be unethical. You know that you can't speak to my clients direct during a deal.'

'Right. Maybe you could speak to them and if they're happy about it they could call me, I can give you my number here.'

'I have to tell you that I know the nature of the problem tonight,' Weiss said. 'And it may be that my clients will consider it a deal breaker. Maybe the whole thing is finished already. What is it you expect me to do?'

Shit. Logan thought fast and tried to talk as he did it – not easy given the time of night and his level of fatigue.

'I understand,' he said. 'But what happened earlier tonight was a mistake. It wasn't supposed to happen. I didn't know about the meeting and so it kind of took me by surprise.'

Silence. Logan said nothing.

'Give me your number,' Weiss said.

He gave him the number and Weiss ended the call.

Logan slumped back in the chair and pulled at the polo shirt plastered to his wet skin. He thought how far his life had fallen in the last few days and wondered if this was how Crawford felt when the terrible truth of his position was made clear to him. A spark of sympathy glowed in him.

But he felt sure that he would not have followed Bob's example in the same circumstances. Cahill would have been the first call he made and that would have set off a chain reaction meltdown. He couldn't decide if he was lucky or cursed to have Cahill on his side.

Logan was jerked from his thoughts by the phone vibrating on the table.

'This is Finch.'

'I know. We met already.'

It wasn't the same man. Logan tried to place the voice but couldn't.

'In your office. It did not go well.'

The tennis pro – Drake.

'I remember and I apologise for that. The importance of the deal was not apparent to me at that time.'

'So you say.'

Logan wasn't getting a good feeling about this call. He wondered what Weiss had meant when he said maybe the deal was finished, trying not to think what that might mean for Ellie.

'Closing the deal was all that mattered to me, Mr Finch,' Drake said. 'But you didn't seem to share my feelings. And then this thing tonight.'

Logan was disturbed by Drake's use of the past tense – *was*.

'Look, it wasn't supposed to happen,' he said, feeling panicked now. 'I mean, it was an accident.'

'Someone had to pay for that in kind. An eye for an eye.'

Jesus, no.

Logan felt his heart slow down and he closed his eyes as the room started to spin.

'Now I need to know that you have our best interests at heart.'

What a cold bastard. Logan opened his mouth, unsure what to say next.

'Dad?'

A girl's voice.

Logan stood quickly, knocking his chair over. His legs felt weak and the room around him shook so hard he was sure he would fall. His throat felt swollen, constricting his breathing.

'Dad, is that you?'

Logan opened his mouth but no sound came out. He saw in his mind the photograph of the girl come alive and she silently mouthed 'Daddy' at him, smiling that wide, gaptoothed grin. Strands of her long dark hair blew across her eyes and she pushed them back with a hand, the daisychain in her other hand moving in the breeze. Then she squinted in the sunlight and mouthed 'Daddy, is that you?' and he heard Penny's voice echo out of her mouth and down through the years.

'There's no one there,' the girl's voice said, sounding as if she had turned her face away.

'Ellie,' Logan said, his voice no more than a whisper. 'Is that you, Ellie?'

And then he heard her start to cry, a sound that grabbed his heart and tore it apart. Unconsciously he grabbed at the shirt over his chest and screwed the material tight into his fist.

'Dad,' she said again, her voice broken by huge sobs.

Logan wanted more than anything he had ever felt before to have her there with him. He wanted to pull her into his arms and tell her it was all okay, that he would never allow her to be hurt. He was debilitated by the depth of his feelings for this girl he had never known.

My blood.

My flesh.

'He took me outside . . . and he . . . he pointed a gun at me and I thought he was going to . . . kill me,' she said, her voice heaving as she cried. 'Help me, Dad. Help me . . .'

Then she was gone.

Drake came back on the line.

'Next time I pull the trigger, Mr Finch,' he said. 'You understand?'

Logan tried to draw a breath but it was a ragged thing, barely filling his lungs. He nodded his head in answer to the question and softly said yes. He felt a thin line of sweat run down past his left eye and wiped at it instinctively.

'We meet and we end this,' Drake said.

Logan felt anger grow in him now and he struggled to keep it in check. Now it wasn't the fear that he had anticipated that was the problem, but instead his rage at this murderer – this torturer of children.

Cool it.

'I can get the final documents to you, deliver them personally. I want you to see that I can do that for you. Then it's just about the money transfers, right?'

No response.

'Look.' Logan heard his voice break slightly on the word and thought that maybe it would be a good sign. 'I need to get her back. Help me to do it and we can all come out of this.'

'At your office,' Drake said finally.

'No. I don't want you back there because the police are

looking at me as a suspect and they might be watching the office.' Logan hoped it sounded convincing.

'That might be wise. Where then?'

'Somewhere public, because I don't want any more misunderstandings like earlier tonight.'

'Agreed.'

'A park – it's called Rouken Glen. There's a bird pond and beyond that a small bridge over a river. Meet me on the bridge at nine this morning.'

'Fine. But let me say this, Mr Finch: there will be no more allowances made for the completion of this transaction. Do you understand? We have a lot of money invested in its conclusion and I will not allow that to be put at risk. If there is a problem tomorrow then that will be the end of it, for everyone. Is that clear?'

'Yes.'

'There will be people with her when we meet. If I don't call them and confirm everything is as you promise, then, notwithstanding my predicament, she will be gone.'

'I said I get it.'

Dial tone.

7

4.00 a.m.

Logan went to the boardroom and pushed the door open. They were all in there waiting for him: Cahill, Judd, Hardy and Washington. Logan sat wearily in the first chair he could find and Cahill leaned forward.

'Are we on?' he asked.

Logan nodded. 'Nine o'clock in the park at the bridge, just like you said.'

Cahill beamed at him and slapped a hand on the table. 'You did good, Logan.'

Logan couldn't muster any enthusiasm, or think of what had just happened as any kind of success, while Ellie's sobs echoed in his mind. Cahill saw his reaction.

'It's all good, right?' he asked.

Logan felt the weight of events bearing down on him and

was tired of it. He wasn't one for religion or fate or superstition, thinking that it was all superstitious crap, but right now he would have been glad to blame it all on some higher power and seek some solace in prayer. Maybe that was the attraction of religion – everyone needed a crutch at some point in their life.

'I spoke to Ellie,' he said.

Cahill waited and none of the others said anything.

'She's alive, at least.' But they had a gun on her, basically torturing her with the fear of death. How can someone do that to a kid?'

'I've seen some shit in my time, let me tell you,' Hardy said from across the table. 'I mean, there's no end to the despair that one human being can inflict on another. That's the truth of it.'

Logan looked over at him, seeing for the first time how war had aged Hardy. He must have been around the same age as Cahill but his face was etched more deeply with lines.

'No one here has seen as much of war as me,' Hardy said, making Logan think he was reading his mind. 'And I've seen far too much of it. You take comfort, Logan, from the fact that she was still able to speak to you. That means we still have a chance to get her back alive and that's about as good as it gets in these situations.'

'Believe it or not,' Washington added, 'she's one of the lucky ones.'

Logan knew it was true, but it didn't make it any easier to bear.

'They're right,' Cahill told him. 'So long as she's still alive we're still in the game, and that's the only thing . . .' He paused, until Logan looked at him. 'The only thing that counts. When we have her back safe, then we can deal with the psychological fallout. For all of us. But right now we need to focus on getting her back and put everything else out of our thoughts.'

'It's easier for you guys,' Logan said. 'I mean, this is what you do. This is what you know. Not me. I'm just a civilian.'

Cahill looked across to Hardy, inviting the veteran to speak again. The significance of this, Hardy's seniority in the group, did not escape Logan.

'It's never easy,' Hardy said. 'But it's a job and that's the only way to think of it.'

'Some job,' Logan said.

'Hey, I know this is some wild shit for you to deal with,' Hardy went on, his voice rising in anger. 'But you have to forget about your own discomfort in all of this and start focusing on that little girl. This is a deal like any of the ones you sit in your office and do. No one ever says to you, hey, buddy, if it troubles you just go home and never mind. You don't have a choice and it's the same for us. Only this time you're in our little world and the stakes are higher than just money and ego. It's literally life and fucking death.'

Cahill put his hand up and Hardy relaxed back in his chair.

'We've all seen people die,' Cahill said.

'Some more than others,' Hardy interrupted.

Cahill sighed and looked again at Hardy. 'Tom, you have to cut Logan some slack, okay?' he said. 'I wasn't going to tell any of you this because it'll just make things harder, but the girl, Ellie, she's Logan's daughter.'

No one said anything for a moment and then Hardy spoke.

'You should have told us before now, Alex. Should have told me, at least.'

'It doesn't change what we need to do,' Cahill said. 'And it might make us more anxious than we need to be when it counts. But you're right, Tom, you do need to know.'

'Fine,' Washington said. 'Now that we have that cleared up and everyone's had a good cry, can we get a fucking move on and do something about it.'

Logan was becoming more aware of the team dynamic as the night wore on and right now he would probably put his life in Washington's hands after Cahill's. He thought that maybe Hardy was not far off needing to get out of this business for the sake of his own sanity and Judd was clearly still learning how it all worked.

'So, Logan,' Cahill said. 'Anything else you can tell us from your calls?'

'Was it too easy?' Logan asked. 'I mean, why did he agree to the first place I suggested for the meeting?'

'Don't know. Two possible reasons: one, he believed you and the location of the meet didn't matter to him. Or he's already decided to kill you and now he knows where you'll be at a specific time.'

'Not really very comforting, Alex.'

Cahill shrugged. 'You never said you wanted comforting.'

'What's the plan now?'

'We've just been covering that,' Judd said, finding his voice. 'We'll run through it with you.'

Logan sat forward and pressed his hands together between his knees to stop them from trembling.

'You don't look so good,' Cahill said.

'I'll get by.'

'Okay,' Judd continued. 'We're going to have you in sight the whole time, Logan, but it'll look suspicious if we all hang around the park individually.'

'You do stand out,' Logan said, his eyes flicking round the table.

'We need to blend in,' Judd said. 'So I've put a call out to Carrie. She's got a dog so I'll do the walk around the pond thing with her so we look like a regular couple.'

'Who's Carrie?' Logan asked.

'The receptionist here,' Cahill replied.

'She's one of you? I mean, she's, like, a CPO or whatever?'

'Uh-huh.'

Of course, Logan thought, why wouldn't she be? The cute Scottish brunette with a secret career as a member of an international security force. It seemed a weirdly apt thing to discover in that room after all that had happened.

'We have five hours to get ready,' Cahill said. 'So now we need to focus. Bails, are you going to pick Carrie up?'

'Yeah. I told her I'd be there at about seven thirty so we can get to the park early and scope it out.'

'Good.'

'How is it going to work after they leave the park?' Logan asked. 'The bad guys, I mean?'

'That's our thing,' Washington said. 'Tom and I will take our most inconspicuous car, a beat-up old thing of some description, and tail them from the park. Hopefully they'll lead us back to where they have the girl.'

Logan noticed that still no one talked about her by name. He could understand it from their perspective: continue to treat her as an object, something to be reclaimed, without any emotional investment. He understood that they would function better on that basis if it all went pear-shaped.

'What about me?' he asked.

'You're driving with me and Bails,' Cahill said. 'We'll meet Tom and Chris at the park and we'll give you cover outside while Bails and Carrie are inside.'

'Cover for what?'

Cahill looked at his men round the table and then back at Logan. 'In case they really have decided to take you out and they're planning to do it before you get there. Or at least before you get out of your car.'

'This is some really scary stuff,' Logan said.

'You bet,' Cahill told him. 'When we're done, we'll meet Bails and Carrie back at our other building to get kitted out for the op, then follow Tom and Chris. They'll keep us posted en route by radio.'

'And then what?'

'Well, once we've scoped the place we'll all meet up and do what we do,' Cahill said.

'We'll take the girl and kill anyone that gets in our way,' Washington added in what Logan was coming to recognise as his usual blunt way.

'Correct,' Cahill added.

Logan was uneasy at the sense of excitement that was building in him now. He wanted to feel scared, but his blood was racing and these guys certainly talked the talk.

'Do I get a gun?' he asked, looking at Cahill expectantly. He regretted asking the question as soon as it was out of his mouth, but he was so caught up in the moment it popped out almost unconsciously. He immediately wanted to take it back, but didn't want to look weak in front of Cahill's men.

Cahill looked a little surprised by the question. He flicked his hair back off his forehead and rubbed at the stubble forming on his chin.

'Sounds like a good idea to me,' Judd said.

'So long as he gets some training in the range before we go,' Washington added.

Cahill gave them the kind of look a teacher might give children misbehaving in his classroom. Judd looked at Washington and Washington shrugged back at him.

'I agree,' Hardy said. 'Look, Alex, if he's going to be there with us, it only makes sense that he's armed and knows how to use the thing. You'd never send one of us in there naked so why do it with Logan?'

'We don't have much time,' Cahill said.

'I know,' Hardy told him. 'We'll do the best we can with what we have, as always.'

'Okay,' Cahill said. 'I don't like it, but it makes sense.'

Logan felt the blood drain from his face and hoped it didn't show too much. His attitude to most things in his career so far, though admittedly less life-threatening than his current

263

situation, was to deal with the scary stuff by taking a deep breath and plunging on with whatever it was. He didn't consider himself brave so much as just willing to do what was necessary.

'Good,' he said weakly.

Cahill continued. 'Tom and Chris, you guys will head off now to get ready for your part. Bails, you try to get some shut-eye before you go get Carrie. Logan, go home and get changed into some of your own clothes. Then get back here and Chris and I will take you over to our other building to get you acquainted with the tools of our trade. After that we're going to my place for some food and then on to the park. Everybody set?'

Judd, Hardy and Washington left the room looking purposeful and not a little serious. Logan felt something settle heavily in the pit of his stomach.

'Let's get it on,' Cahill said.

8

4.31 a.m.

Logan walked back to his flat, glad of the chance to breathe in some cold, clear air and take a break from the madness that was CPO. How on earth those people operated unseen in the middle of the city was a marvel. The phrase 'hide in plain sight' no longer seemed like a cliché.

When he got to the lobby of his building, Logan tried to push the memory of the intimidation by the two thugs from his mind, but when he did that the image that replaced it was the tall man's head snapping back and falling bloodily on to the floor of the lavatory at the bar. He was sure he would never forget that.

In the flat, Logan put some food down for Stella, then quickly undressed and dumped his clothes on the floor before trying to blast all thoughts from his head by alternating hot and cold water in the shower. He lasted a few minutes and then gave up, his skin tingling and blotchy.

He towelled dry in the main living area and then found the jeans he'd been wearing early that morning – yesterday morning, he corrected himself in his head – and pulled them up over a pair of white stretch boxers. Rummaging through his wardrobe he found the clothes he thought would fit the bill for the day ahead – a plain green T-shirt and a similarly coloured zip-up fleece he'd bought at the Gap store in the Buchanan Galleries a couple of months back. He finished the outfit with chunky blue trainers, not quite hill-walking material but more robust than your average pair of Nike running shoes.

Coffee seemed like what was needed before he headed back to the CPO office, so he switched the machine on and sat on one of the stools to wait for it to heat up. As he sat down, he felt something in one of his back pockets. He reached round and pulled out the photo of the girl who had his eyes. He had forgotten where he had put it and the sight of her hit him like a physical blow to his sternum, knocking the breath out of his lungs. He leaned over on to the breakfast bar and dropped the photo on the counter top.

He thought that he heard the gentle lapping of waves on a shore and people talking and laughing. The girl's hair fluttered in a gentle breeze rising up off the sea behind her and she squinted in the bright sunlight. He wanted to be there with her, to pick her up and swing her round while she screamed and laughed in his arms.

The strength of his feelings scorched through his head. He'd never really thought seriously about having children before; it seemed like something other people did. Cahill and Crawford. Not him. But now, staring at the picture of her . . . *his daughter* . . . and having heard her voice for the first time, he felt an incredible surge of contradictory feelings: love and fear and everything in between. Is this how it feels when you see them being born, he wondered. That's how it struck him: as if she had just been born right in front of him – a fully grown baby of eleven years old.

Logan pressed his hands over the photo, trying to smooth it out. He put it more carefully back into his pocket and quickly downed a mug of coffee.

After that, he went to his desk, pulled his laptop from its bag and waited for it to boot up. He had direct access to the office network via a secure extranet connection. The firm's IT team had spent the best part of four hours sorting it out for him a year ago. It was great when he wanted to get on with something in peace and quiet without phones ringing and e-mails popping up every two minutes.

He clicked on the desktop icon of the firm's logo and typed in his user name and password. After a few seconds' delay, he was logged on and went straight to the contract document that he needed for the meeting that morning. Logan saw that Crawford had already worked it up extensively from his first rough draft and was glad because it meant he wouldn't have to do too much to get it into a format that would look credible. He worked at it quickly for about half an hour and then printed off two copies. He stuffed them in a battered black record bag, slung it over his shoulder and then headed out of the flat.

9

4.39 a.m.

Irvine was trying to keep awake by listening to a Madonna song on Xfm with the volume turned right up and cursing her own stupidity for not buying some pro-plus pills or something similar. It hadn't occurred to her that she might be waiting for Finch all night. Chalk that one up to experience, she thought.

She had come close to going home about an hour ago, and been feeling pretty stupid about it, but the remnants of her Lucozade and the last bite of her Snickers bar re-energised her.

Now, she was finally losing the battle to stay awake, her head nodding as sleep overtook her, and decided to get some air. She walked along the street away from her car and then turned to come back, and saw Logan walking along the street from the city centre. She stopped where she was and watched him, hoping that if she remained still his eyes wouldn't be drawn to her. Plus, it was dark and cold and his main aim was probably to get home.

The first thing she noticed was that he was not drunk; quite the opposite, striding purposefully along. And then she saw that he was not in his suit, but some casual gear with an insignia on it she couldn't make out.

When Logan had gone inside the building, she got back in her car and picked up her mobile phone, intending to call Moore. Then she realised that he would not be in his office at this time of the morning and that she was alone.

'Okay, Becky,' she said under her breath. 'This is what you're here for so just relax and wait for him to come back out.'

It was around forty minutes later that Logan came out of the building. She noticed that he had changed again and had a casual bag slung over his shoulder. He looked as if he was going to be walking and that immediately caused Irvine a problem. Should she follow on foot, which would be spectacularly conspicuous on the empty streets, or drive past him in her car, park and see where he went? The second option seemed marginally better.

Logan got to the corner of his building and turned to head up the hill. Irvine's first thought was that he was going to the Kennedy Boyd office. She waited until he was out of sight, started the car and pulled across the street to head past him as he went up the hill. He had not seen her car yet and so she thought she would be safe enough doing that.

She passed him about halfway up the hill, looking the other way as she drew level with his position. At the junction at the top of the hill, she went straight through and up to the next junction at Blythswood Square. From there she drove past the front entrance to the Kennedy Boyd office, and then doubled back round past the Pitt Street HQ, finally stopping outside the Malmaison Hotel. She realised she'd made a mistake when Logan came into view and started walking towards her and not to the front entrance of his office.

He's going to the garage behind the office to get his car. Nice thinking, Becky.

She had no choice but to sit still and hope that he didn't look at her. The ramp to the garage was about twenty feet from the front of her car and he went straight to it and down, apparently without noticing her.

Irvine started the car again, ready to follow Logan when he came out of the garage, which he did about a minute later.

She followed him into the centre of the city at what she thought was a discreet distance until he stopped on St Vincent Street outside number 123. She watched him get out of the car, grab his bag and go inside the building, after waiting a moment for the night guard to let him in. Ah, so he was known there.

Logan *must* have been at the Bar Room, she thought. He was one of the men whom the bouncer had seen heading down this way after the shooting. But who was it with him – the American from the meeting at the office? She didn't think so, because of the age description. The American was wearing well, but was definitely in his forties.

Christ, she was confused.

She switched off the engine and sat for a moment and then, on impulse, got out and ran across to the building. The security guard at the front desk was a woman of indeterminate age with an alarmingly ruddy complexion. The doors were locked but Irvine tapped on the glass to get her attention and then held up her ID for her to see. The woman opened the door and stepped back to let Irvine in. Irvine didn't want to be there for too long in case Logan came back out, so she asked quickly if the guard knew whom he was going to see.

'He was with one o' them CPO people earlier,' the guard said.

She said nothing else, as though Irvine was supposed to know what CPO was.

'What's CPO?' Irvine asked, slightly exasperated.

'Some sort o' private security outfit. There's a bunch of Americans up there on the third floor, and I think it's run by this guy who looks like Robert Redford, I swear.'

Irvine thanked her and left the building secure in the knowledge that Logan was with the American she met in his office.

Back in her car, Irvine took out her notebook and started writing down what she now knew, not that it took her any closer to understanding what on earth was going on with Logan Finch. She wrote people's names and locations in little boxes and drew lines between them to see the connections. She ended up with what looked like a random collection of lines on the page. She closed the notebook and put it on the front passenger seat.

There was some movement on the street ahead of her and she looked out of the windscreen. She saw a silver BMW X5 pull to a stop at the traffic lights ahead, coming up from the side of the CPO building. It was about forty feet from her and she could make out three men inside, although from this distance she could not be sure if Logan was one of the occupants.

She had another decision to make – follow the BMW and hope it was Logan, or wait here. She rationalised it in her head. Logan had gone home, got changed, picked up something in that bag and come back here. Why? The obvious answer was that he was going on somewhere from the office building. There were no other cars on the street and so the odds were that he was in the BMW.

It turned left as the lights changed to green, heading directly away from her up the hill. She started the car and followed, pulling through the red light at her side of the crossroads. They turned left again at the next junction and drove south over the River Clyde, eventually ending up cruising through a heavily commercialised area, packed with warehouses and cash 'n' carrys, and on to Scotland Street. It was a long, straight road so she slowed to drop further back. The brake lights of the BMW flashed brightly after it passed the school and it came to a complete stop outside an old warehouse. There was no sign on any part of the building and from the outside it looked unused.

Irvine pulled to the side of the road and watched as an electrically controlled gate opened in the warehouse and the BMW drove inside. As the vehicle turned, she saw the front passenger in profile. It was Logan. The gate clanked slowly shut behind them as the first of the early morning traffic rolled by on the motorway overpass at the end of the street.

10

5.25 a.m.

Logan followed Cahill and Washington out of the car and waited while Cahill punched a five-digit code into a keypad beside an impressively heavy-looking metal door. A light on the keypad changed from red to green and Cahill inserted a key into the door's manual lock, turned it and pushed the door open. Logan had expected a cavernous old wreck of a building inside, but instead he found himself in a wide corridor with spotlights embedded in the concrete floor and freshly painted grey walls. He followed Washington and Cahill and waited when Cahill stopped at another door with a keypad and entered what looked to Logan like a completely different code. There was a soft beep and the door swung inward.

Logan stepped up to the opening and saw Cahill and Washington in what looked like a narrow cupboard. Then

Cahill pushed at the back wall. It swung into a big, square room. Logan smelled something metallic and organic in the air.

'You weren't kidding, then?' Logan asked.

Cahill turned and frowned at him. 'About what?'

'When you said you had an armoury.'

'No,' Cahill said. 'I mean, why would I kid about something like that?'

Logan had nothing to say. He followed Cahill into the room behind the false cupboard and saw that every spare inch of wall space was taken up by weapons of some sort. He saw handguns, rifles, knives and a number of solid wood cabinets and drawer units.

'Wow,' he said. 'How did you get this stuff in here? Without, you know, getting arrested?'

'We were very careful,' Washington said, deadpan.

'No shit,' Logan said. 'But isn't this illegal?'

Cahill raised an eyebrow. 'Logan, you're so naïve. The government makes the law and controls the country and sometimes they need people like us to look after them. Don't you think they can do what they want when it's necessary or expedient? When someone is doing something that assists them?'

'I never really thought about it. Don't they have MI6 or the secret service or something for all that?'

'Sure they do. But they also have private contractors like us.'

Cahill went left to a line of handguns resting on long pins on one wall. He moved his hand along the line and pulled one of the smaller weapons off its perch — a dark, square-looking pistol. The barrel of the gun was no longer than the depth of its handle and it looked to Logan like a toy compared with some of the other handguns on display.

Cahill moved his fingers quickly over the weapon, clicking a small safety catch up and cocking the hammer back. Then, turning the pistol on its side, he pulled back the slide on the top, exposing the bullet chamber. He held the gun up in front of his face and looked inside the chamber, checking to make sure it was empty. When he was done, he released the slide and hammer, clicked the safety catch back down and held it out by the barrel for Logan to take.

Logan hesitated for a moment and then wrapped his fingers round the hand grip, feeling the cold, dark strength of the thing and breathing in its oily fragrance. It didn't look very big wrapped in his hand but still had some heft to it.

'How's it feel?' Cahill asked.

Logan looked at him, allowed his right hand holding the pistol to drop to his thigh and then returned it to waist height.

'Not too heavy, but solid,' he said. 'Kind of right.'

Cahill smiled.

'Is that wrong?' Logan asked him.

'I'd have been worried if you'd said anything different.'

Cahill went over to a narrow cupboard that stretched the full height of the room and rummaged around inside, coming back with a small box of what Logan assumed was ammunition for the weapon nestled in his palm. Then he took a belt with a dark holster from a hook on the wall to the right of the entrance door and slung it over his shoulder.

'This way,' he said to Logan, going back out of the room.

They moved down the corridor and turned right, and Cahill opened yet another secure door into a cupboard with another false wall. This room was longer and narrower than the previous one and had more weapons arranged neatly on the walls on either side of the door. The rest of the room comprised two separate shooting ranges, each about twenty-five metres long with target boards in the shape of a man's upper body and head at the far end. The targets were hanging on metal rails suspended from the ceiling and were electrically controlled, allowing them to be moved closer to or further from the shooting position as necessary. It looked to Logan like a film set; built for big kids to play pretend with plastic guns. He found it hard to accept that this whole operation went on unnoticed not far from the heart of Glasgow's city centre.

'This is too weird, Alex.'

'I know. It's great, isn't it?' Cahill beamed at him and walked to the enclosed booth at the head of the left hand range.

He set the box of ammunition and the belted holster on the counter and waved at Logan to join him. Washington went to one of the walls and lifted a large pistol from its perch.

'Right, I'm giving the simple stuff to you,' Cahill told Logan. 'But I really don't want you to have to use it. I mean, if you have to shoot someone, you shoot to kill. That movie stuff of shooting the bad guy in the leg is just bullshit, you know. I mean, use this thing properly and you won't be at the business end of it.'

'Okay.'

Cahill took the pistol from Logan, showed him the safety catch and then pushed a separate catch to release the magazine, which slid out of the handgrip. He pushed the magazine back into the handgrip until it locked in place.

'Do as I just did,' he said, handing the pistol back to Logan.

Logan carefully repeated what he'd just seen, allowing the magazine to fall into his left hand. Cahill handed him a bullet from the box of ammunition. It had a smooth, cylindrical case tipped with a rounded nose made of lead. The nose was slightly flattened at the tip.

'Lay the bullet flat against that piece of metal on the top of the magazine there,' Cahill said, pointing. 'It's spring loaded, so push it down against the pressure of the spring until it clicks in below the lip.'

Logan did what he was told.

'Good,' Cahill told him. 'Easy when you know how, right? Load another five rounds now.'

Logan filled the magazine with bullets from the box on the counter and looked expectantly at Cahill.

'Safety on?' Cahill asked.

Logan looked down at the pistol, saw that the catch was on and nodded.

'Right,' Cahill said. 'Just put this holster rig on like a regular belt with the grip facing back on your strong side. You're right-handed?'

Logan nodded as he put the belt round his waist and buckled it before sliding the pistol into the tight holster. He felt a little lopsided with the extra weight. Washington walked past them and into the booth on the other range, next to the one Logan and Cahill were in.

'Nothing fancy about this,' Cahill told him. 'Pull the weapon out and level it at your target.'

He pointed down the range at the target. Logan wasn't sure what he was meant to do until Cahill looked sideways at him.

'Now would be good,' Cahill said.

Logan reached down with his right hand and pulled the weapon out of its holster. It came up and out without any catch and he straightened his arm and pointed down the range.

'No,' Cahill said. 'Not like that. This is a nine-millimetre pistol and it will pull up on you a bit so you have to hold it correctly. What you need to do is put your left hand under the hand grip to give you a stable shooting platform. Spread your legs out a bit and bend at the knees.'

Logan did as he was told.

'How's that feel?' Cahill asked.

'Good. I mean it feels solid.'

'Now, the trigger on this has two pressure points and you need to squeeze it smoothly through both, okay?'

Logan nodded.

'When you've fired off a round, the pistol will naturally return to the starting position after it pulls up.'

Logan nodded again, his face set unknowingly in a frown.

'You need to know that handguns are not the most accurate things to use,' Cahill went on. 'To aim it properly what you want to do is focus on the target and then blur the foresight at the end of the barrel when you've aligned it with the target.'

He tapped his index finger on the small, raised sight at the end of the barrel. 'It will feel a little strange because you'll automatically want to use the sight more, but you'll get used to it.'

Logan tried it out, looking down the range, and nodded.

'When you're ready to fire, squeeze the trigger like I said rather than pulling at it. If you pull at it, you'll likely find that you'll jerk it, pull the weapon to the side and you'll miss the target.'

Cahill took two sets of ear defenders from a hook on the wall of the booth and offered one to Logan.

'These walls are thoroughly soundproofed,' he said. 'But you'll still need these.'

'Shouldn't I get used to the sound of it?' Logan asked. 'In case, you know, I actually have to fire the thing in anger?'

'No. The sound of firing a weapon within the confines of a range is entirely different from firing outdoors. In here, the sound is amplified by the narrow space. It's very loud and it resonates, so you need to wear the defenders. When you're outside the sound is much less noisy and it dissipates instantly. Think of it like a large tree branch snapping rather than an explosion. There's no resonance at all.'

Logan took a set of defenders from Cahill and slipped them on over his ears, instantly dulling his hearing.

'Secure the weapon and let's try it for size,' Cahill said loudly, putting his own ear defenders on.

Logan checked the weapon to make sure the safety was on and then reholstered it. Cahill tapped him on the back and shouted for him to go.

Logan pulled the weapon from the holster and took up the firing stance Cahill had explained to him. He squeezed the trigger, which stopped short of firing. He looked over at Cahill, who pulled the defenders away from his ears.

'Safety,' Cahill said.

Logan nodded, feeling pretty stupid, and went through the process again. He felt he got the thing out and the safety off in decent time and squeezed off the first round at the target.

Boom

It *was* loud, even with the ear defenders on.

'Keep going,' Cahill shouted.

Boom

Boom

Boom

Boom

Boom

Click

'Secure the weapon again,' Cahill shouted. He pressed the button to bring the target forward and it clanked slowly towards them on the overhead rail. Logan smelled cordite in the air, like a freshly struck match.

'I think you might have done okay, Logan,' Cahill said.

Logan saw that he had hit the body shape on the target with only two of the six rounds fired. One of them had gone low, hitting around what would have been the top of the legs. The other was about waist level.

'Not bad,' Cahill said.

Logan thought it was crap and said so.

'Look,' Cahill told him. 'You need to fire a handgun several times to get used to it before you even think about any kind of accuracy. I mean, the fact that you hit the target more than once is impressive in itself. Just focus on your technique, okay?'

Cahill loaded up again, this time with a full magazine of twelve rounds. He sent the same target back to the end of the range.

Logan had similar results this time, with four rounds hitting the target. He tried again with another full clip and did a little better, missing with only half of his shots.

Cahill brought the target back to the booth and replaced it with a new one, which he sent whirring back along the rail.

'Now I'm going to get Chris in the next booth to shoot some rounds across your field of fire to simulate some of what it's like to be in the middle of something. You'll be entirely safe but I won't tell you when he's going to shoot so it'll come as a surprise.'

Logan felt sweat begin to bead on his forehead and his pulse quicken. He nodded without saying anything and Cahill slipped round the wall of the booth into the next one to speak to Washington. Logan waited for a moment, unsure when he was supposed to start.

Boom

Boom

Washington fired past Logan's booth. Logan was startled for a moment, then pulled his weapon from the holster and as he got into his stance Washington fired three more times. Just as the third shot sounded, Logan fired off five rounds of his own.

He lowered his weapon slightly and Washington fired another volley. Logan felt his heart thud against his ribs and he fired this time until his magazine was empty.

Cahill came back round to Logan's booth and brought the fresh target up. Eight rounds had hit it with varying degrees of accuracy.

'That'll do,' he said.

'Are you sure?' Logan asked. 'I mean, it's still pretty wild.'

'If you weren't good enough, I wouldn't let you out of here with that thing. But it'll be a lot different if it all kicks off. The key always is to find cover and make yourself safe and wait for support. This is not the wild west and you are not Billy the fucking Kid. Got it?'

Logan nodded. It was the most serious he had ever seen Cahill.

'But,' Cahill added, 'I am Wyatt fucking Earp and if you get in the middle of the shit I will be right there with you.'

11

5.55 a.m.

Washington tidied the gun range and locked up while Cahill and Logan went back to the car in the loading bay of the warehouse. Cahill opened the rear hatch and told Logan to stow his newly acquired gun and holster rig in the floor, under the cover for the spare wheel.

Logan noticed for the first time just how cold it was and was glad to get back inside the car, where the climate control was set at something approaching a comfortable temperature. He had a sudden nagging feeling that he'd forgotten something and was about to open the door to go back into the building when he realised what it was.

'We need to go back to your office and get my bag,' he told Cahill. 'I forgot to bring it with me and it has the contract in it.'

Cahill nodded okay but said nothing.

'Interesting bunch of guys you have,' Logan said.

'Yeah.' Cahill smiled. 'You need to have the spread of youth and experience in this job. They're all pretty good.'

'What's the story with Tom? He seems kind of intense.'

Cahill fiddled with the heating controls, and Logan thought he was just buying time to avoid talking about Hardy.

'I've known him the longest,' he said eventually. 'We were in Delta Force together for a while so we go back a ways.'

'That much I had worked out.'

Cahill shifted in his seat and turned to look out of the side window. Logan realised he wasn't going to get much out of him on Hardy and decided to wait and ask Washington later if he got the chance.

'Chris seems like a good guy,' he said. 'I mean, he's pretty straightforward.'

Cahill turned back to him. 'He's the only one I had to recruit, really. The other guys I knew personally or came on board on a recommendation.'

'Bails told me he got the call to join from Chris,' Logan said. 'I suppose that means you trusted Chris by that point?'

'Absolutely. He'd been with me about nine months when he told me Bails would be a good hire and I had learned to trust his judgement by then. All of this . . .' he waved his hands around, '. . . this stuff with Ellie. It's pretty unusual. I mean, we're not in the business of going into war zones like Iraq or anything. Our bread and butter is corporate and government contracts.'

'Quite a lot of bread, by the look of it,' Logan said.

'I charge more per day than any corporate lawyer in Scotland, that's for sure,' Cahill said.

'So, how do you go about recruiting for this kind of thing?' Logan asked. 'I mean, I don't suppose you can just go to a regular recruitment consultant or put an ad in the paper?'

'Actually, you'd be surprised. We did both to get Chris. You just use sort of coded language so that the people who know about these things can work out what the job really is. Makes it easier to weed out those that don't suit.'

'What was Chris doing before he joined up with CPO?'

'He came out of the army after a tour in Afghanistan not long before Bails. They were in the same unit but their tours were different, although they overlapped some.'

'Yeah, Bails said.'

'He was single when he got out and went to Vegas as part of a casino security gig. He met his wife there – she's English and was on a girls' only holiday at the time. So he ditched the casino job, followed her over to the UK and got hired by a private bank in London to head up their security. It wasn't really his thing, I don't think – too much emphasis on the internet security side of things. He's more a physical kind of guy.'

'That doesn't surprise me,' Logan said.

'Anyway, I guess the bank thing wasn't doing it for him either, which is why he answered my ad. Still, he brought the bank on board as a CPO client and they pay pretty well.'

'Does he live locally? I mean, it must have been a big move for his wife.'

'It was, but they were still in that early phase where she

was happy to follow him anywhere. She's an accountant and it was easy enough for her to get a job up here. Before the baby came along, that is.'

'I didn't have him pegged as a family man,' Logan said.

'Why? I've got a family.'

'I know, but it's different when you're the boss. It just seems like a difficult profession to fit into a normal kind of life and maybe it suits loners a bit better.'

'The opposite is true so far as I'm concerned,' Cahill said. 'I don't want gung-ho types who are loose with their own safety when I'm in it with them. If they've got something to go home to then they've got something to make sure they stay safe for.'

'What about Bails?'

'He's young but he's very cautious. Plus, it's good to have a bit of a mixture because it keeps everybody fresh.'

'Even Tom Hardy?'

Cahill looked to his right as Washington came out of the building and locked the main door.

'It's a long story with Tom,' he said. 'He's had it rough his whole life.'

There seemed little chance of Cahill's opening up any further about Hardy, so Logan sat with him in silence, only the thrum of the car's big engine and the gentle sound of the climate control filling the vacuum.

Washington climbed into the back seat and slammed the door shut.

'Let's go,' he shouted.

*　　　*　　　*

Cahill turned the wheel to take the car down into the underground garage at the CPO building and watched in the rear-view mirror as Irvine's car passed behind them, her brake lights going on just as she went out of sight. He'd been watching her back there since they left for Scotland Street and still hadn't decided what to do about her. For now.

They bumped over the speed inhibitor on the steep slope down into the garage and then pulled into one of the reserved spaces.

'Chris,' Cahill said. 'You go get ready and we'll meet back here. I'm going to take Logan to my place to give him a chance to get some rest first.'

'Okay,' Washington said, opening his door and walking briskly towards the bank of lifts.

'I'll go up with Chris and pick up my bag,' Logan said, jumping out of the car and running to catch up with Washington at the lift.

'What's the story with Alex and Tom?' Logan asked once the lift doors had slid shut.

'The boss his usual tight-lipped self?' Washington asked with a smile.

'Yes,' Logan said, feeling a little embarrassed at his lack of guile in raising the subject.

'It's up to Tom and the boss to tell you the whole story,' Washington said. 'But I will say this: Tom kind of looks up to Alex even though Tom's a bit older. I don't know all the details but Tom came from a rough background and the army was his way out. They were pretty tight in the service and from what I hear Tom saved Alex's ass one time. And still carries the scars from it.'

The lift slowed to a stop on the third floor and they went out into the CPO reception area. Washington turned to Logan.

'I gotta go get ready,' he said. 'Listen, don't press the boss too much on Tom, okay? If he's going to tell you the whole story he'll do it in his own time.'

'Does he have any family here?' Logan asked. 'Tom, I mean.'

'No. His wife stayed put back in Texas when he came here with Alex and from the way he talks about her, I don't see them getting back together. He's got a son in college, though, and he stays in touch with him.'

Logan held out his hand and Washington shook it firmly.

'I appreciate what you're all doing for me,' Logan told him.

'This is more than just a job,' Washington said. 'And Alex is way more than just a boss. We're all soldiers and for a soldier the only thing that counts is the guy next to you and the guy next to him. When you're in the desert or wherever and you're receiving hostile fire you're not thinking about God and country or any of the so-called reasons you're there. The only thing is getting out of it alive. I mean, nothing else compares to it. Nothing.'

Logan nodded, seeing the depth of Washington's emotion.

'You're one of us now,' Washington continued. 'And we look after our own.'

He paused and looked solemnly at Logan.

'And that means you have to look out for us too,' he said. 'You understand?'

Logan nodded.

'Okay, then. Let's go do this thing.'

12

6.08 a.m.

Ellie had not been able to sleep after the combined effect of being forced outside and made to think she was going to be killed and then talking all too briefly with her dad. Back in her room, she went straight back to the window to continue her efforts at removing the nails from the boards, but had to sit down to relax when she found her hands shaking uncontrollably. She closed her eyes but it brought back the almost physical memory of how her breath had hitched in her throat and her heart had stuttered and beaten erratically. She lay down on the bed and after a while she began to breathe more easily and felt ready to continue. She went back to her task with renewed vigour, almost immune now to the fear of being discovered. The sight of that gun pointed at her face had brought home more forcefully than ever the realisation that she had to get out of there.

By the time Ellie had worked all but the last nail out of the second board the skin of her thumb and forefinger was split and bleeding from the effort. She lay back on her bed and sucked at the injured fingers to ease the pain and staunch the blood and then fell asleep, to dream of her mother singing her to sleep as a baby. She slept briefly and woke as pain throbbed in her fingers, wiping at the tears the dream had produced.

It was odd that with so much having happened in the last couple of days, and her focus on trying to get out of there, the memory of her mother had started to fade. It terrified her and she wanted desperately to have a photo or something to cling to.

She did have something, though, and reached under her pillow to pull the photograph of her dad out. It was still dark inside and she couldn't really see it well, even after her eyes had fully adjusted to the blackness.

She put the photo to her mouth and tried to inhale the smell of him, but there was nothing but the rank stench of her own sweat and blood. She imagined he would smell like the sea, of salt air and a clean, fresh breeze. Despite never having known him, she held on to his image as the only light of hope in that awful place and tried to remember the sound of his voice from the phone call. She felt the tears well up again and her chin trembled.

There was more noise out in the cabin and then footsteps approached her door. She sat up, still holding on to the photo and determined not to hide it. She felt stronger for having it with her as the door swung open and Drake came in with the other man behind him.

Drake switched on the light and Ellie had to shield her eyes from the glare for a few moments. She felt someone sit on the side of the bed and then heard Drake's voice.

'You're a very lucky girl, Ellie,' he said. 'Your daddy wants to give me what I need now so maybe we'll be able to let you out of here soon.'

He smiled at her but she saw through the smile and down into the dark depths of his eyes where no light shone. She did not believe that they would let her go. She was certain of it now, after the events outside.

'You don't look happy,' he said.

Ellie shrugged but said nothing.

'I understand. It's been a difficult time for you.'

He stood and looked over at the window. Ellie's heart seemed to stop and then hammered fast and hard in her chest.

Please don't see it.

Please don't see it.

Please don't see it.

He looked back at her and she tried her best to keep the emotion out of her face. He leaned down close to her as he spoke.

'I will go to see your daddy and then come back here. More of my men are coming here too, just in case your daddy has any stupid ideas about trying to find you. If I am not back when they get here, it will not be good for you. Understand?'

Ellie tried her best to hold it in, but all the emotions dammed up inside her suddenly burst through her defences and she cried uncontrollably. Hot tears streaked down her face.

'Okay?' he asked again.

Ellie couldn't form the word so just nodded her head.

'I'm not sure it's such a good idea meeting where he wanted to meet,' Sergei told Drake when they were back in the main living area of the cabin. 'I mean what if he's been in touch with the police and is setting us up?'

'He won't,' Drake said.

'How can you be sure?'

'I heard it in his voice, Sergei. He wants that girl back and he's not going to do anything to risk it now. He's just a soft lawyer.'

'Not so soft,' Sergei said. 'Or did you forget so soon about Vas?'

Drake was tired of this, of fighting with Sergei, and he had lost one of his oldest friends.

'Sergei, I know you're trying to rile me but it will make things easier if you start to accept things as they are.'

'Assuming Gabriel is going to give any of us time after this fuck-up, *old friend.*'

Drake ignored the sarcasm. 'Let's get this done, okay, and then we can see where we go from there. I'm going to call Gabriel and tell him what's happening, maybe give him something to smile about.'

'I'll go get the car ready,' Sergei said.

After Sergei had gone outside, Drake went to Katrina's room and found her sitting pensively on the edge of her bed.

'Tell me it will be okay, Yuri,' she said.

'It will be okay.'

She smiled, unsure whether he was gently mocking her. They had been through a lot together and she knew him well enough not to look for any more reassurance.

Drake moved into the room and sat beside her on the bed. Tentatively, he put his arm round her waist and pulled her closer to him, tilting his head until it rested against hers. She was not used to such sensitivity from him and it unsettled her.

'Are you frightened of this man?' she asked. 'After what happened to Vasiliy?'

'No.'

'Are you going to kill him?' She paused before asking the question she really wanted to ask. 'And the girl?'

Drake stood but made no effort to leave the room.

'I don't know,' he said finally.

'About which one?' Katrina asked, turning her head and looking up at him.

He looked at her but said nothing. She was unable to read his eyes and he said no more as he left the room.

Ellie had listened intently to what was going on in the cabin until she heard the two men talking as they went outside together to the car. She was alone now with the woman, she was certain of it. She went to work on the last nail in the second board as soon as the men were gone. The woman had a radio on at the front of the house and Ellie could hear her moving around and singing to herself. Ellie wondered how it was that a woman could do this to her with these men. She could not understand it.

The last nail proved much harder than the previous ones and Ellie wondered if that meant that the nails in the next board were all going to be as difficult. She hoped not, as she was sure she could get out after she had three of the five boards removed. The window itself could be pushed up from the bottom and then she would be able to squeeze out, drop to the ground and run. It was the thought of her freedom that kept her working through the pain as the effect of the drugs started to wear thin again.

As she worked, she placed the photo of her dad on the window sill, glancing at it and trying to imagine what he would look like now.

Her mum had always been happy to talk to her about him after that first time she asked why the other girls at nursery school had a mummy and a daddy and she did not. Her mum told her then that she had had to leave Scotland where her dad lived but she thought she would go back soon to see him so that they would all be together. But she had not been able to go back as she had planned, and the longer time went on the more difficult it became. Ellie sensed sadness in her mum whenever she asked about her dad, but not like she was angry at him. It was more like she missed him.

As the years passed and they moved around they frequently talked about him, even when her mum was going out to dinner and stuff with other men. She sensed that her mum never really forgot about her dad and the other men were never around for too long. She thought of them as temporary only and her mum never talked about getting her a new dad, as if it was not a possibility that ever crossed her mind.

On the day that her mum told her she had finally decided to go back to see Ellie's dad it had seemed natural to Ellie, as if it was always going to happen one day. Even so, her mum seemed to come to the decision quickly and without any planning. But she was happy about it and Ellie was too, and that was really all that mattered.

The nail finally popped loose and Ellie eased the second board off the window and put it on the floor next to the first one. She bent and looked out of the window, wanting to open it and smell the fresh air but afraid to do that before she was ready to go. The glass was cracked and warped, but in the growing light of the winter morning she could see trees and then the ground sloping away down to the water where they had taken her earlier.

Ellie put her face against the glass and strained to look as far to each side as she could. There was nothing to the right, but to the left she saw lots of trees and then a road leading through the woods and into a grassy area beyond. She thought she could also make out some small cabins at the far end of the grassy area and a larger wooden structure beyond them.

Ellie put the two boards back in place and pressed the nails in to hold them. Then she went to work on the third board.

Only one to go.

13

6.54 a.m.

Logan had tried to sleep on the drive north to the gentle suburb of Bearsden where Cahill lived, but his mind was too full and he ended up simply staring out of the side window as the city rushed by.

They pulled off the main road on to a narrow side street lined with houses built in the 1920s and 1930s. Cahill's two-storey detached villa looked modest from the street, but Logan knew that it had been extended substantially at the rear and still had a pretty big garden back there as well.

Cahill braked hard and turned into the drive. Irvine's plain Mondeo passed behind them on the street, its brake lights burning red as it slowed. Logan took hold of the door handle as Cahill switched the engine off.

'We've got a bit of a problem,' Cahill said. 'That cop, the

woman, she's been following us since we went to the range at Scotland Street.'

Logan swivelled in his seat, looking out of the back window almost instinctively.

'No,' Cahill said, shaking his head. 'She's gone past and probably stopped further up the street.'

'How did you know?' Logan asked, turning back to Cahill.

Cahill smiled. 'She went straight through a red light to follow us after we left the office. I mean, it was pretty obvious. First mistake she made was sitting in her car on the street outside the office with her lights off. As soon as we turned the corner she switched her lights on and that immediately drew my attention to her. Then she accelerated and went through the lights on red. Pretty amateurish, but then cops don't really get taught that kind of stuff. It's bread and butter for me.'

'What do we do about it?'

'Well, we can just ignore her and let her keep doing what she's doing. But that's not really a viable option given what we're going to do.'

Logan nodded, acutely aware of how absurd it seemed to simply accept the military-style operation that was planned and not even question it now.

'Or,' Cahill went on, 'we can take her on a bit of a mystery tour out into the country and lose her out there.'

'Or we bring her in on it,' Logan finished for him.

Cahill nodded. 'Correct.'

Logan's first thought was to go with the last option. He wasn't sure why or how it had happened, but he felt a connection with Irvine and he tended to trust his feelings.

'It's the most dangerous option,' Cahill said, reading Logan's thoughts in his face. 'But if you think she'll be with us on it, then I'm prepared to go against my instincts and bring her in. And anyway, she might be able to help us.'

'She'll have some weapons training, presumably?'

'Shit, Logan. I don't mean that she's coming on the op with us. There's just no way that's going to happen. But it would be useful to have a cop on our side because we're going to have to come up with an explanation for how we found Ellie. How *you* found her.'

It sounded to Logan as if Cahill had something in mind already.

'How do I find her?' he asked.

'The best thing is to keep it simple, you know,' Cahill told him. 'The more elaborate you make it, the less credible it will seem and the easier it will be to slip up in telling the story.'

Logan nodded, following the logic so far.

'So we make it almost stupidly easy,' Cahill said. 'She just turns up at your flat and that's it.'

Logan frowned. 'You're right,' he told Cahill. 'Stupid is the operative word. I mean, how is that going to work?'

'Simplicity, like I said. Let's say, for argument's sake, that Penny brings her home to Glasgow with the intention of coming to see you, okay. So she knows who you are and possibly even where you live. Even if she doesn't have the address, it'd be reasonably easy for a girl of her age to look you up in the phone book. With me so far?'

'Okay, but how do we explain where she's been since Penny . . .' He couldn't quite bring himself to say the words.

'That's the genius of it,' Cahill said. 'We don't.'

'What?' Logan was completely at a loss. 'She's just been wandering the streets undetected for a couple of days in her jammies?'

'Who knows?' Cahill said, throwing his hands up. 'We can't explain it because the first you know of her is she turns up at your door. She's dressed in some kind of warm clothes from her own wardrobe, she's probably beat up and that's as much as you know.'

Logan was starting to get it now. 'So any awkward questions anyone asks about how a little girl survived out there I can just say "I don't know"?'

Cahill nodded.

'How do we get her clothes?'

Cahill smiled. It took Logan a moment to work it out and Cahill let him get there on his own.

'Irvine,' he said finally.

'She's assigned to the case so nothing suspicious about her going back to the house,' Cahill said.

'I guess we have the answer to what we do about her, then. But when do we bring her in on it?'

'I'm still working on that part,' Cahill said, opening his door and stepping out on to the drive.

Logan sat quietly on the sofa in Cahill's big study at the back of the house. It was part of the extension and had a wide window looking out into the garden, and was furnished with a metal desk and two sofas facing one another in front of it. Cahill sat on the sofa opposite Logan, his foot tapping on the oak flooring. Samantha Cahill came into the room from the kitchen with two big mugs of coffee. She gave one to her husband and then sat next to Logan to sip at hers. Logan had a glass of water that he held in both hands, leaning forward with his elbows resting on his knees. The room still smelled of cut oak from when the floor had been fitted.

'It'll be okay, Logan,' Sam said to him. 'This is what Alex does.'

Logan turned to look at her, still surprised at how much younger than her true age of forty-one she looked. Her mother, whom he had met a few times, was the same; must be in the genes. Sam was small, only about five two, with dark shoulder-length hair and striking blue eyes, and she always smelled great. Logan smiled at her.

'He's told me that already,' he said. 'But how do you live with it, all this crazy stuff?'

Sam looked over at her husband and shrugged. 'Well, it's not really like this all the time. He's away a lot, that's for sure, but it's mostly just babysitting for politicians and film stars. Nothing . . . violent.'

'Yeah,' Logan said. 'He told me that as well. It only took him five years or so. But then it seems that lots of people have been lying to me, so I'm getting used to it.'

Sam sighed. 'Logan, he never really lied to—'

He stopped her with a wave of one hand. 'I know, Sam. It's just that I've had a rough few days and you can't blame me for taking it out on someone.'

'I suppose.'

They sat quietly for a couple of minutes before Cahill stood and said he was going to rustle up some breakfast.

'You just used the phrase "rustle up",' Logan said, smiling broadly and starting to laugh.

'Yeah, so?'

'Wyatt fucking Earp.'

Sam laughed too. Cahill gave them the finger, then turned and went into the kitchen. Logan finished his water and sat back on the couch.

'This must be weird for you,' Sam said to him. 'I mean, finding out you have a daughter and that she's eleven. God knows, it's hard enough to get to know them when you bring them up from babies, but that must be a real kick in the guts.'

Logan nodded and looked at the photo sitting on the desk of Cahill's two girls. They were on a sunny beach, and he wondered if it was from the time when Jodie, the eldest, had gone missing. He asked Sam if it was. She looked at the picture and Logan saw her face shift and change, the memory of that day still a painful wound for her.

'No, that was another time,' she said. 'I hope this ends for you like that day did for us, with Ellie in your arms.'

'Yeah, but even if it does how am I supposed to relate to her? We'll still be strangers.'

'I know you, Logan. It'll work out fine.'

'Assuming they don't kill her.'

Sam put her hands on top of his and squeezed. 'Alex will do this, Logan. And so will you. She's coming back.'

Logan knew that she was trying to be positive, but he couldn't share her optimism. Nothing about this situation had turned out well so far. Penny was dead, one of the bad guys was dead and he imagined that they wouldn't be the only ones when it was all done and dusted.

He stood and walked to the desk, picking up the photograph there and looking at it, trying to imagine what it must be like to have a daughter. He put it back on the desk and reached into his back pocket for the photo of Ellie. Sam Cahill looked at him with a frown, unsure of what it was he had in his hand. He went back and sat beside her, handing her the crumpled photo.

Sam looked at it for a moment and then looked at Logan. 'Is that her?' she asked.

Logan nodded. 'They came to threaten me and dropped that on the floor. I didn't even know who she was and I didn't take care of it at first.'

He took it from Sam and put it on his thigh, pressing on it and trying to smooth it out with his hand. Sam recognised the symbolism in his actions and it moved her.

'She's got your eyes,' she said. 'No mistaking she's yours.'

'I know. I hope that makes it easier . . . when she's back here. Safe.'

'Just take it slowly, Logan. We'll help you get through it.'

He slipped the photo back into his pocket. She noticed how carefully he did it, as if it might break if he was too rough. He slumped back on the couch and rubbed hard at his eyes, dark circles smudged on the skin below.

'Don't be so down,' she told him. 'There will be life after this is over, you know. And we will definitely need to get you a woman.'

Sam nudged him and then stood and went into the kitchen. Logan sat on the couch, thinking about Ellie, about Irvine, and about where his life was going after this day.

Assuming he was still alive at the end of it.

14

8.03 a.m.

Irvine turned her mobile phone over in her hands, wondering whether she should check in now with Moore, and maybe even ask for some support. She was sure she could argue a good case for it, especially if she linked Logan and the American to what happened at the pub.

Someone rapped their knuckles on the passenger window of her car and she started, dropping the phone on the floor. She looked over and recognised the American, and then saw Logan standing behind him. She looked at Logan and he smiled weakly at her, shrugging his shoulders. The American motioned with his hand for her to unlock the door, which she did. He pulled the door open and sat in the front passenger seat, with Logan getting in the back directly behind him.

'Detective,' Cahill said, nodding at her.

Irvine felt heat rising in her cheeks and hated that she had been caught by him.

'I suppose you're going to tell me that you've known right from the start that I was following you?' she asked.

'Sure,' he said. 'I'm happy to give you some tips for your next stakeout if you like.'

Irvine couldn't tell if he was being sincere or not so she said nothing.

Cahill turned in his seat to face her and Irvine glanced back at Logan, noticing how his eyes darted away when she looked at him.

'I don't suppose I can convince you to go home and forget about us?' Cahill asked.

'You're right,' she told him. 'You can't.'

'Okay, then maybe I can persuade you to help us.' He paused for effect, enjoying the confusion in Irvine's face.

'I'm a police officer,' she said after a moment. 'And I'm investigating the murder of a woman and the disappearance of her child. For all I know the two of you are mixed up in the whole thing and I'm not prepared to risk my career for you.'

Logan wasn't convinced by Irvine's apparent indignation. Her voice lacked conviction. Cahill had insisted that he was the best one to win her over, but there was a personality clash that was getting in the way and Cahill was enjoying the game he was playing too much. It was Logan's daughter whose life was at risk and he decided to take the direct approach.

'We know who has her,' he said, cutting across Cahill as he started to respond to Irvine. 'Ellie, I mean.'

Both Cahill and Irvine turned their heads sharply to face him.

'And we're going to get her back,' he finished.

Irvine watched him closely, looking for any sign that he was lying. He held her gaze disconcertingly and she was the one who had to look away, turning to Cahill.

'He's right,' Cahill said to her. 'He might be fucking stupid, but he's not wrong.' He turned to Logan. 'This seems to be your show now, so you can run with it, buddy.'

Logan shifted to the middle of the back seat and leaned forward, resting his elbows on the backs of the front seats. His face was only a short distance from Irvine's and when she turned to him she saw the fatigue etched on his features. She thought he looked a lot older this morning than he had the first time they had met.

Logan hadn't really noticed before, but Irvine looked young for a detective and he thought that must mean she was both ambitious and good at what she did. The police force was, after all, still a male-dominated world.

'How much can I tell you?' he asked her.

Cahill viewed the exchange between his friend and the detective in silence, watching them both closely and seeing something between them that was more than just a cop doing her job. His innate caution meant that he would have told the cop as little as possible, but he said nothing, content to let Logan make the decision.

'Have you killed anyone?' Irvine asked Logan, not looking at him.

'No.'

'Has he?' she said, flicking her eyes at Cahill. 'And don't lie because this is too important, okay.'

'Probably,' Logan said. 'I mean, he used to be a soldier.'

Irvine exhaled and looked down before fixing her eyes on Logan again. 'Has he killed anyone in the last twenty-four hours?'

Logan felt comfortable talking to Irvine even in these circumstances, which was pretty weird given where they were and what was happening.

'No,' he said. 'But last night in town one of his team killed one of the gang that has Ellie.'

Irvine did not react.

'Just as he was about to stick a knife in me.'

Irvine looked at Cahill, who remained impassive. She remembered again the man lying on the floor of the lavatory with blood pooled around his head.

Irvine knew Logan must be telling the truth, but beyond that was feeling increasingly lost. She was torn between the logical side of her mind, which stressed her commitment to her duty as a police officer, and the emotional side of her that wanted to save a little girl's life no matter what it took.

She turned back to Logan, and was startled by the intensity in his eyes. 'This was in a place on West Nile Street?'

Logan nodded.

'What do you expect me to do with that information?' she asked.

'That's up to you.'

Irvine pulled her door open and stepped outside, walking

away from the front of the car and then turning to look back at them.

'What do you think?' Logan asked Cahill.

'She's on board.'

'That's what I thought.'

They watched her pacing in front of the car, her breath billowing out in the cold air.

'If this thing works out,' Cahill said, 'you could do a lot worse than her.'

This time it was Logan feeling the heat in his face.

'There's a lot to get done before then,' he said. 'And anyway, didn't you see the wedding ring on her finger?'

'Of course I did,' Cahill replied slowly. 'But she's been out all night chasing us around and you'll notice she hasn't got her partner with her so this is on her own time. No one does that just out of devotion to the job.'

Logan had noticed all of that and felt his cheeks continue to burn as he saw the logic in what Cahill was saying.

'She might not be ready to admit it yet,' Cahill went on, 'but she feels a personal stake in this; and that's down to Ellie *and* to you. I'm good at reading body language and I can see how you react to each other.'

Logan found it difficult to imagine sustaining a relationship if he was going to have to devote time to Ellie and help her adjust to what had happened.

'Listen,' Cahill said. 'We'll get through this and then you need to start living again. Penny's gone and you're going to need all the emotional support you can get to bring Ellie up after what she's been through.'

'You are the single most positive prick I have ever met,' Logan told Cahill. 'And that's a compliment.'

'Think positive, plan ahead and do what you have to. There's not much to it beyond that.'

Irvine walked back to the car, got in and closed the door.

'There's a problem,' she said.

'What?' Cahill asked.

'One of the doormen at the pub saw two guys leaving not long after . . .' she searched for the right words, 'it happened. And he remembers them walking down on to St Vincent Street.'

'So?' Logan said.

Cahill leaned back in his seat, knowing immediately what was wrong.

'The city centre is monitored twenty-four/seven by CCTV,' Irvine said. 'And there will be coverage of you and this other man going into his building.' She jabbed a finger at Cahill. 'Plus, the bar has a camera at the entrance so the odds are they will have your faces on film.'

Logan slumped back, rubbing his hands over his face and then up through his hair.

'We're totally fucked,' he said. 'They'll be coming for me and Bails before we get a chance to do anything.'

'They don't have you on *film*,' Cahill said. 'All CCTV stuff is digital now and most of it is accessed on secure extranet sites.'

'What does that even mean?' Logan asked angrily.

'Logan,' Cahill said, 'you saw what Bruce did earlier, right? Well, he can access anything that's out there – including CCTV archives for the bar and the city centre cameras.'

'You can't just hack into a police system and erase records,' Irvine said.

'Yes we can. And it can be made to look like a system screw-up, nothing more.'

'That's illegal.'

'Sure it is. But so what, detective? I mean, the life of a little girl – Logan's daughter – might depend on us being able to keep your colleagues out of our hair and I am willing to do absolutely whatever needs to be done to achieve that. Is that a problem for you?'

Irvine knew that if she played it straight and involved Liam Moore the girl might never be found, or at least she might not be found alive. On the other hand, if she committed to what Cahill was proposing she might end up in jail herself.

'This is time for the big boys and girls,' Cahill told her. 'We need you to show some balls, detective.'

Logan rested his hand on the top of Irvine's seat.

'This is my daughter,' he told her. 'She's being held by some bad men. The same men who killed her mother and I'm pretty sure one of them came to the bar last night to kill me.'

Irvine turned her head to look at him.

'Alex here is the only chance I have of getting her back and we all know that. Let us do this. Help us do this.'

Irvine held his gaze for a while and then nodded.

'Okay,' she said. 'What can I do?'

'First,' Cahill said, 'we need to get on top of this CCTV footage. If you can give my hacker access details it will speed things up.'

'Access details?' Irvine asked.

'Yeah,' Cahill said. 'You know, the stuff we need to get in. Passwords and the like.'

'Christ,' Irvine said, realising just how deep she was in.

'In for a penny, in for a pound,' Cahill said.

'I get it, okay,' Irvine said, exasperated by his exuberance. 'Get him on the phone and I'll tell him what I can.'

'Come on in the house and we'll do it from there,' Cahill said, turning to leave the car.

'But I don't want to know his name or where he is or anything else,' Irvine said. 'The less I know the better it'll be for everyone.'

'You did the right thing,' Cahill told her, opening his door to get out of the car.

Irvine looked back at Logan. He nodded and then opened his door.

Irvine shivered, unsure if it was from the cold air or from fear of what lay ahead.

15

8.58 a.m.

After a short, faintly surreal phone call in Cahill's study with Bruce the hacker, Cahill gave Irvine a summary of what they were planning and how they were going to use the meeting this morning to find out where Ellie was being held. Then he outlined how they intended to explain Ellie's reappearance.

'Can you get back into the house, Ellie's house, and get some clothes for her to change into?' he asked.

'I think so. I've been in a couple of times already and I'm one of the lead detectives so no one will think anything of it if I go back again.'

'Did you . . .' Logan tried to find the right words for what he wanted to ask, 'get a sense of what she was like?'

Irvine hesitated before she spoke. 'I don't know. Like any

girl, I suppose. She likes clothes, that I do know. A bit of a tomboy, but cool with it.'

Logan smiled, thinking that Cahill was right about Irvine. She seemed to have a personal investment in this and that would probably be good for them all in the end.

'Logan's not a professional like you,' Irvine said to Cahill, trying to change the subject. 'You can't just send him into the park alone with these men.'

'It has to be me,' Logan told her. 'They have to think that I'm alone and desperate so that they're not on guard.'

'If they think they're still in control,' Cahill added, 'we might have a better chance of being able to tail them. They're criminals, not soldiers or anything, and people like that think the rest of us will be scared of them and what they can do so they get sloppy. It's why they mostly all get caught in the end.'

'But what if Ellie's, you know, already dead?' she said, glancing at Logan. 'And they kill Logan as well. Have you thought of that?'

'She's not dead,' Logan said firmly.

'You have to face that possibility,' Irvine said. 'I'm sorry, but—'

'I've spoken to her,' Logan said. 'Last night. She's alive.'

Irvine paused. 'That's good, then,' she said softly.

'We'll be as close to Logan as we can be without getting made,' Cahill said. 'Plus, he'll have a weapon.'

'I've had some training,' Logan added quickly as Irvine turned to him to complain.

'Jesus,' she said, shaking her head. 'This is too much. Can't you just, I don't know, put a tracking device in Logan's bag and follow them that way? Wouldn't that be safer?'

'No good,' Cahill said. 'They're not that dumb and they would find a tracker if we put one in there. This is the best we can do. Okay, it's not perfect, but then operations like this never are. You do what you can with the circumstances you're given.'

'I suppose,' Irvine conceded. 'And what happens when you find out where she is? I mean, they won't just hand her over if you ask politely.'

'That part you don't need to know about,' Cahill said.

'Yes I do.'

'No. You don't. And I'm not discussing it any further with you.' He stood to leave and held a hand out to Irvine, cutting off any further complaints. 'It's for your own benefit,' he told her.

She didn't want to accept that he was right, but let it go anyway.

Irvine drove behind Logan and Cahill as they all headed back towards the city. The traffic was, as ever at that time of the morning, a real hassle, but it eventually thinned out when they got through the centre and started heading south on the motorway. She eased back a little and followed them up an off ramp after a couple of miles. They went left from there, past the entrance to the big garden centre at Rouken Glen Park, and then turned right to go along the side of the park. About halfway along the road, the X5 slowed and turned left into a tree-lined street with big, expensive houses on either side. Then it turned again and pulled to a stop behind a pretty crappy-looking estate car with two people in the front seats.

Irvine stopped behind them and waited, unsure of what to do until Cahill stepped down from the car and motioned for her to follow. She jogged to catch up with Logan and Cahill as they got into the back of the car and squeezed in beside Logan. There was just about enough room for the three of them.

The two men in the front seat craned round to look at her.

'Detective, this is Chris Washington and Tom Hardy,' Cahill said. 'Boys, this is Detective Irvine of the Strathclyde police force. Say hello to each other.'

Hardy nodded and Washington raised a hand in greeting. Irvine said hello, feeling comforted by just how tough and professional the two men in the front appeared. They wore thin blue jackets over plain black T-shirts and black combat trousers and looked very, very serious.

Logan had noticed a plain canvas cover draped over the contents of the boot of the car and he asked what was back there.

'Stuff,' Washington said. 'You know, body armour, helmets, guns and flash-bangs.'

'What's a flash-bang?' Logan asked.

'You never read any Tom Clancy?' Cahill asked.

'No.'

Cahill rolled his eyes.

'Stun grenades, for want of a better description,' Washington explained. 'They make a lot of light and noise to momentarily stun the bad guys so we can take them down. Flash bang!'

He shouted 'Flash bang!' and opened and closed his hands quickly. Logan just stared at him.

'And they are really fucking bright and fucking noisy,' Hardy added, a little redundantly Logan thought.

'Not that you'll ever know,' Cahill said. 'We do the dirty stuff and you wait in the car.'

'Fine by me. But I still want a gun to take in there with me.'

Cahill reached into the back of the car and brought out the same compact nine-millimetre handgun that Logan had used in the range. This time it was nestled in a black vinyl holster, no belt.

'Undo your belt and slip this on,' Cahill said. 'And listen to me good, okay.'

Logan nodded, feeling like a schoolboy being lectured to.

'You do not let them search your person in any way,' Cahill said. 'If they move to do that, you tell them that you have a weapon and that it is there for your protection only. That you do not want to engage them in violence.'

Logan nodded again.

'But make no mistake,' Cahill went on. 'If it all goes to shit then you shoot first and run like the fucking devil himself is chasing you. Like Tam o' Shanter. Got it?'

Logan was impressed that Cahill had learned something during his time in Scotland and didn't have the heart to tell him it was the witch, not the devil, who chased Tam and grabbed poor Meg's tail.

'And you'll be there as soon as it happens?' he asked.

'No,' Cahill said. 'If it happens it'll be too quick and you're on your own. Bails and Carrie will be as close as they can but you will have to look after yourself.' He produced a tiny radio microphone and fitted it under the collar of Logan's polo shirt, then pushed a small earpiece into his own ear.

'I'll be able to hear you,' he said. 'But I can't give you an earpiece because they'll see it and then we'll be fucked.'

Logan nodded and set his mouth in a tight line.

They waited in the warm car for about half an hour with little talk and only the sound of the car's radio breaking the quiet. Cahill finally said that it was time and Irvine opened the door to let Logan out. He had forgotten how cold it was and their breath billowed up and out of their mouths and noses, mingling in the air above their heads before evaporating. Irvine zipped up Logan's fleece top as he slung the record bag with the contract in it over his shoulder.

'Be careful,' she said.

'I can't do that,' he told her. 'My safety comes second to hers at the moment. If I have to choose between being careful and getting her back, then careful loses.'

Irvine dropped her hands to her sides and they stood awkwardly again.

'You'd better go now,' she said.

Logan walked away from the car and towards the park, hugely aware of the weight of the handgun resting on his hip under the fleece. Behind him, Irvine got back in the car beside Cahill and blew warm air on to her hands.

At the main road, Logan stood on the pavement opposite the park gates and waited for the traffic to thin out. It was busy with commuters – rich commuters, in flash German motors.

'Beemers and Mercs and Porsches, oh my,' he said softly into his collar for Cahill's benefit, smiling as he did it. 'We are a long way from Kansas, Toto.'

He jogged across the road at the first break in the traffic and moved quickly into the park. He started to walk anti-clockwise round the pond, heading for the path leading to the bridge at the top right corner. A light but persistent drizzling rain started, smearing his vision and misting the park. He passed a young mum pushing a pram and a teenage couple walking hand in hand, and shivering in the cold. A single swan glided imperiously in the middle of the pond, its beak held high as it looked scornfully down on the other birds.

Logan looked across to the path on the far side of the pond and was relieved to see Judd and Carrie walking behind the Labrador. He knew they were just putting on a show, but felt a momentary pang of grief for the life he had lost with Penny – a life they never had. They had never enjoyed these kinds of moments together as Ellie grew up. He spoke again to Cahill, this time keeping his head up so as not to arouse suspicion if anyone was watching.

'I see them,' he said. 'Bails and Carrie. I'll be at the path to the bridge in a few more seconds. I don't see anybody that might be with these guys. I'm going quiet now until I get there.'

He reached the turn towards the bridge and sneaked a last quick glance towards his guardian angels. They were rounding the top of the pond, moving just a bit more quickly.

Logan turned right and saw the two men leaning against the left hand railing of the bridge, staring downriver. It was Drake and the shorter of the two men from the foyer of his building. The short one looked his way and stepped away from the railing, starting to walk towards him. Logan kept moving forward despite the screaming urge in his brain to turn and run. Ellie's voice sounded in his head and it propelled him on.

As he closed in on the bridge the noise of the water rushing over the rocks below increased and the drizzle twisted in the wind, blurring everything like a watercolour painting of the real thing – all soft edges and bleeding colours. And the short man kept right on striding towards him, with Drake not moving.

Logan realised he was going to be searched. He stopped, pushed the record bag round into the small of his back and lifted his hooded top to reveal the gun on his hip. He put his left hand up, palm out. The short man stopped and his brow creased into a heavy frown. He clenched his right hand into a fist and released it again, his breath steaming out of his nostrils like a bull's.

Drake stepped forward, his right hand disappearing under the long wool coat he wore.

Logan sensed an electric charge sizzle through the wet air and his lungs felt as if they were filling with water instead of air.

At that moment, the teenage couple turned on to the path. The girl screamed when she saw Drake pull a gun from his coat and they turned and ran back out of sight.

Logan pulled the bag over his head and the short man moved forward to take it from him before retreating back to the bridge to join Drake. Logan watched Drake put his gun away and take the contract out and start to flip through it, all sixty pages.

'It's all there,' Logan shouted. 'We don't have much time now after what just happened. Those kids will have called the police and they're going to be here soon.'

He heard his voice slip back into the broad Ayrshire accent of his childhood – 'they're gonnae be here'.

Drake scanned the pages at the end of the document, pulled out a pen and signed it where Logan had marked it with one of those little sticky 'sign here' pointers – a small yellow label with a picture of a hand holding a pen. He shoved it back into the bag and walked over to Logan, stopping about six feet away. The short man watched from the bridge.

'Where did you get the gun?' Drake asked.

Logan was not prepared for the question and tried to hold the man's gaze while he raced through possible answers in his head.

'You are stronger than you appear, Mr Finch. I'll pay you that compliment at least.'

Logan figured Drake had taken his silence for strength. Well, he'd grab any little piece of luck he could.

'This isn't about who's stronger or better,' he said. 'You

won, okay. The deal's on, you'll get your money and I'll just have to hope that no one ever finds out. Because if they do, I'll be out of a job and in jail.'

'That's not my concern.'

'I know that,' Logan said, starting to feel angry at the cold bastard. 'You just want your money.'

The man nodded.

'And I want the girl.'

Drake threw the bag at Logan's feet and started backing away from him. Logan moved forward, matching him step for step.

'I *want* the girl,' he said again, aware that the short man was now moving fast towards him. He hoped that Judd and Carrie held their ground and didn't break cover. He didn't want to fuck it up now.

The short man passed Drake and closed in on Logan, his hand moving round behind his back. Logan sharply quickened his pace, pulled his gun out of its holster and pressed it against the short man's forehead.

Drake stopped moving and pulled his own gun out from his coat, pointing it at Logan's chest. Logan thought he heard sirens in the far distance.

Hold your nerve.

'I want the girl,' he said, pushing the gun harder into the short man's head to make the point and trying to control the tremors he felt in his stomach.

'After the money is transferred and moved out of the country,' Drake told him. 'That way I know it's safe.'

'You'll kill her,' Logan said, a ragged edge in his voice

now as his thoughts were drowned out by the memory of Ellie crying.

'You don't have a choice,' Drake said.

Logan wanted more than anything just to do it, right there and then; to pull the trigger on the short man and erase him from the world. And then take his chances with Drake. Instead, he pushed the short man's head back with the gun and stepped away.

'If she dies, I won't rest until I find you. Wherever you are.'

Both men smiled back at Logan, clearly believing themselves safe in the knowledge that they would never be found by this lawyer, a pretend tough guy with a gun and a short fuse.

Logan reached down to lift the bag from the ground and the two men turned and walked away from him. He put the bag over his shoulder and watched them go. Except they didn't just walk, they swaggered. Logan spoke into his collar.

'Alex, tell Tom and Chris to look for them at the north exit of the park, one short and one regular.'

He paused for a beat, watching them move further away and feeling his anger boiling over. He wanted to do something so that he would feel less impotent. He spoke into the radio transmitter again.

'I'm going to make some noise now, Alex,' Logan said. 'But don't worry. Everything worked out okay.'

He lifted the gun, pointed it down into the muddy ground in front of him and fired six shots. Smoke and fire belched from the mouth of the gun and swirled in the mist of the rain. Dirt and stone kicked up violently, splattering his jeans with the earth's blood.

The two men turned sharply and for a moment Logan imagined that he saw fear in their eyes. But they were too far away now to really tell. Drake lifted his own gun and trained it on him. Logan stood still and stared at them as they became indistinct in the blurring rain. He slid the gun back into its holster, turned, and headed back to the pond.

16

9.20 a.m.

Judd and Carrie met Logan at the junction of the two paths and guided him to the nearest bench where he sat heavily, clasping his hands tightly together to stop them from shaking. He heard raised voices and looked up to see Cahill running fast towards him with Irvine following. There was no one else left in the now deserted park. It was an odd moment in a strange week.

Carrie stepped round Cahill and blocked Irvine's path to the bench. Irvine saw something in Carrie's eyes and stopped ten feet away, her cheeks red and her breathing laboured. Logan looked up and told her it was okay, waving her back towards the park entrance as the sound of approaching sirens grew louder.

'Boss,' Judd said to Cahill, 'we need to book. Right now.'

Irvine brushed past Carrie and sat on the edge of the bench, looking at the ground and still breathing heavily. Her shoulders slumped as she rested her elbows on her knees.

'It's okay,' Logan said.

She angled her head to the side and looked at him from the corner of her eye.

'It is far from okay, Logan. You're just in so deep you don't realise it any more, running around out here with guns.'

She sighed before she spoke again.

'Listen to me. I don't know what the hell I'm talking about.'

She looked round at the grave faces surrounding her and at the gun safely holstered again on Logan's hip. She met his eyes.

'Boss,' Judd said, his voice rising in pitch to match the sirens. 'We have to fucking book.'

Cahill nodded and gestured for Logan to stand. 'Let's go, boys and girls,' he said.

'You're going to kill all of them when you find them, aren't you?' Irvine said, standing to face Cahill.

'I told you already that I'm not discussing it with you.'

'This isn't a game,' Irvine said, almost shouting now. 'A little girl's life is at stake and you're going to get her killed. I can't believe I've let this go on so long already and I'll probably get the sack for it, but let me end it now. Let me call my boss.'

'Doing that will get the girl killed,' Cahill said. 'And I know more about this kind of operation than any cop so just let it be and let's move.'

'We are leaving right fucking now,' Judd said to Logan, grabbing him by the shoulders and pulling him up. 'Move it.'

'Logan?' Irvine pleaded.

Judd pushed Logan in the back and turned to speak to Irvine. 'Lady, no offence okay, but you are so far out of your depth and you are fucking drowning.'

'I'm beginning to realise that,' she said.

Logan walked back to her, hunkering down in front of her.

'Alex is right,' he said. 'I mean, these are not amateurs and they know how this stuff works. This is what they do and I believe Alex when he says that they do it better than anyone. I also believe that they are the only hope my little girl has and that they will not stop until she is safe.'

Irvine looked in his eyes and believed him.

'We all need to get out of here,' Judd shouted. He turned and ran towards the gates, leaving them to follow. Irvine stood and ran her hands through her wet hair. The low cloud cover broke in the east and watery light seeped through the grey rain. She wanted a rainbow to form but it never came.

Logan waited, wanting her to say something – anything.

'Go,' she said. 'And make sure you bring her back safe.'

'I'll see you later?' Logan asked.

She nodded and then ran down the path and over the bridge, praying that she would get out of the park before her fellow officers arrived.

Logan caught up with Judd as they came out of the park and Cahill's car slid to a stop at the kerb. Judd opened the passenger door and pushed Logan in before slamming it shut and sprinting up the hill towards a fast-reversing red Audi driven by Carrie.

Cahill followed her on to the A77 and turned right, away from town and towards Newton Mearns, guessing that the sirens were the armed-response teams from town reacting to the reports of guns in the park. Logan sat upright and pulled his seat belt into place.

'Do we have them?' he asked.

Cahill shook his head. 'Haven't heard.'

Logan felt his stomach rise and swallowed it back down.

Cahill punched a speed dial button on the phone handset fixed to the dashboard and the dialling sound filled the car from the speakers mounted above the windscreen. It rang five times and then clicked on to Washington's voicemail.

'Fuck,' Cahill said, punching the end button and then hitting speed dial for Hardy.

The phone rang loudly again and Logan fought hard to keep his breakfast down.

'Boss?' Hardy's voice came on.

'Yeah, it's me. Status?'

'We have them. Heading north.'

'Copy that,' Cahill said. 'We'll be on your tail as soon as we can.'

'Copy.'

The dial tone sounded before Cahill cut it off.

Logan closed his eyes and punched the dashboard in celebration.

Cahill phoned Judd's mobile. 'We got them,' he shouted.

'Let's double back on to the motorway and get ready to go after these fuckers, Bails.'

'Copy that, boss.'

Cahill looked over at Logan and smiled. 'We're in the game now.'

'Will we get her?'

'I can't promise that.'

'Fuck you,' Logan said. 'Promise me.'

'It won't mean anything if I do. It'll just be words.'

'Promise me.'

Cahill looked again at Logan.

'We'll get her.'

17

10.02 a.m.

Rush hour was over and traffic was light heading back along the motorway into the city, so they made good time. No one said anything until they were through the outer gate and in the courtyard of the building on Scotland Street. Cahill was out first and motioned for everyone to come to him.

'This is it now,' he told them. 'Just like we've done before. It makes no difference that I'm invested personally in the outcome. We keep it strictly professional.'

Nods all round.

'Okay. You know how this is done – violence of thought and action. You all have to appreciate that this operation is not like previous jobs; it is not officially sanctioned in any way. That means that if it gets traced back to us then we face serious jail time. Anyone wants to pull out, this is the last time I ask.'

Silence.

'Good fucking job,' Cahill said.

Logan cleared his throat, wanting to say something but not quite sure what.

'Look, you guys, I just wanted to say . . . well, to say thanks, you know? I could never ask you to do this for me and it means everything to me that you are standing behind Alex. I don't really know what it's like to go into something like this and even just firing that gun in anger in the park made my legs weak, so . . .'

'You did good back there,' Judd told him. 'Real good, okay? You leave the rest of it to us now, you hear. We're going to get your girl.'

'Thanks,' Logan said. 'That's all I want to say. Just thanks.'

Once inside, they moved quickly through the building to the bigger of the two armouries and everyone went about the business of suiting up quickly and smoothly. Mortal business was about to be done and there was no big show about it.

Carrie was the first to get into her combats and pull on her belt and holster. Then she busied herself loading two heavy canvas bags with the weaponry they were taking with them – small black automatic rifles, more flash-bangs and what looked to Logan like long strips of rope. When he asked what they were, Carrie told him they were shaped explosives for taking out doors.

Cahill threw a pair of black combat trousers at Logan and he pulled them on after self-consciously dropping his jeans. He stood uncomfortably while Cahill and Judd checked their handguns, holstered them and then helped Carrie with the final packing of the gear. He bent to pick up his jeans and felt the photograph of Ellie in one of the pockets. He took it out, looked at it quickly and put it in one of the side pockets of his combats.

He was beginning to realise now how people could become obsessed with guns. Their inherent power was apparent even when they were just inert metal things, silent and unused in a canvas bag. There was a dark beauty to them that could be mesmerising.

Logan heard beeps as someone punched the entry code into the door and two CPO team members he had not seen before came in to take the kit bags out to the car. Following them out, Logan saw that they had already loaded some additional gear – ballistic vests and helmets with plastic goggles strapped to them. He hadn't even been aware of all of this pre-planning going on, which made it all the more impressive.

Carrie directed the loaders where to store the bags of equipment and pulled the rear door of the X5 down when they were done.

'Mount up,' Cahill said.

Judd got in the driver's side with Cahill next to him and Logan climbed in the rear after Carrie. Judd gunned the big engine and roared out on to the street as Cahill turned the dash-mounted phone on and punched in Hardy's number. He picked up on the second ring and his voice filled the vehicle.

'We're on the trail, boss. We have a visual on the subjects, copy.'

'Copy,' Cahill said. 'Lead us on down the road.'

18

10.17 a.m.

This was the end, she was sure of it.

Ellie thought she felt the air in the room change when she pulled the second nail out of the third board. It felt lighter, less oppressive. She knew it was probably just a draught of air coming in through the loose-fitting wooden window frame, but it was enough to lighten her spirits. She felt gooseflesh rise up on her arms and legs and welcomed the sensation.

Two more nails to go, Ellie told herself, and then I'll be out of this place and away from these people. She pushed everything else from her mind, including the reality of being outside at this time of year and in this weather wearing nothing but a flimsy pair of pyjamas. The fantasy she created in her mind's eye saw her running a short distance to one of the other cabins she had seen out of the window, where she would be sheltered by a friendly family while they called the police. Nice and neat.

A smile twitched at the corners of her mouth but was quickly pushed away as a rolling wave of pain washed through her head from her swollen face. She moved to the bed and sat with her head bowed, waiting for this latest burst to ease. After a moment, she felt it subside and breathed in long and hard.

Ellie had no idea how badly her face was damaged. At first, with the pain and the swelling being entirely new to her, she was sure that she was very seriously hurt. But now, after a couple of days, the swelling seemed to have peaked and, she thought, might even have reduced a little. The vision on the injured side of her face appeared to have opened up a bit this morning, although the pain was still pretty intense.

She could hear the woman moving around in the front part of the cabin and sometimes she thought she also heard some music. The woman rarely came in to see her, except when she was with one of the men. She never made eye contact with Ellie.

'Got to finish it,' Ellie whispered to herself. 'Got to do it today.'

She stood and waited to see if any more pain or nausea would set in. Her head felt light for a moment and she swayed a little unsteadily when she stood.

'Got to do it now,' she said. 'Come on.'

She went to the window again and pulled at the end of the board where she had already removed the two nails. She pulled it out and away from the frame of the window, trying to loosen the nails on the other side so that it would be easier for her to get them out. Then she sucked at the raw ends of her fingers, tasting the metallic tang of her own blood. It was a taste she hoped never to have to endure again.

Ellie worked her fingernails under the head of the bottom nail and pulled. It slid right out. She had not been expecting that result and had pulled with a lot more force than she needed. She stumbled back against the wall and heard the thud she made as she collided with it. She closed her eyes and held her breath. Through the wall she heard the music continuing and hoped it had covered the sound of her mistake.

Then she heard quick footsteps and the door being unlocked. She glanced quickly at the window and saw that the free end of the third board rested against the top edge of the one beneath it. She was glad she had left the bottom two in place, but anyone looking closely would see that the third one was loose.

The door handle moved and Ellie pushed off the wall and stood between the door and the window, hoping to hide the results of her hard work.

The woman stopped just inside the door with her hand still gripping the handle. She looked at Ellie and then around the small room.

'What are you doing?'

Ellie grasped for an explanation. 'I was just . . .'

'What? What are you doing?' The woman started to move towards Ellie.

'I was trying to exercise,' Ellie said.

The woman stopped and looked at her.

'But I got dizzy and I fell. I'm sorry. Please don't hurt me.'

Ellie couldn't tell if the woman believed her and started to panic when she moved into the room and took hold of her arm. But then her face seemed to soften slightly and she guided Ellie over to the bed and sat her down.

'Then don't exercise, stupid girl. You're hurt and you need to rest.'

Ellie lowered her head and nodded.

The woman sighed and stood over Ellie. When Ellie looked up, the woman looked away towards the window.

Please don't.

Please don't.

Please don't.

A frown creased the woman's forehead.

Nonononononononono.

Then Ellie heard the phone ringing in the front of the cabin. The woman looked down at Ellie and narrowed her eyes.

'No more exercising, stupid girl.'

Ellie nodded and slumped back on the bed after the woman left. She tried to hold the tears back, but they came anyway – running down her face and into her hair.

19

10.38 a.m.

'We're still running along the A82 Loch Lomond road, copy.' Hardy's voice filled the car's interior.

'Copy that,' Cahill acknowledged. 'What kind of time are you making?'

'Uh, steady at just below sixty. Staying within the speed limits all the way.'

'Okay. We're going to try to close the gap some but still stay close to the limits. We don't want to have to explain our load to some traffic cops.'

'Copy. Where are you now?'

'Just coming up to the Erskine Bridge. I'd guess we're thirty minutes or so behind you. How's the traffic?'

'Good. Busy enough for a tail.'

'Okay. I'll check back in ten.'

Cahill ended the call and turned in his seat to speak to Logan. 'Are there any secluded spots along the loch?'

'Probably some,' Logan said. 'But I don't really know it too well.'

Cahill's skin looked taut on his face.

'Would they stay this close to the city, and in such a public spot?' Logan asked.

'Maybe,' Cahill said.

'Has some kind of sense about it,' Carrie added. 'I mean, it's close to the city if they need to move quickly and it's not too far from the airport. I can see it being attractive to them.'

'I wouldn't choose it,' Judd said. 'And I don't think they would. I think they'd want to be more remote, somewhere easier to move around unseen.'

'This time of year,' Logan said, 'could be a lot of places like that.'

Judd slowed the car, taking the exit for the bridge, and Logan noticed snow starting to fall lightly outside.

'Glad we brought the four-wheel drive,' Judd said.

When they were up on the bridge, Logan looked along the river and wondered just how far Ellie was from here. Although the snow was still light where they were, he saw darker clouds moving down from the north and the far distance was already obscured by the approaching weather front.

'This is going to be bad,' Carrie said, following Logan's gaze.

The phone rang and Cahill punched the button to answer it.

'Okay, we just changed direction,' Hardy's voice came on again. 'Left at Tarbet, heading west now on the, ah . . .'

'A83.' Washington's voice came on the line.

'Where does that take us?' Judd asked.

Cahill had a road atlas on his lap and traced his finger along the A82 to the junction with the A83 at Tarbet. He followed that west and then spoke.

'Over to the eastern edge of Loch Fyne, around the north tip and then right down the western side to the foot.'

'Copy that,' Hardy said. 'Beginning to look like we might be in for the long haul. Anyone know this route, because we don't?'

Cahill looked expectantly at the Scottish passengers in the rear of the car.

'I think they might be heading for Oban,' Logan said. 'Not the quickest route, but it gets there just the same.'

'If it's a long way round,' Cahill said, tracing the road to Oban, 'it's probably not the final destination. And I think it might be too far for them.'

'Where then?' Logan asked.

'I'd guess somewhere beside one of the lochs,' Cahill said, still looking down at the atlas. 'That would make sense because there will be remote spots along the way. There's Loch Fyne and then Loch Awe before they get to Oban.'

'I'll be back in touch, copy,' Hardy said.

The dial tone sounded and Cahill switched the phone off again.

They motored along at a steady sixty-eight, hoping to stay under any police speed checks. Cahill wanted to be as close to Hardy and Washington as possible when they reached the end of the road so that they could all move quickly together. The worst case scenario was sending the two point men in on their own. He didn't want them exposed without back-up. But sometimes that was just the way it worked out.

The snow started to thicken once they were past Tarbet and heading to the north tip of Loch Fyne. Cahill hoped that the weather would slow their targets down and enable them to close the gap even more. The big BMW might be hard on petrol, but it would make lighter work of the snow.

Loch Fyne wasn't wide at its northernmost end and as they travelled along the east side they could see over to the west where the road curved round the tip. Beyond that, it was starting to look as though they were going to hit some very serious snow as the cloud cover darkened with every mile.

'Nice scenery,' Judd said.

'Not today,' Logan told him.

The next call came.

'We're turning north again towards some place called Lochgilphead,' Hardy said. 'Pretty tough going now in this weather. We're stuck at fifty.'

Judd was maintaining his speed.

'Copy,' Cahill said. 'We're closing in on you so shouldn't be too far behind when we need to be.'

'Good. I see signs now for the A816 and Oban.'

Cahill was again concentrating on the atlas and found what he was looking for.

'Oban's too far and too public,' he said. 'I think they'll be heading for somewhere before that. If you check the map

341

you'll see that a narrow road comes off the A816 just south of Loch Awe and then runs along the loch side. My money would be on that.'

'Copy. I see that.'

'How's the traffic?'

'Pretty thin now. We're staying as far back as we can but we're going to have to risk staying tight in this weather.'

'Do the best you can.'

'You know we will.'

The dial tone again.

Logan was coming to hate that sound.

Hardy called to confirm that they took the Loch Awe turn-off as Cahill had anticipated. By that time, Logan reckoned they were no more than ten miles behind the leading car. He wanted to be closer and felt his heart rate rise as the odometer clicked over with the slowly passing miles. There had been less chat in the car and contact with Hardy and Washington had been infrequent as they followed along behind.

Cahill called Hardy back after deciding that now was the time to maintain constant contact between the two teams.

'Keep this phone line open from here on in,' he told Hardy. 'And activate your radios when you get to the site. We should be in range about ten minutes after that.'

'Copy, will do. This road is a complete bitch in this weather. Lots of twists and turns. They could be stopped ahead of us and we wouldn't know it until we slammed into their rear.'

'We do what we can,' Cahill told him.

*　　*　　*

In the banged-up old estate, Washington's hands were tight on the wheel as the rear end of the car slewed round each bend in the road. Then the terrain started to dip and rise and the road narrowed to a single track with trees on either side. The tarmac stopped and Washington felt even less traction as they slid along on snow and gravel.

They struggled up a short, steep hill and then pitched down the other side, towards a ninety-degree left turn. There was nothing but a solid line of trees in front of them beyond the edge of the road. Hardy looked further ahead and thought he saw the red glow of brake lights through the snow.

Washington pressed his foot down on the brake, but nothing happened. The car slid forward without slowing. The tree line loomed large. Hardy looked at Washington; like, hit the fucking brakes already.

Washington pumped his foot on the brake, trying to simulate an ABS system. The tyres gripped a little and he turned the wheel. The car turned halfway and then started to slide sideways.

'Oh, shit,' Hardy yelled.

Washington pumped the brake again but nothing happened. They were fifteen feet from the trees when Washington lifted his foot off the brake and pulled the wheel round the other way, turning into the slide. The front end levelled with the rear and just when it looked as if they were about to crunch off the road and into the trees, Washington turned left again and guided the car round the corner, the rear wheels still slipping even at walking speed.

'We're okay,' Hardy said for the benefit of those following behind.

The road went straight for a short distance and then bent round to the right. As they cleared this shallower bend with no difficulty, they saw a steep hill rising to three plateaus at roughly equal intervals.

'This is going to hurt,' Washington said, looking at Hardy.

He gunned the engine and, after a second of wheel spin, the tyres gripped and pushed the car up to the first plateau. On the second stage, Washington felt the wheels start to spin just as they made it on to the plateau and he hunched forward in his seat, willing the old beast to make it up the last stage.

Hardy leaned back in his seat, one hand gripping the seat and the other braced against the dashboard in front of him. If we lose this now, he thought, we lose the girl.

The wheels started to spin halfway up and the car skittered from side to side as the wheels fought for purchase on the mix of snow and gravel.

'Come on, you old bastard,' Hardy shouted, banging his hand in the dash.

Washington saw the final plateau just a few metres further ahead but then felt the wheels spin freely and the car started to lose speed rapidly. He saw what looked like a passing space on the left just at the edge of the plateau and because it was under the shelter of the trees there was more gravel and less snow. He whipped the wheel to the left, pressed his foot down and hoped for the best. The car lurched forward with one last effort and the front wheels gripped the exposed gravel and pulled the car up and off the hill.

Hardy looked at Washington and they both laughed, Washington punching the wheel.

'What the fuck is going on?' Cahill shouted over the open phone line.

'Sorry, boss,' Washington said. 'That is one bitch of a road. Watch the sharp left turn about six miles in and then the three-stage hill. Should be okay for you guys, but watch it all the same.'

'Copy,' Cahill said. 'You still have sight of the subjects?'

'Uh, no we don't,' Hardy said. 'But there're no turn-offs so we're going straight on.'

'Watch yourselves, you hear?'

'Copy.'

20

12.15 p.m.

After leaving the park, Irvine had gone home to get changed out of her wet clothes and clean up before going to the house on May Terrace. She was grateful to be alone and called Liam Moore to say that she had not seen Logan all night and was taking the day off to catch up on her rest. He told her that was fine, but said little else before hanging up on her.

She hated lying to Moore, but she had made her choice and had to carry through with it all the way now – no matter what the consequences.

After a quick shower, she did her best to hide the tiredness in her face with make-up. She had not slept in a long time, though she was unsure of precisely how long it had been, and the best she could do was to make herself look as if she had had a particularly rough night on the town.

'Great,' she said aloud.

The house on May Terrace was still under twenty-four-hour guard which meant that Irvine did not have to go into the office and get the house keys out of evidence. It would have been a hard task trying to explain that one away.

The same PC at the door let her into the house with no questions and she went again to Ellie's bedroom on the first floor.

There was an eerie sense of emptiness, more so than the last time she had been there. Maybe it was because she knew that Ellie was not just missing, but was being held by the same men who had visited so much violence upon her mother. She tried to shake the feeling that the room was going to remain empty long after today.

She opened the wardrobe, but instead of picking out some clothes she reached up for the journal again. She found it and lifted it down, being careful to hold it level for fear of dropping the daisychain and causing it more damage. She was still no closer to understanding the significance of the reference to summer 2003, but felt sure it was something that might be useful to have at the end of all this. Perhaps something that would allow Logan to make a connection with Ellie. She set the journal on the bed and then considered which clothes to take.

For the story to appear credible, in so far as that was at all possible, the clothes had to be something that Ellie would have picked in a hurry, so a nice, matching set was to be avoided. Irvine sifted through what was there and settled on a pair of old jeans, a T-shirt and a hooded jogging top. She grabbed some underwear, socks and the nearest pair of shoes and closed the wardrobe, setting all the clothes together on the bed.

It then occurred to her that she had no way of getting the stuff out of the house and past the officer at the front door.

'Shit.'

She cursed her own stupidity for not having thought this through. She was in so much of a rush to get here that she had not considered the practicalities.

She went to the window and looked out on to the street, searching for inspiration but not really sure what she was expecting to find out there. The street was empty at this time of day, with all the residents out at work. Her car sat alone at the kerb.

She still had her evidence kit in the boot of her car. That was the only option. Treat the clothes and the journal as evidence, bag it and take it out in plain sight.

She went downstairs and past the officer, explaining that she had some further evidence to take in and that she'd be back in a minute. The officer nodded and said nothing.

She grabbed two evidence bags from her car, together with a pair of latex gloves and evidence tags, and then walked calmly back into the house. She wrote out two pretty basic tags that would stand up to scrutiny if the PC wanted to look at them and then put the clothes and journal in separate bags. They looked convincing enough, she thought.

Irvine got out and back to her car with no trouble, and even took the time to thank the PC for his help. She drove sedately back across the city, feeling guilty and not wanting to attract any attention to herself. The journey passed without incident until she was back home where she ran to the bathroom and threw up. When her stomach was empty, she dry-heaved and then sat on the floor, wiping tears from her eyes from the effort.

When she felt strong enough, she got up and went to her bedroom to change clothes, leaving her suit lying on the floor in a crumpled heap and falling back on to the bed.

Here I am, she thought, stuck in a failing marriage with a baby to look after and I just committed a serious crime to assist in the likely killing of suspects in a murder-kidnap plot.

What the hell am I doing?

She didn't have an answer and didn't even really know what was going on. She had trusted her future career to men she had not even met until a couple of days ago.

It suddenly hit her that she had no idea how Logan found out who had taken Ellie, much less had been able to make contact with them to arrange the meeting this morning. Her professional, inquisitive nature had disappeared completely in the adrenalin rush of the night, no doubt reinforced by the combination of too much garage-bought sugar and not enough sleep.

She tried to convince herself that she had allowed them to draw her into this as she sat in the car with the Americans and their guns.

That's rubbish, Becky, and you know it.

Okay, maybe she was trying too hard to ignore the real reason for it – her emotional response to Logan's situation, and to the fate of the little girl she didn't even know. It struck her as incredible that she had come to this in such a short period. Was she getting too caught up in Logan's emotions and the shock of what had happened to him? Maybe seeing Ellie's room and reading her journal had brought her closer to the girl as well. Too close to maintain professional detachment?

Irvine sat up and took the photo frame from the table beside her bed. It held a wedding photograph of her and Tom, all bright sunshine and wide smiles. She tried to recall how she had felt that day and could not.

She wondered how it had changed so much between her and Tom and found it difficult to understand it, except the cliché of growing up together and then growing apart. It wouldn't be much comfort to the wee man when she had to explain it all to him later. Irvine tried to imagine the conversation.

It's okay, son, she would say. *I just got fed up with your dad and all his annoying habits. And then this kind of vulnerable and exciting guy came along and we got sort of caught up in this murder slash kidnap slash Hollywood bullshit.*

Yeah, that would work.

She went back downstairs and sat on the couch looking at the two evidence bags on the floor. Then she had a thought.

She went to get her notebook from her handbag and flicked through it until she found Logan's mobile number. She had jotted it down from the business card they had found at the house. She punched the number into her phone and waited while it rang.

21

12.35 p.m.

Judd took the turn-off for Loch Awe and Cahill told him to stop when they were out of sight of the main road. Judd slowed and pulled off the road and into the woods, branches snapping under the big tyres. They came to rest behind a line of trees, partially hidden from the track just in case anyone came past.

'We get ready here so there's no delay when we hit the target site,' Cahill said, stepping out of the car and bowing his head into the wind and snow.

Logan's mobile phone vibrated in his back pocket and he saw that the number calling was not recognised from his address book. He clicked to answer.

'It's Becky Irvine.'

She sounded odd to Logan.

'Oh, hi,' he said, not really sure what else to say but feeling better that she had called.

'I don't know why I'm ringing you,' she said. 'It's just that, well . . .'

The line went quiet.

'What?' Logan asked.

Cahill turned back to face him and Logan mouthed 'Irvine' at him.

'I don't understand what's happening,' Irvine said. 'I mean all of it. How you know where Ellie is and how you set up that meeting in the park today.'

'I'm not involved in anything illegal,' Logan said, and then realised how stupid that sounded. 'Not intentionally, anyway.'

Irvine laughed. 'This is so weird,' she said.

'I know,' he told her. 'Listen, I'll explain it all later. As soon as we've got Ellie back.'

'Okay.' She paused. 'I got her clothes so if you bring her over to my place you can pick them up.' She gave him the address and then fell silent. Cahill signalled to Logan that he ought to get moving.

'Look, Becky, I have to go now,' he said.

'I know. Look after yourself.'

Logan said goodbye and clicked to end the call.

'What was that all about?' Cahill asked.

'She just called to say she had clothes for Ellie and that we should go to her place to pick them up. That was all.'

'I told you about her,' Cahill said.

Logan didn't know how to respond.

*   *   *

They all huddled together under the raised rear hatch of the car while Cahill and Judd sorted quickly through the gear and organised it in neat piles for each team member. Logan thought his little pile looked pretty pathetic next to the others: a ballistic vest and helmet with goggles, a waist belt and holster for his handgun and a communications rig with a mike and an earpiece. The others had the same but also knee and elbow pads, small automatic rifles, flash-bang grenades, an additional handgun for back-up and cold weather gloves.

When Cahill was ready, he activated the communications gear and tested it with Judd; it seemed to be working okay where they were but there was no signal from Hardy or Washington. Logan asked if something was wrong.

'No,' Cahill told him. 'If we'd had more time and knew the site we could have set up a command post and a proper comms system so we could transmit everything that came out of these headsets.' He tapped at his earpiece. 'But as it is, we need to be pretty close to each other to hear. The range of the headsets alone is tiny.'

Logan watched Cahill and Judd check all the weapons while Carrie helped him on with his vest and helmet. She fiddled with his radio headset until it was in place and then the four of them cross-checked each other. Logan stood uncomfortably in the biting wind rubbing at his arms while the three professionals did a final cross-check on their own gear. It didn't quite seem real to him, not in the way it had been at the bar when Judd came gliding in to save his neck. This was like being inside a film and he looked up through the trees to watch thick flakes of snow drift down from the dark sky.

About eight miles ahead, Washington slowed the old estate to a crawl as they approached a clearing in the trees. He looked at Hardy, who nodded to indicate that they should stop here. He pulled the car off to the side and went as deep into the covering foliage as possible. They didn't want to risk being seen by the men they were following and he and Hardy were both ready for what might be a long yomp through the snow to get to their target.

They got out and went through the same routine as the others, and were fully geared up in about three minutes. Hardy called over the radio for contact with Cahill, but there was no response.

'Must still be too far away,' Washington said.

Hardy nodded and went back into the car to use the phone. He told Cahill that they were going to be on foot now and out of contact until they were in range for the radios to work. Then he and Washington exchanged a quick hand-slap, kind of a low five, and Hardy, the more experienced soldier, moved out in front with Washington three feet behind. They passed slowly through the trees, staying parallel to the road but far enough off it to escape detection if their prey decided to come back and check their backs.

After half a mile, Hardy held up his hand and pointed ahead through the trees to a big wooden structure on the right. It looked empty, and there were no lights on anywhere. They moved towards it and saw an open area with a row of small cabins just behind it and then some more cabins in the woods about two hundred yards away. Hardy pointed over to the side of the building and motioned for Washington to follow him there, where they would be hidden from anyone in the cabins.

'We need to check the place and find out where they are,' Hardy said.

Washington pulled his goggles down and nodded. They went to the front end of the building and Hardy lay on the snow and peered round the corner. The sky was dark with clouds and the snow reduced visibility in the middle to long distance. He slowly scanned all the cabins in his sight line and then pulled back and stood, turning to Washington.

'Can't see any cars. The nearest cabins along the loch front are empty, but I'm not sure about the ones in the woods. Plus, I don't know how far they go. Could be miles for all we know and they're right at the end.'

Washington's face looked pinched, his mouth shut tight. 'How about if we move down to the loch's edge and use the cabins there for cover? Approach the woods that way.'

Hardy thought for a second and then nodded. 'Good call. Let's do it.'

They moved back along the building with Hardy on point. They came to a window and passed below it at a crouch. On the other side, Washington stood and peered in. It was a reception area as far as he could tell, with a curved wooden desk and some chairs. It looked as if it hadn't been occupied for some time. He looked again and saw a sign on the desk with prices for the cabins. It was headed: *Rates 2002–2003.*

He tapped Hardy on the shoulder and told him what he'd seen.

'Been closed for a while,' Hardy said. 'That means no civilians. First bit of good news.'

He motioned with his hand for them to move on, then stopped again at the end of the building and went flat on his belly to look out and check the terrain. The ground continued on a level for twenty feet and then sloped away down to the water's edge. Trees were dotted along the top edge of the slope and more down along the edge of the loch.

Bad news/good news scenario.

They had twenty feet of open ground to cover, but then the slope and the trees would give them shelter as they moved to check the cabins in the woods from behind.

Hardy sat up with his back against the wooden wall of the building. 'On the ground or run it?' he asked Washington.

'Run it.'

Hardy nodded. 'First, let's go back and get a look inside one of these cabins to check the layout.'

They went through the woods, quickly covering the ground to the closest cabin. Washington tried the door but it was locked. Hardy found a broken window, reached in to unlatch it and then pushed it open. They went inside, finding themselves in the main bedroom with a door opening out into the hall. Washington paced out the hall and counted that it was over twenty feet long. There were three doors – one on the right for the main bedroom and two on the left for smaller bedrooms. The living and kitchen areas were combined in one space that the hall opened out into at the front. There was a shorter hall, maybe eight feet long, leading from the living area to the front door with the bathroom and a small cupboard on opposite sides of it.

They left the cabin, moved back to the main building and then ran out to cover the open ground to the loch.

Cahill tried the radio again one last time after they had finished gearing up and reloading the car with the surplus equipment. He shook his head at Logan – nothing.

Judd heard the low rumble of the engine of a Range Rover before anyone else and quickly stepped round the X5 so that he was hidden by it from the road. He crouched down behind one of the big wheels and motioned for everyone else to get down too. Logan instinctively dropped on to the ground where he was, and then saw Cahill and Carrie move quickly and quietly to join Judd. He felt stupid, but at least he was pretty much hidden from the road.

The Range Rover burst past them along the road, going north at a fair rip. Judd was up and round the car looking after it.

'Looked like four,' he said to Cahill. 'Two in front and two in back. All men.'

'Shit,' Cahill said. 'Back-up?'

Judd nodded. 'Most likely. Who else would be out here in this weather and driving a fifty grand car?'

'Fuck. Let's go. Carrie, try them on the radio again.'

Logan started to feel it was unravelling as he heard Carrie's voice in his earpiece calling for Hardy and Washington. There was no response.

'This is what happens,' Cahill said, turning to Logan. 'It never goes according to plan. You adapt.'

Judd reversed back on to the road and the car bolted forward, its heavy wheels digging deep into the snow and gripping tight.

22

12.45 p.m.

Ellie was dozing on her bed when she heard the car pull up and stop. She froze, caught between wanting to get to the window and pull all the boards off, jump out and just run or staying put to see what happened. She heard Drake's voice and then the other man, the one that scared her so much, as they walked towards the cabin.

She sat up and swung her feet out on to the floor and looked over at the window. She had worked the final nail on the third board about halfway out last time before she took a rest. She was just too tired to go on. Before lying on the bed, she had put all the nails back in place and it looked fine to her now. No sign of her hard work, except for her raw fingers. She clasped her hands behind her back and stood as footsteps approached her door and a key turned in the lock.

Drake came in alone and closed the door. He looked a little surprised to see her standing there. She heard the other man talking to the woman through the walls of her room.

'Would you like to sit?' Drake asked.

She shook her head. She never wanted to sit on that bed again if she could help it. She wanted him to finish what he had to say and leave. Then she would be gone.

He shrugged and sat on the bed behind her. It made her uncomfortable having him back there and so she turned to face him.

'Your daddy did what he was told this time,' he said, but with no hint of pleasure in his voice. 'That means that this should all be over soon.'

'How soon?'

He looked at her for a moment, trying to understand where her strength came from. He shook his head and sighed.

'If I get my money today then that will be it.' He smiled. 'And this will be over for you.'

She tried to read his eyes but they were closed to her. He stood and left without saying anything else.

Ellie did not move. She listened to him speaking softly to the other man outside her door but could not hear what was said. Then a phone rang and they both moved away into the front part of the cabin.

Ellie looked at the window, her face empty of any emotion.

'Hello, Gabriel,' Drake said into the phone as Sergei followed him into the living area. 'It's all done. The money should be through tomorrow.'

'Good,' Gabriel said. 'Tell Sergei he can do what he likes with the girl now. I want Finch to know what happens when he fucks with me. Wait there till he's done and then dump her body in the loch.'

Drake watched Sergei as he sat beside Katrina on the couch, his eyes locked on Drake and a smile spreading on his face. Drake wondered if Sergei had been in touch with Gabriel for this – to satiate his craving.

'Is that a problem for you, Mr Drake?' Gabriel asked.

'No.'

'Because if it is, the others will be with you shortly and they can clean up after you.'

Drake was conscious of the threat in Gabriel's words – do what I say or you'll be 'cleaned up' along with the girl. He had no problem with killing the girl and sending the message, but he wasn't in the business of torture and was sickened by Sergei's desires.

'I said it isn't a problem, Gabriel.'

'I know Sergei can be . . . difficult. But he has his uses. I hope you're not getting squeamish now.'

Drake felt Gabriel was taunting him. Maybe he *had* spoken to Sergei and the others were coming here with orders to take him out so that Sergei could take his place.

'It's not a problem,' he said. 'Leave it with me.'

He hung up before Gabriel could speak again, something that would undoubtedly have repercussions later.

'What's up, *boss*?' Sergei asked.

Drake put the phone in his back pocket, ignoring Sergei and thinking now about how he was going to kill his old friend and then the girl. There would be no coup today.

'So,' Sergei went on. 'Do I get to have some fun at last? Do I get to play with her?'

'What happened to you, Sergei?' Drake asked. 'What happened to us?'

'You got soft, Yuri,' Sergei said, standing. 'You forgot where you came from and who your friends really are.'

'No, Sergei,' Drake said. 'You just forgot what it's like to be human.'

Sergei laughed and brushed past him.

'Where are you going?'

'For some air. It stinks in here.'

After he had gone, Drake sat next to Katrina. 'Gabriel said to give the girl to Sergei and to kill her when he's done.'

Katrina sat forward, grasping Drake's hands in her own. 'We can't, Yuri.'

'I know.'

'So what's going to happen?'

'I'm going to kill that fat fuck and then I'm going to drug the girl before I shoot her. She doesn't need any more pain.'

'Yuri . . .'

'It's done,' he said, cutting off her complaint. 'There's nothing I can do to stop it. And anyway, Gabriel's right about it. We need to send a message out that this is what happens if you screw with us.'

'Let me come with you when you give her the drugs. Maybe that way she'll be more relaxed and it won't be a struggle.'

Drake nodded. First, though, he had to deal with Sergei.

23

12.50 p.m.

Logan was surprised how well the X5 handled the rough road and the snow. He'd always thought of it as a pretend off-roader; a big bus for the yummy mummies to take the kids to their private schools. But it was doing okay under Judd's expert guidance.

'Take it easy, Bails,' Cahill told him. 'Watch out for that Range Rover.'

Judd didn't reply, his eyes fixed on the road ahead and his hands moving deftly round the wheel.

Cahill spoke into his mike.

'Hardy, do you copy?'

Nothing.

'Washington, do you copy?'

Nothing.

He repeated again.

Silence.

Logan rested his right hand on the butt of the gun holstered on his hip and shifted uncomfortably in the bulky vest. He could feel sweat forming under the helmet and his scalp felt hot and itchy.

'Hardy, Washington, do you copy?'

Somebody answer, please.

Hardy maintained his position on point after they scrambled down the slope to the water. They progressed slowly along the loch, moving separately from tree to tree and covering each other at every turn. No point in taking unnecessary risks this close to their objective.

They looked up at the loch-front cabins they passed and confirmed their first impressions: they were all empty. Most were in poor repair also, with broken windows and cracked wood.

They passed the final loch-front cabin and saw the tree line marking the start of the woods up ahead. Hardy was behind Washington at this point, covering his position from the narrow trunk of a silver birch tree. Water lapped gently at the rocks along the edge of the loch and the snow continued to fall heavily, coating the ground and making it slick underfoot. They were wearing all weather boots with good rubber soles, but still had to be careful.

Washington pointed at Hardy and then motioned with his hand for Hardy to make the first move off the loch side and up the slope towards the woods. Hardy nodded back at him and sprinted out past Washington, coming to rest behind a pine tree halfway up the slope. Washington followed quickly, huffing out air as he ran past Hardy's position before going flat on to his belly just below the top of the slope. He turned on to his back and waved Hardy on.

They lay together for a few seconds to catch their breath. Hardy tapped his earpiece and Washington nodded in agreement.

'Cahill, do you copy?' Hardy whispered into his mike.

Nothing but empty airwaves.

Hardy shook his head at Washington and then started to crawl up to the top of the slope to look out into the woods. Washington stayed where he was, his rifle gripped tightly against his chest where his heart thumped hard, pumping blood and adrenalin through his hot veins.

Judd guided the BMW down through the ninety-degree bend and then up the hill that had caused the old estate to expend so much effort. It was no problem on four-wheel drive.

Cahill continued to try to contact the others, with no success.

'Christ,' he said, exasperated. 'How far away can we be?'

'We'll get them, Alex,' Carrie said.

Judd drove slowly now, scanning each side of the road. Logan leaned forward and strained to peer through the snow at the road ahead. It looked as if the trees widened out up ahead and then Judd tapped Cahill on the arm and pointed into the woods. Logan didn't see anything until the car veered off the road and took out some thick bushes, exposing the estate car's position.

Judd stopped the car and they sat with the engine idling.

'Hardy, do you copy?' Cahill said.

Logan heard a faint echo and a crackle in his earpiece.

Cahill repeated his call.

Nothing.

Hardy paused at the top of the slope, looking along the line of cabins. He saw what looked like the front end of the car they had been following jutting out behind a cabin about a hundred feet away through the woods. It had been hidden from their initial vantage point behind the reception building but he was sure of what he now saw. There was a short, fat man pacing outside the cabin blowing on his hands. Hardy watched until the man went back into the cabin and then moved slowly back down the slope and nodded to Washington.

'The car is about a hundred feet along the top edge of the slope,' he told him. 'It's parked beside a cabin with boarded-up windows.'

Washington nodded, trying to breathe slowly to control his heart rate. Hardy pointed past him along the slope and Washington nodded.

They moved back down to the loch and went quickly from tree to tree, counting out the hundred feet and covering the ground smoothly and rapidly.

When they reckoned they'd covered the right distance, they went on to their bellies at the bottom of the slope and inched up towards the top edge. It seemed agonisingly slow but in reality only took about fifteen seconds. They paused beneath the ridge and checked their rifles. Moving together, they looked up over the lip.

The car was parked about thirty feet away and ten feet out from the cabin. Two windows faced them, both boarded up. From their earlier look at the other cabin they reckoned those windows belonged to the two smaller bedrooms. They couldn't see any movement. Hardy looked back through the woods, counting the number of cabins. He looked at Washington and held up five fingers and then one. Washington checked and nodded. Cahill would need to know this to target the right cabin.

Sergei sat in the chair by the window, rubbing his hands together. He saw Katrina filling a syringe with a sedative.

'What are you doing with that?' he asked. 'And where's Yuri?'

She looked over her shoulder at him but said nothing. Sergei stood and walked to her, grabbing the hand that held the syringe.

'I said, what—'

Drake came down the corridor into the living area, raised his arm and shot Sergei in the face. Katrina screamed as blood sprayed her face and hair. Sergei's body crashed to the floor, blood pumping from a ragged hole in his cheek and pouring from his mouth. His hands scratched at the wound, as if trying to claw the bullet out, and blood gurgled in his throat.

Drake walked over to him and pushed Katrina back, pointing the gun at Sergei's head. Sergei raised his hands protectively.

Drake shot him twice in the head, the second bullet taking off the top half of one of his fingers before entering his skull.

Drake stared at Sergei's ruined face, feeling nothing but contempt.

Ellie waited until she heard the one who had gone outside come back in and then went to work on the boards on the window as quickly as she could while still remaining quiet. She had wrapped two of the bed sheets around her, one at her waist and one diagonally across her body. She wanted some extra cover in this weather.

Time to go.

Ellie removed the bottom two boards easily and set them down on the bed before the sound of the first gunshot cracked through the cabin. She stifled a scream and tried to concentrate on getting the final nail out of the third board. Her hands shook violently, but she kept going and eventually it came loose.

Two more shots followed, making her flinch.

Now they're going to kill me.

Panic rose in her almost uncontrollably. She tried to breathe to calm herself and make sure she did this right, but her hands continued to shake as the board came free and she almost dropped it.

She tried to breathe again but her throat felt tight and a tear spilled out over her cheek. She put her face to the exposed window, felt the cold air and saw the snow falling.

Now.

*   *   *

Cahill told Judd and Carrie to go outside and find some cover to camouflage the two cars, then tried the radio again.

'This is Cahill. Hardy, do you copy?'

The radio crackled. Then Hardy's voice came on. 'Copy, boss. We got them.'

A jolt of electricity passed through Logan.

'Clarify,' Cahill said.

'We have a visual on the cabin. Subjects' car parked outside. No movement inside.'

Judd and Carrie came quickly back to them.

'How do we find you?' Cahill asked.

'You see the main building?'

'Copy that.'

'There's a slope down to the water from behind it. Move along the shore, past the loch-side cabins, and you'll reach the woods. Subjects are in the sixth cabin in from the tree line, copy?'

'Copy. We're at your car now and will be with you soon. But listen, there's—'

Cahill was about to warn them about the Range Rover approaching their position when he heard the first gunshot. It was faint, but unmistakable. Logan started to ask what it was, but Cahill held his hand up to cut him off.

'Shot fired,' Hardy said over the radio.

'Copy,' Cahill replied. 'What can you see?'

Silence.

Logan felt on the edge of panic.

Hardy spoke again, his voice high and sharp. 'Movement in the cabin at the window.'

Logan tensed.

Two more shots.

'It's the girl,' Hardy said. 'She's opening the window.'

Cahill didn't hesitate. He shouted, his voice piercingly loud in Logan's earpiece.

'Take her, take her, take her.'

Washington was up fast and over the edge of the slope. Hardy rested his weight on his elbows and trained his rifle at the cabin, sweeping along it to find a target.

Washington waved at the girl framed in the half-open window and she looked at him with wide eyes.

Take her.

Then the headlights of the Range Rover cut through the trees and Washington went down, his face cracking hard on the solid ground beneath the snow. He bit through his lower lip and tasted blood in his mouth.

The girl looked at him and he saw tears well in her eyes. He was only ten feet away.

So far.

He looked left and saw the Range Rover weaving quickly through the trees as it approached the cabin. He waved at the girl, motioning for her to get back, to close the window and stay inside. Then he buried his face in the snow and hoped he would not be seen as the Range Rover turned off the road and its lights swept over his position.

Hardy stayed where he was for a fraction longer before sliding back down the slope. The last thing he saw was the girl's face warping and splintering behind the old glass as she pulled the window down. His heart jack-hammered inside his ribcage.

24

12.55 p.m.

Washington lay still, not even risking a glance up to see where the Range Rover was. He heard its engine rev lower as it slowed and the sound of soft, new snow crunching as it was compacted under the vehicle's weight. The snow continued to fall heavily and he felt it land on his neck and face before melting on his warm skin.

The engine idled and then cut off and he heard the sound of men's voices and laughter. It sounded like four distinct voices, all with English accents. He guessed they had stopped behind or beside the other car, judging by the direction of their voices, and they probably hadn't heard the gunshots.

The men moved in towards the cabin, closer to his position, and he heard the door swing open on rusted hinges. It closed loudly and their voices were immediately muffled by the wooden structure. He stayed where he was, waiting for Hardy to let him know when it was clear.

Time stretched interminably.

'Okay, buddy.' Hardy's voice finally sounded in his earpiece. 'Move on back to me real slow. You should be clear but just keep it low.'

Washington looked up and saw that the girl had placed some wooden boards across the inside of the window. Smart girl, he thought. She knows we're here but she's covering her tracks until it's safe.

He moved backwards on his stomach through the snow, keeping his eyes trained on the cabin. When he felt the top edge of the slope he raised up on his knees and moved quickly back down beside Hardy and blew out a long breath. Hardy patted him on the shoulder and then spoke to Cahill.

Cahill knew from experience that when you send your men into a hot zone, you maintain radio silence until they are ready to talk to you.

Except sometimes you never heard their voices again.

Logan couldn't understand why no one was talking but he kept quiet and waited for Cahill to break the silence, his entire body rigid with tension. He started when Hardy's voice sounded in his earpiece.

'Cahill, you copy?'

'Copy, Tom. What's your status?'

'We didn't get her.'

Logan's muscles refused to relax and he heard his heart beating as blood rushed in his head.

We didn't get her.

'Copy,' Cahill said. 'The Range Rover get in your way?'

'Yeah. Chris got exposed halfway to the cabin and had to hit the ground. We're both okay and no one saw us. Still set to go.'

Cahill turned in his seat to speak to the others.

'This doesn't change anything,' he said. 'Our plan was always to take them by force so nothing's changed. This was just a little local excitement, nothing more.'

Logan almost laughed at the euphemism but it came out more like a barked cough.

'You have a feel for the cabin layout?' Cahill asked Hardy.

'Copy that. We had a look at one we passed earlier. Two windows facing our position which I think will be bedrooms. There's only one entrance and that's to the right as we look at it. There's a short hallway as you go in, opening out to the living area with another hallway leading off that to the back; two bedrooms off to the left and one door on the right for the main bedroom.'

'What about a kitchen?' Judd asked.

'Place is too small for all of that,' Hardy told them. 'It's open-plan in the living area.'

'Copy that,' Cahill said. 'There's a risk that not all the cabins are the same but we can only go with our best guess at this point.'

'The girl's in the last room on the left of the hallway, at the back. Her window is boarded up on the inside and she replaced the boards when the Range Rover arrived.'

Logan realised that Ellie must have worked the boards off

and had been meaning to get out on her own when Hardy and Washington showed up. Jesus, she was going to make a break for it all alone in this weather and probably without even knowing where she was. She was tough, that was for sure. It made him smile until he realised that if they had not been there she would have died either from exposure or because the bad guys would have caught her.

'She must have been desperate,' he said.

Cahill looked at him and nodded. 'Yeah, but brave with it. I don't know many eleven year olds who'd try that.'

Hardy spoke again. 'What's the assault plan, boss?'

'We agree it now so that when we get to your position we're ready to go. No waiting.'

'Copy.'

'Hardy, you and me are going to position ourselves on either side of the door. Washington, I want you at the window of the bedroom that the girl is not in. Judd and Carrie take the other side where we assume there will be at least two more windows. Logan, you wait at the slope. Your job is to get Ellie when she comes out that window because I have no doubt that's what she'll do. She'll be looking for us this time.'

Logan had anticipated waiting in the car while they went and got her. It felt as if someone had traced a cold blade down his spine and he shifted in his seat and swallowed a bubble of fear that rose up from his gut.

Cahill looked at him for an acknowledgement. He nodded; he had to be there for her now, no matter what it took. No matter how scared he was.

'On my count of three,' Cahill went on, 'I want flash-bangs in all the windows you're covering. Tom and I will blow the door with a shaped charge at the same time and then I want you all after us as we go in. The girl is our priority. We assume the bad guys will congregate in the living area. Tom and I will stay there and put down anyone who moves in the hallway or in the room. Chris, Carrie and Bails will clear the other rooms off the hall and then come to back us up.'

Nods all round.

'We need to neutralise all the bad guys. So if any of them book it out of there, Chris and Bails will hunt them. The rest of us will move back to the vehicles and get the fuck out of Dodge.'

Logan felt his head go light as the buzz of adrenalin kicked in. No wonder young men wanted to be soldiers — what a rush.

'Any questions?' Cahill asked.

After a chorus of nos, they left the BMW with the engine running and the heater on full blast. Judd quickly went to the estate and started it up to do the same. Then they moved out and down the slope to the loch side.

Ellie sat on the bed with her hands clasped between her legs and rocked slowly back and forth, trying her best to hold the flood of tears back.

They're here for me.

She unfolded the photograph of her dad and looked at his face. It seemed unfamiliar and wrong somehow. She was frightened that her fantasy of him would not match the reality and it chilled her. Tears leaked out and she squeezed her eyes shut to stop them.

The men from the new car were shouting and arguing with the others and she knew they must be here to kill her now that it was over. She could hear Drake's voice and the woman, but not the other one. Maybe he was the one that got shot.

I don't want to die.

That phrase repeated in her head and she willed herself to stand again and move to the window. She wanted to rip the boards off, jump out and run, but something held her back. Instead, she loosened one end of the bottom board and looked out through the narrow gap, watching for her rescuers.

Gabriel's men had come to the cabin thinking that it was a simple clean-up job, but instead they found Sergei dead on the floor with the girl still alive in her room. Drake stood by the window, the warm gun still in his hand and a thin tendril of smoke curling from it into the air. He'd sent Katrina to the main bedroom to get her out of the way when he heard the car stop outside.

'What the fuck,' the largest of the four men said, staring at Sergei's body. 'How did this happen?'

Drake watched them impassively and said nothing. The two men standing furthest from him held single-barrel pump-action shotguns across their bodies and the other two had bulges under their jackets indicating that they had pistols in shoulder rigs. He didn't recognise any of them but knew that he was going to have to be very careful and very lucky to get out of this situation alive.

'Well?' the big man asked again.

One of the men behind him turned his shotgun towards Drake. He in turn raised his pistol to aim back.

'Hold it,' the big man said, raising his hands. 'Just fucking hold it.'

'We're all in this together,' Drake said, still keeping his gun trained on the man with the shotgun. 'Sergei is gone now and there's no need for anyone else to join him.'

'We can work it out,' the big man said. 'Sure we can.'

'Then let's talk,' Drake said.

Logan, Cahill and the others moved past the main building and quickly along the loch, certain that Hardy would warn them if there was any risk of being seen from the cabin. Logan saw the two men ahead, lying below the top edge of the slope and waving them on.

This is it, he told himself. There will be no pause and no second chances when we reach their position.

It took all his will to ensure his legs kept moving forward and he tried not to think of the consequences if anything went wrong.

They reached the bottom of the slope and moved up to meet the other two. Cahill crouched below them and the others followed his lead.

'Hands in,' Cahill said, holding his arm straight out with his palm open and facing down.

They all placed their hands on top of his. Logan was the last one and he hesitated a fraction before doing it.

'Be smart, be quick and put your man down,' Cahill said.

He pulled his hand away and the others did the same.

'On three.'

Cahill held his gloved left hand up with the first three fingers showing. He counted them down and then moved fast up the slope.

Logan waited until they were all gone and then went to the top of the slope.

I'll try to make it right, Ellie. If you give me the chance I'll make it right.

He crouched down and watched as the people he had trusted with the life of his daughter moved in on the cabin.

25

1.30 p.m.

Washington went low and crouched under the window of the room next to Ellie's. Cahill and Hardy went to the front door of the cabin where the cars were parked. Judd and Carrie went round the back, heading for the far side.

Logan could only see Washington from his position. He looked at the other window and saw the boards there start to come down from the inside. He caught a glimpse of Ellie's face and instinctively started to move towards the window; towards his daughter.

Washington saw Logan move and waved him back. Logan ignored him.

The window started to move up and Ellie was slowly revealed. Logan quickened his pace.

Washington watched helplessly.

Cahill's voice came over the radio, low and urgent.

'On my mark. Three, two, one. Go, go, go.'

Washington stood and threw a metal stun grenade full force through the window. Logan heard other windows shatter on the far side and then the sound of the door being blown in. An instant later, six sharp, successive explosions went off in close order.

Boom-Boom-Boom-Boom-Boom-Boom

Logan saw light flash as bright as the sun through the windows and then Cahill and his people started to move.

Inside, Drake and the four men fell to the floor as windows shattered, the stun grenades erupted around them and the front door exploded.

Drake was dazed from the grenade flashes but he heard the roar of the shotguns as Gabriel's men fired blind. He pressed himself to the floor, started to crawl along the back hall towards where he thought the main bedroom was and prayed that Katrina was safe.

He heard footsteps outside the cabin.

Brrrraaaatt

Automatic rifles stuttered from the doorway.

Brrrrrraaatttt-brrrrrattttt

Two more bursts sounded and Drake heard the wet thud of bullets hitting flesh and men screaming behind him.

In her room, Ellie pushed the window up until it was fully open and started to climb out.

*   *   *

After their initial burst of fire, Cahill moved into the short front hall of the cabin at a crouch with Hardy beside him. They saw movement straight ahead through the smoke and both fired.

Brrrraaaatttttt-bbbbrrrrraaattttt-brraattt

Something flashed back at them and Cahill heard the unmistakable roar of a shotgun.

Boom

Then another.

Boom

Wood splintered where the shotgun shells ripped into the walls.

'Bails and Carrie,' Cahill shouted. 'Get back round to the side and put some grenades in the windows. Do it now.'

Washington came through the door behind Cahill and Hardy and went down on his belly, firing as soon as he was in position.

Brrrraaaattttt

Judd and Carrie were behind Washington when they got Cahill's order and immediately sprinted back round to the side of the cabin facing away from the loch. They each went to one of the two windows and pulled the pins on their fully armed grenades. Judd counted down silently from three using his fingers and then they threw the grenades into the building, Judd shouting a warning as he crouched down for cover.

'Fire in the hole.'

Cahill, Hardy and Washington put their heads down and covered up with their arms.

Boom-Boom

The grenades went off in quick succession and Cahill felt their concussive force shake the cabin.

Logan thought, this is what war sounds like.

Then he saw Ellie come up to the window and perch unsteadily on the ledge, searching for someone to help her. He scrambled up, slipping on the snow, and ran to the window, grabbing her under the arms to lift her out.

She's so light.

She came out and wrapped her arms tightly round his neck. He was acutely aware that if one of the bad guys came out at him he wouldn't be able to clear his gun from the holster.

Drake's vision had started to clear when the grenade came into the main bedroom through the window and landed beside Katrina. She was sitting on the floor with her back to him, still confused from the initial stun grenade. She picked the small device up. Drake screamed at her and then it exploded, ripping through her body and decapitating her.

Drake's head slammed into the floor from the force of the explosion, although he had been shielded from the worst of it by her body. He turned on his back and fired through the wall below the window, hoping to hit whoever had thrown the grenade.

Logan heard more gunfire after the grenades went off and this time it sounded to him like the handgun he'd fired at the CPO range.

Bang

Bang

Bang

Bang

Carrie's voice sounded in his earpiece. 'Taking fire through the walls. Returning fire.'

Brrrrraaaattt-brrrraaaatttt

Logan turned and ran back towards the slope as best he could while holding on to Ellie. She was sobbing uncontrollably into his neck. Her hot tears soaked his skin, seeping down through the years and the flesh and muscle and entering into the marrow of his bones.

Let us get through this, please.

Drake was barely finished shooting at the wall when he heard the return fire from the automatic rifle and bullets crashed through the walls and floor of the bedroom from below the window. Wood splinters spiked into his face.

Drake wiped blood from his eyes and crawled quickly along the floor away from the window and towards the girl's room. He could see the door five feet ahead of him across the hallway. The lock had been forced open by the impact of a shotgun round. Two of Gabriel's men lay on the floor at the mouth of the back hall, their bodies shredded by bullets. The other two, including the big man, were lying behind the bodies, trying to shield themselves from the assault.

The rifles from the front hall chattered to life again.

Brrrrraaatttt-brrrraattt

The big man looked up and fired across the living area.

Boom

He pumped the slide and fired again.

Boom

Pumped and fired.

Boom

Logan could see the safety of the slope ahead, but it seemed to always be just too far away. Behind him, more gunfire sounded in the cabin and Logan felt the ground shake under his feet. He lost his footing and turned as he fell, taking the force of the impact on his back so as to protect Ellie. The fall winded him momentarily and he gasped for breath.

Cahill's voice came through the radio. 'Logan, did you get Ellie? Are you clear?'

Logan tried to speak but couldn't.

Cahill spoke again, his voice rising in pitch. 'Logan, copy goddammit.'

'Copy, yes. I've got her. I've got her.'

Cahill fired at the shapes ahead of him and Hardy did the same. Then they both advanced across the living area while Washington provided cover fire. The sound of their rifles filled the air.

A single shotgun round boomed back at them, harmlessly going high and shattering wood in the ceiling over their heads.

'Clean the area,' Cahill said.

The three of them fired simultaneously and the noise in the tight confines of the small cabin was deafening.

*　　*　　*

Drake watched as the two surviving men were cut to pieces by the automatic gunfire. He heard the soldiers, because that was how he thought of their attackers, moving towards his position. He had no choice now but to move.

He rose up on to his feet, unsteady from the after-effects of the grenade explosion, and ran towards the door of the girl's room.

Cahill saw the man dart across the back hall, barely ten feet from him and fired without aiming, strafing bullets along the floor and up the wall.

The man crashed into and through a door without stopping, although Cahill thought he saw a burst of red as one of his bullets hit home.

Drake stumbled into Ellie's room, feeling pain rip through him as Cahill's bullet bit into his left arm. It hung limply by his side, the muscle torn and the bone shattered. He saw that Ellie was not there and his eyes moved to the open window. Ignoring the pain, he went to the window and climbed out, seeing someone running ahead of him with the girl in his arms. He stopped, steadied himself and fired at the moving figure.

Cahill heard the sound of Drake moving around in the room down the hall and then it went quiet.

'I think one got out,' he said. 'I'm after him.'

'I'm coming round to you,' Carrie said.

*　　*　　*

Logan heard and ran desperately for the slope. There was a noise behind him but he dared not look back.

The impact of the bullet came a fraction before he heard the shot and then he was at the slope.

Another bullet bit into him and he dropped Ellie and fell forward, feeling the pain jagged across his back as he tumbled down.

'Who fired? Who fired?' Cahill's voice sounded strained.

'I got hit,' Logan shouted. 'Fuck it hurts.'

'Everyone out. Cover them. Cover.'

Logan put a hand out and came to rest at the bottom of the slope. Ellie was ten feet above him at the top edge, her eyes wide, tears and dirt streaking her face. She looked from Logan back to the cabin and saw Drake coming towards her, leaving a trail of his blood in the fresh snow.

She started to slip and slide down towards Logan. She didn't know who he was, who any of these people were, with their helmets and goggles and guns. But she knew they were here to help her. To save her.

Logan watched her, paralysed by pain and yearning.

'Where is he?' Cahill shouted the question over the radio.

Drake stumbled at the edge of the slope, weak from his injury, and fell forward. He held a black handgun and his face and shirt were soaked in blood and matter, not all of it his own. He landed heavily and dropped the gun, shouting out in pain.

Ellie turned and screamed when she saw him. Drake reached out and grabbed her leg with his good hand.

'He went down the hill,' Carrie said as she came round the

corner of the cabin and saw Drake falling. 'They're all down there.'

'Fucking move, now,' Cahill screamed, panic in his voice now. 'Everyone.'

Logan tried to sit up but pain bolted raggedly through his body.

Above him, Ellie kicked out and pulled herself free of Drake's grip. Drake clawed at the gun beside him with his right hand, struggling to hold it in the wet snow.

Logan reached down and pulled his handgun from its holster, remembering to flick the safety off. He looked up the slope and saw Drake grabbing for his gun. Ellie screamed at Logan.

Logan fired and missed.

He fired again.

Snow and dirt kicked up beside Drake.

Drake finally closed his fingers round the gun as Ellie got within touching distance of Logan at the bottom of the slope.

Logan fired.

Missed.

Drake swung his arm round unsteadily, trying to focus his sight on Ellie.

Not now. Not so close.

Logan fired three times.

The last bullet punched a hole in Drake's chest, smashed through his collarbone and exited the top of his shoulder, taking out a chunk of flesh.

Drake dropped the gun as his blood sprayed the snow red.

Ellie slid down into Logan's arms.

Cahill came over the edge of the slope and Logan gave him a weak thumbs up.

The others joined Cahill, their chests heaving and their breath pluming in the air.

Drake tried to pull his body up on blood-slicked hands.

Cahill walked down the slope and raised his weapon until it was levelled at Drake's head.

Logan closed his eyes and heard the hot metallic stutter of the rifle.

'Torch this fucking place,' Cahill said. 'Burn it all down.'

26

2.30 p.m.

Irvine was sleeping on the couch in her living room when the phone rang. She grabbed at it and answered quickly, her eyes half open and her head groggy from the afternoon sleep.

'It's Logan.'

She waited for him to speak again.

'We got her,' he said. 'We got Ellie.'

He sounded exhausted and his voice cracked as he said her name. She could hear the sound of a car engine in the background.

'Is everyone okay?' she asked.

'Nothing a hot bath won't cure.'

'And Ellie?'

He paused.

'Logan?'

'She's going to be fine. She's been through hell, but she's alive.'

'God,' she said. 'It sounds bad.'

Logan laughed, or at least that's what she thought it was supposed to be though it didn't sound like anything she'd heard before.

'No. She's fine. It's okay.'

'You sound shattered,' she said.

'That's because I am.'

'And . . .' She realised she didn't know how to ask the question. 'What happened? To them.'

'I don't want to talk about it right now. I mean, they don't matter to me. All that matters is we got her and we all got out of there.'

'Where is "there"? Why can't you tell me what happened?'

'Just leave it for now, Becky, okay?'

She felt bad for having pushed him and didn't like the pain in his voice. He was clearly tired and the strain of the last few days was obviously getting to him. She knew this wasn't the time for any kind of real conversation.

'Listen,' she said. 'Get some rest and then bring her here and we'll get it sorted.'

'Okay.'

The dial tone sounded in her ear.

Irvine called Tom next and asked him to pick up the wee man and take him to Tom's parents' house. He sounded annoyed but agreed when she said some people were coming round on business. She had expected him to be angrier after she'd been out all night, and wondered if perhaps the realisation that their marriage was over had now occurred to him.

Life is so messy.

They had moved quickly to the cars after getting Drake's body back to the cabin and setting the fire and got out of there as fast as they could. Logan carried Ellie all the way and then climbed into the back seat of the BMW with her clinging to him, still with his helmet and goggles on. Judd got in the driver's seat with Cahill beside him.

'Go,' Cahill said quietly, a mixture of exhaustion and relief in his voice.

Ellie said nothing and lay across the seat shaking from the cold and from fear. Cahill handed Logan a blanket from the floor in the front of the car and Logan draped it over her. She stopped shaking and was asleep five minutes later and it was only then that Logan realised he still had the goggles and helmet on. He pulled them off and rubbed his hands over his sweat-soaked hair and face.

The winter night descended rapidly as they drove back to the city and Logan cradled Ellie's head on his lap as she slept. He held his hand out to Cahill who reached back and grabbed it tight.

'We made it,' Logan said.

'Fucking-A we did. You did good, Logan, real good. You saved her.'

'No, you did. I was just there at the end.'

'Someone had to be.'

Logan smiled and put his head back on the rest, the fatigue of the last few days suddenly hitting him all at once. After calling Irvine he slept until Cahill shook him awake at a petrol station just outside Dumbarton. Judd was at the pump and the others were all out of the estate car and stretching, their joints groaning and popping.

'Want something to eat?' Cahill asked.

Logan tried to shift his weight without disturbing Ellie. Pain coursed across his back and he winced.

'Those vests are good,' Cahill told him. 'But it'll hurt for a few days.'

Logan pulled strands of hair off Ellie's face and only now noticed the swelling and discoloration at her eye. He felt as if it had been done to him and sucked in a breath as emotion knotted his stomach.

Cahill leaned over to look at the injury.

'She'll be fine. I have a guy, a doctor, who can look at her when we get back.'

Logan nodded and stroked her hair.

'She's alive, Logan. That's all that matters.'

Logan knew he was right, but wondered all the same where it would go from here.

He looked up at Cahill as a stray thought struck him.

'What do I tell my parents?'

Cahill shrugged.

'Fucked if I know.'

Cahill called ahead to the doctor and asked him to meet them at the building on Scotland Street. He didn't say too much and Logan guessed that the doctor knew about CPO and didn't need to ask.

They got to the building at around six and Carrie and Judd went in first followed by Cahill, Logan and Ellie. She was still asleep as Logan carried her out of the car and inside.

A forty-something man with short grey hair and wearing blue medical scrubs met them in the corridor. Cahill didn't tell Logan the doctor's name and he knew by now not to ask.

The doctor asked Logan to take Ellie through to the first aid room, which turned out to be a small, but very well equipped, medical centre. This place was always surprising. The doctor then asked them to wait outside while he examined her. Logan started to argue with him, but Cahill pulled him away.

'Let him take care of her, okay,' Cahill said. 'He needs space and you need to get cleaned up. You can see her when you're both ready.'

Logan nodded and followed Cahill to a bathroom, where he washed his hands and face in a sink and started to feel like himself again. They went to a kitchen nearby and got some coffee before heading back to the medical centre to sit side by side on the floor outside the room, sipping at the coffee and not talking. Logan tried not to think about exactly what the examination might uncover.

Judd came by after a few minutes and told them there was something they needed to hear. Cahill stood, helping Logan up as his back had started to stiffen even further, and they went to another room round a corner.

There was a circular table with six chairs in the room and a conference phone was on in the middle of the table.

'Go ahead, Bruce,' Judd said.

'Listen, I haven't finished what I've been doing yet, but . . .'

'Spit it out, Bruce,' Cahill said.

'Okay. I've been looking into this Gabriel Weiss character . . .'

'Who told you to do that?' Cahill said angrily. 'You don't go poking around and risk alerting these people without my say-so.'

Judd held his hand up. 'Relax, Alex,' he said. 'It was me.'

Cahill glowered at him and then told Bruce to go on.

'It was strictly secure, official channels,' Bruce said, defending Judd. 'No street contacts or anything like that.'

'Fine,' Cahill said, not really sounding as if he meant it.

'Anyway, I got a hit through Interpol.'

'Sounds serious,' Logan said.

'Yeah, it is,' Bruce said. 'They've got an open investigation over in France. Some heavy hitter guy from the US, a real gangster type but not mobbed up, got his throat cut in Paris. They think it's connected to some international racketeering involving drugs, prostitutes, gun-running et cetera. All the usual charming stuff, you know. Anyway, there's some intelligence that the UK is being used to wash the money from this outfit and that there are Russians involved.'

'Proper pan-global operation?' Cahill said.

'Yeah, but that's as much as I could get really. My source wasn't willing to say too much else.'

'So what's the point?'

'Well, he did tell me the Interpol code name for their investigation. In fact when I told him the name of the guy I was asking about, he made a real point of saying that he couldn't tell me anything except the code name – Project White Angel.'

He paused for effect and Cahill and Logan looked at each other, confused.

'Gabriel Weiss,' Judd said, with heavy emphasis.

'Gabriel the archangel,' Bruce said. 'And Weiss means white in German.'

Cahill pulled out a chair and sat down. 'Thanks, Bruce,' he said, clicking the phone off.

Logan and Judd sat down at the table.

'I thought he was just a dirty lawyer,' Logan said.

'It's a nice, respectable cover to have,' Judd said. 'Allows him to travel internationally and to enjoy the finer things in life without arousing suspicion.'

Cahill rubbed his eyes and sighed, then turned to Logan. 'You just risked your life for that little girl,' he said.

Logan nodded.

'So,' Cahill went on, 'you don't want to have to look over your shoulder for the rest of your life wondering if this guy is going to come after you, do you?'

'I thought you said I wouldn't have to,' Logan said. 'That all of that Russian mafia talk was bullshit.'

'It is, but this is different,' Cahill said. 'Those guys up at the cabin were obviously just foot soldiers and there will be more of them, without question. This changes things and we have to adapt to whatever information we have.'

'How?'

'You have two options,' Cahill said. 'One, you tell the police that you think the deal with Bob is wrong and give them Weiss's name. Let them chase him down.'

'But that would bring them in to look at the whole thing and that might lead to what happened at the loch today,' Logan said. 'Plus who's to say they would get him before he gets to me?'

'Right,' Cahill said. 'Or, two, we call Weiss and tell him that his guys are gone and they're not coming back, but that you and Bob will complete the deal and send him some nice, clean money if he forgets about it. Call it even.'

Logan stared at Cahill. 'You're crazy,' he said.

'Am I? You want to destroy all of what we did today because you're the last honest lawyer? You want all the deaths to have been for nothing?'

Logan opened his mouth to protest.

'You want to see your daughter killed in front of you? Because that's what men like this do if you cross them.'

Logan looked to Judd for support, but he remained quiet.

'Welcome to the real world, Logan,' Cahill said. 'To the dirty, stinking shithole that we live in where expediency rules above all else. You want to have a chance at a life with Ellie, then put your ethics in your back pocket and do this.'

'You want me to help fund these monsters?' Logan shouted. 'Maybe help them kill and . . . and God knows what else?'

'Yes. There's no other option.'

Logan stood quickly, his chair scraping back on the polished concrete floor.

There was a knock at the door and the doctor looked in. 'I'm done,' he said.

'How is she?' Logan asked.

'She's generally in good shape. A couple of broken ribs which I've strapped up as best I can.'

'What about her face?' Logan asked.

'Nothing broken. It'll take time to heal, but no long-term damage. I've cleaned and dressed it and given her a good strong painkiller to numb it for a bit.'

Logan picked his coffee cup up from the table and swirled the remains around, not wanting to ask the next question and wondering whether he was going to throw up.

'Anything else?' Cahill asked.

Logan closed his eyes and held his breath.

'No. Nothing.'

Logan breathed again.

'She's asking for her father,' the doctor said. He paused and looked at Cahill. 'I didn't know what to say, I mean, is he dead?'

Logan laughed. 'He's been reborn,' he said bitterly, standing and walking past Cahill out of the room.

27

6.30 p.m.

Logan walked into the first aid room and closed the door. Ellie sat with her back to him, dressed now in a CPO polo shirt and combats that were way too big for her. She leaned slightly to one side, favouring her injured ribs.

The room seemed to shrink and the air thinned. She turned her head sideways at the sound of the door clicking shut but didn't look at him. He saw the white dressing over her swollen face and went forward slowly. As he came round the padded bench she was sitting on, he saw that she had a grubby old photograph held in her hands. Still she didn't look at him.

'What have you got there?' he asked, unable to make out who was in the picture.

She sniffed and drew a hand across her nose. Logan smiled; just like a kid to wipe her nose with her hand like that.

'It's my dad,' she said, her accent a mix of influences but with a faint trace of Scotland still there.

Logan looked at the photograph again and fell into his past.

Penny's skin warm beneath his hand.

The new life growing, unknown to him, in her womb.

Her smile creasing the skin at the corners of her eyes.

Standing in the rain on Byres Road at the end of it all.

He reached down into the side pocket of his combats and pulled out the creased photo of Ellie. He tried to flatten it some more in the palm of his hand and a tear splashed in its centre. He wiped his eyes and cleared his throat, unsure that he would be able to speak.

'Snap,' he said, reaching out and placing his photo of her gently on top of the one she held.

She looked down, her brown hair falling forward. Then she pulled it back from her face and stood to face him.

They looked at each other then for the first time.

Her chin trembled and creased as tears welled in her eyes.

Logan felt his own tears spill out on to his cheeks.

'Hi, Ellie,' he said, his voice cracked and broken. His hands twitched at his sides, wanting to grab hold of her and pull her into his chest. To enclose her in his being and never let her go.

The photographs fell from her hand and came to rest side by side on the floor, next to small specks of her blood.

Logan felt as if his heart would burst.

She stood there, not moving, with tears now running down her cheeks. Both of them unsure what to do. What to say.

'They killed my mum,' she said, her voice faltering. 'Those men.'

'I know. But they can't hurt you now. You're safe.'

'But who's going to look after me?'

Her body heaved and she sobbed openly. Logan stepped forward and gingerly lifted her into his arms. She put her arms round him and held him tight. He pulled her in until their faces touched, their tears running together.

It felt as if they stayed that way for an hour, but it was no more than a minute. Logan lowered her until her feet were on the floor, then wiped the tears from her cheeks with his hands.

'We're going to be okay, you and me,' he said.

Ellie looked at him uncertainly and he realised that, beyond the raw emotion of the day, they were still strangers.

'Can you wait here for a second?' he said. 'I'll be right back.'

She nodded and he helped her back up on to the bench.

Cahill and Judd were still sitting at the table in the meeting room when Logan came back.

'How's she doing?' Cahill asked.

'She looks good considering,' Logan said, conscious that his eyes were damp and probably bloodshot but not caring. 'Make the call,' he said. 'Tell Weiss I'll do it and that he can have his fucking money.'

He turned without waiting for a reply and went back to Ellie.

To his daughter.

28

8.05 p.m.

Cahill stopped the car outside Irvine's house with Logan in the passenger seat and Ellie asleep again in the back, covered by a tartan travel rug. The porch light went on outside the house and the front door opened. Logan and Cahill got out and walked over to meet Irvine at the gate. She closed the door behind her and walked down to them, pulling her coat closed over a pink tracksuit and carrying the two evidence bags she had filled with clothes and Ellie's journal. She went straight to Logan, dropped the bags and wrapped her arms round him. It felt more maternal than anything else, but in the aftermath of the day's events he no longer knew how to feel about anything.

'I'm fine,' he said.

'Where is she?' Irvine asked, ignoring Cahill's presence.

Logan turned his head and inclined it back to the X5 parked at the kerb. 'In the car,' he said.

She looked then at Cahill. 'Did you kill them all?'

'Yes.'

'It was that easy for you?' Irvine asked, feeling uncommonly angry with him but not really sure why. 'You didn't even blink at the question.'

'Why the fuck should I?' Cahill replied sharply. 'They brought it on themselves. We're professional soldiers and they were just fucking criminals. It wasn't a fair fight. Who gives a fuck.'

Irvine tried to read Cahill's eyes in the shadows cast by the street lights but could not.

'Where are the bodies?'

'You don't need to know,' Cahill said.

'It's better that way,' Logan added, trying to soften it.

'Sounds nice and easy.'

Logan shrugged, not sure what else to say.

'It was,' Cahill said.

Irvine sighed at him and shivered in the cold. She looked past Logan at the car. 'Let me see her.'

She picked up the bags, gave the one with the clothes in it to Cahill and pushed between them to get to the car without waiting for a reply. She cupped her hands on the glass and looked in as Logan and Cahill came up behind her. Ellie opened her eyes and sat up, staring uncertainly at the three of them.

Irvine stepped back as Logan opened the door.

'This lady is a police officer,' he said. 'She helped us find you.'

'Thank you,' Ellie said to Irvine.

Irvine sat on the edge of the back seat. Ellie looked at Logan and he smiled, telling her it was okay.

Irvine reached out and pushed Ellie's hair back off her face, wincing at the extensive bruising visible around the dressing at the damaged eye. 'That looks like it hurts,' she said.

'It's getting better now,' Ellie told her.

Irvine smiled and untied the evidence bag, reaching in to get the journal. She handed it to Ellie, who traced her fingers over the embossed cover design.

'I got that from your room,' Irvine said. 'I thought you might like it back.'

Ellie opened the journal to the back and saw the broken daisychain. She pushed the broken ends apart and then closed the book.

'Did you make that in the summer, like you wrote in the book?' Irvine asked, trying to ignore the tears she felt building in her for breaking this precious thing.

Ellie nodded. 'I got this then as well,' she said, showing Irvine the photograph of Logan. 'That was when my mum first told me about him, about my dad.'

Irvine saw how young Logan looked in the picture, so different from now, and realised the significance of the date – summer 2003.

'You can fix the flowers,' she said hopefully.

'It doesn't matter,' Ellie said. 'That's baby stuff and I'm not a baby any more.'

Irvine put her hand on Ellie's neck and kissed her forehead.

She stood and Cahill closed Ellie's door before moving round to get in the car and start the engine up.

Logan walked with Irvine back to the gate.

'I'm sorry I broke it,' she told him. 'I thought she'd like to have it, you know?'

'She's had a tough few days,' Logan said. 'She doesn't mean it.'

'Maybe she's right. She's *not* a baby any more.'

Logan looked back at the car and watched Ellie flick through the journal. He wondered if she was trying to find Penny in there, or at least the memory of her.

'I'm sorry for how I reacted,' Irvine said. 'You did the right thing by her. You and Alex.'

'I'm not sure you really believe that,' he said.

She grabbed his hands and told him again they'd done the right thing. He felt the moment between them, certain that she felt it too. But it was the wrong time, the wrong place, in so many different ways.

'We got her,' he said. 'We got my little girl. That's all that matters.' He looked back at Ellie again. 'And she needs all that I can give her right now,' he said.

Irvine placed her hands on his face. 'I know,' she said, and turned to go back to the house.

Logan watched her for a moment and then went to the car.

As soon as Logan closed his door, Cahill pulled away along the street and Ellie leaned forward and waved to Irvine as she stood watching them from her door. It all seemed so normal to Logan, as if the last three days had never really happened.

Then Ellie turned to him and he saw the dressing on her face and the memory of her mother's death dulling the surface of her eyes.

We have so far to go, Ellie. So far.

'Where are we going now?' she asked him.

'We're going home, honey.'

She smiled weakly at him and her eyes sparked to life for an instant.

It's a start, he thought.

Good enough.

Don't miss the next thrilling GJ Moffat novel . . .

Fallout

Logan Finch has made a new life for himself with his daughter, Ellie. But a blossoming relationship with DC Rebecca Irvine is about to be put to the test when Irvine's old flame, drug-addicted rock star Roddy Hale, enters her life again.

And there's the small matter of a professional killer following her every move.

Alex Cahill, close-protection operative and ex-US army special-forces soldier, hates babysitting celebrities. Maybe this time will be different. Tara Byrne is a Scots girl about to break into Hollywood and is back in Scotland for the premiere of a low-budget film as a favour for a friend. She is the target of a disturbed stalker and needs Cahill and his team to watch her back.

As the clouds roll in to blanket the sky at the end of an Indian summer, violence erupts all around, putting everyone at risk. For Logan, there are impossible choices to be made; between his best friend and the woman he loves. Between who lives and who dies.

Available soon from all good bookshops and online.

ISBN: 978 0 7553 1853 7